Threads

An American Tapestry

G L O R I A   W A L D R O N   H U K L E

authorHOUSE®

AuthorHouse™
1663 Liberty Drive
Bloomington, IN 47403
www.authorhouse.com
Phone: 1-800-839-8640

First published by AuthorHouse 5/6/2009

ISBN: 978-1-4389-7415-6 (sc)
ISBN: 978-1-4389-7416-3 (hc)

Library of Congress Control Number: 2009904403

Printed in the United States of America
Bloomington, Indiana

This book is printed on acid-free paper.

For John
A Promise Kept

"Keep us, O God, from pettiness; let us be large in thought,
in word, in deed.
Let us be done with faultfinding and leave off self-seeking.
May we put away all pretenses and meet each other face to face,
without self-pity, and without prejudice.
May we never be hasty in judgment and always be generous.
Let us take time for all things.
Make us to grow calm, serene and gentle.
Teach us to put into action our better impulses, straightforward
and unafraid.
Grant that we may realize it is the little things that create
differences,
that in the big things of life we are at one.
And may we strive to touch and to know the great, common
heart of us all;
And, oh Lord God, let us forget not to be kind."

Mary Stuart (1542-1587)
known as
Mary Queen of Scots

Margaret Vandenberg, the tall, plain-featured Colonial offspring of Holland-born immigrant Gerrit Vandenberg and his Native American wife, stands at the threshold of a door positioned midway down the corridor of her life. Reaching for the latch, Margaret reflects upon the often-read words of the Scottish queen, feeling a kinship to the woman, and in many ways an affinity to the doomed monarch. Like Queen Mary, she herself leaves behind many rooms filled with heartbreak and unanswered questions, but Margaret will step forward unafraid. She has placed all misgivings in God's hands.

INTRODUCTION

English commander Colonel Richard Nichols sailed into New Amsterdam's harbor in September of 1664, intent upon dislodging Dutch ownership of the New Netherland colony. He was successful. Within days, and without a shot fired, the strategically positioned choice inlet became England's New York harbor.

In October of that same year, all Dutchmen living within the New York colony were required to take the English "Oath of Allegiance" to King Charles, as well as to his royal brother, James, Duke of York. Those who took the oath were allowed to keep their land properties and their arms. Those who refused to put their signature to the document were given six months to change their minds before being stripped of property, arms and their adopted country.

In 1665, all Dutch West India Company properties were confiscated. To James, Duke of York, went the city's company storehouse, the store itself, the weigh-house, and the pride of New Netherland, the Company Great Farm which was located near Broadway on Manhattan Island. This property would be known as The Duke's Farm until 1685, when James II, a converted Catholic, ascended the throne and it became the King's Farm. A few years later saw England's "Glorious Revolution" and the Catholic King of England, Scotland, and Ireland was replaced by his Protestant daughter, Queen Mary, and Protestant son-in-law, William of Orange. In 1694 Mary died of smallpox. William ruled solely until his death in 1702, after which he was succeeded by Queen Anne, James's second daughter, who in 1705 granted the land to Trinity Church.

Today, Trinity Church (chartered in 1697) stands as an enduring beacon of hope amid the reconstruction at Ground Zero. Combined with St. Paul's Chapel, built in 1766, the church is the oldest in Manhattan.

With the arrival of Colonel Nichols in 1664, Dutch people residing on the tip of the island of Manhattan sometimes found it awkward cohabitating on a daily basis with their new English government. Some returned to their European homeland, however, most chose to remain rooted to the North American soil that they had come to love during the forty-plus years of Dutch rule. These first New Yorkers, men such as the Baron Resolved Waldron, reluctantly pledged allegiance to the English king, but sought to retain their Colonial properties, faith, craft, business, language, and personal customs. With this objective in mind, and the tolerant blessing of England's king, several Dutch families such as the Waldron's, the Meyndert's, the Tourner's, the Jansen's, and the Verveelen's, moved three hours walking distance from the tip of Manhattan Island to the small village of New Haarlem (known as Harlem after 1664) where the declared official English language would be heard less often. Waldron, who was the first constable of Harlem under English rule, laid the cornerstone for the Dutch church there in March of 1685. This church endured until it was burned during the Revolutionary War. Waldron had established his large family upon an extensive farm, a multiple acre slice of what would ultimately be known in modern times as the Carnegie Hill District of Manhattan. Resolved Waldron died at Harlem in the year 1690.

Peter Stuyvesant, the former Director General of the New Netherland Colony, remained in his adopted land and eventually settled comfortably at his beloved country estate which is today the site of Saint Mark's Church in lower Manhattan. He and Colonel Nichols, staunch enemies in the past, became good friends, often visiting one another. Stuyvesant died at his New York estate at eighty. He and his family are buried within the catacombs beneath St. Mark's Church.

As the decades passed, second and third generation Dutch and English married, uniting families of the two Old World enemies. Many of these new American, Anglo-Dutch colonists also solidified their status in the New World by doing something more that would have been unthinkable to many of their fatherland grandparents. Dutchmen married native Indian women, strengthening their new position as landowners in their forbearers' adopted country.

Manhattan colonials ventured north into what is known today as the Hudson River Valley, early on traveling beyond Kingston, their eyes settling upon Albany, the well-established center for the fur trading business. In 1701, young, Manhattan born Peter Waldron, the first son of William Waldron, and grandson of Resolved Waldron, saw opportunities not to be missed in the rapidly growing northern frontier city of Albany. Together with his wife, Catharina Vandenberg Waldron, infant daughter, Engeltie (Elizabeth), and an African American slave woman called Sarah, Peter Waldron, a bricklayer who also dabbled in the fur trade, settled his budding family within a modest brick house, typical for an Albany tradesman. Later, Waldron would purchase land and a country house north of Albany at the settlement then called Half Moon, now present day Waterford. Eventually, Peter and Catharina Waldron's children grew to number ten, and their descendants today number in the thousands.

By the turn of the eighteenth century a new breed of adventurous settlers had created vast farming estates throughout the Hudson Valley region. The new wave of land barons had become masters to African born and American born slaves; yet in the upper regions of New York around Albany, following Europe's feudal system example, quite often they were themselves answerable to a master as tenants on the lands owned by the 'Patroon Landlords' such as the Van Rensselaer's. The tenant farmers cleared the land, and built homes and barns to which they held full ownership, but continued to lease the land upon which their dwellings had been built, paying the rent with a portion of their livestock and crops. They also gave a specified amount of days of their own labor as partial payment.

As the first quarter of the eighteenth century in the American Colonies drew to a close, the bloody terror of King William's war (1689-1697) and Queen Anne's War (1702-1713) had ended. Despite threat of random attacks against Albany by bands of combined renegade forces consisting of French soldiers and Huron Indians stationed in and around Montreal, the European war was over.

Within the New York Colony, the troubles that flared up in 1712 with rebellious Negro slaves in New York City had been quelled subsequent to a long list of new and very severe restrictions. Included within the new rules was a death penalty that was put upon the heads of escaped slaves who were found forty or more miles north of Albany, who authorities feared might pass information about their former household into the hands of the French enemy.

For the most part though, the restoration of order enabled a pause for a time of reflection and a time of peace that would last some thirty years. Colonial traders rekindled old alliances with the powerful Iroquois. Shopkeepers filled their shelves. Crops grew undisturbed in the rich soil of the river valley farms.

The American-bred Colonials were a tough-spirited group, who were quickly developing a unique, unprecedented voice. Begun as a tentative whisper, fifty years later their fervent shouts for independence would change the course of world history. America was unintentionally headed away from being a *colony* and toward becoming a *country*.

In 1684 New York became a royal colony. Under English rule, colonists were free to worship within their own congregations, ministered to by their own clergy whom each congregation financed. Calvinism as it had been known in New York during the Dutch days under Peter Stuyvesant's strict rules was changing, yet the Protestant Dutch Church remained strong, especially in the Dutch-speaking upper North River (Hudson River) Valley region of New York. For now though, while the Anglican Church reigned supreme, and was lenient during the first quarter of the eighteenth century, Dutch Calvinism began a split into two distinctive branches: those Dutch Colonials who wished to remain completely loyal to the Classis of Amsterdam, and others who leaned more toward a new, warmhearted, evangelical piety. This very early wave of religious renewal, which began in Europe, instigated many questions among America's uniquely blended Colonials, such as the morality of holding slaves, African or native born. The most paramount question among Christians of this time period was the issue of whether or not baptism should confer freedom.

* * * *

"The unique mix and growing independent character of these early New York Hudson Valley colonials, both European, African, and Native American, and their influence upon today's American culture, formed the inspiration for my third novel. As with the other two (*Manhattan Seeds of the Big Apple* and *The Diary of a Northern Moon*), the struggle as well as triumph of the unsung American is at the heart of my story."

Gloria Waldron Hukle

PROLOGUE

Margaret Vandenberg was the sole daughter of Holland born immigrant Gerrit Vandenberg, a wealthy, New York, North River Valley landowner.

Gerrit Vandenberg had been married twice. His first marriage to a Dutch Colonial woman had produced a son, Teunis, later sometimes called Anthony by the English. His second marriage to a Lenape Indian yielded a son, John, and a daughter, Margaret. In 1711 after a prolonged illness, Gerrit died and his last will and testament was revealed. Asserting his formidable presence from beyond the grave, the New York land baron continued in the Dutch custom of his fatherland by bequeathing his vast country estate, as well as all the surrounding lands he owned, equally among his three children. Unlike English primogeniture, where everything went to the eldest son, distributing property equally among all the children of the deceased was a common practice of the Dutch, and the Dutch inheritance laws had held in the New York colony under English rule.

When Vandenberg's will was made public, some who completely understood the inheritance laws of the Dutch were still shocked by the equal distribution. The question of rights surfaced not so much for the generous allowance allotted equally, but because it was generally accepted by most that Vandenberg's eldest son, Teunis, was the only offspring from what was considered a legitimate church sanctified marriage. Other than the oblique reference to Gerrit's *squaw woman*, outside of the farm, Margaret and John's mother's Christian name, Ruth, given at the time of her baptism, was rarely mentioned. Ruth preceded her husband in death by a number of years. Few if any acknowledged her as a wife of Gerrit Vandenberg.

When Gerrit Vandenberg passed into the hands of the Almighty, court officials upheld the will yet agreed that undoubtedly the deceased's second union with the Indian would bring future turmoil within his mixed family. Both of the younger children and their Indian mother had been baptized within the true faith, yet it was understood by all that no Indian, Mulatto, or Negro, be that person a slave or free, were capable of a good perception of the scriptures. Vandenberg's intentions in seeing to the education of his children had been praiseworthy, but the fact remained that two of his children were half-breed, therefore considered Indians and not white within society. It was preposterous, many said, to believe that two Indians would be capable of standing equal beside their elder brother to manage their father's fortune. What could be thought of children raised up as babes in the village of their mother's people? Neighbors thought it would have been better for his Indian children had Vandenberg married appropriately after the Indian woman died, but Vandenberg had not married a third time. Trouble was bound to happen as everyone had said it would, and it did. But trouble came faster than anticipated, and didn't come from where his neighbors suspected it would.

A few years after the passing of the elder Vandenberg, his son, Teunis, succumbed to a smallpox epidemic, after which Gerrit's younger son, John, abandoned his inheritance to wander the western frontier. Margaret Vandenberg, unmarried, now well past thirty years of age, was left to solely administer her father's magnanimous legacy.

However, during the latter part of 1722, Margaret's single-handed manner of plantation control was jolted as John returned with a wife, a business partner, new ideas, and an eagerness to take up the staff.

As all Colonists dreamed of peace and prosperity, siblings John and Margaret Vandenberg's differing visions produced conflicts, prompting unexpected catalysts that would reroute their lives and the lives of their progeny forever.

Chapter 1

1723
The New York Colony

Margaret Vandenberg closed the bottom section of the Dutch style front door, snapping the wrought iron latch into place. The top half of the door being left open, a gentle, yet unlikely, July breeze brushed her face as her dark eyes pensively trailed the departing census taker's carriage. The wheels rattled precariously over the long, yellow bricked, tree lined drive that connected Vandenberg manor to the dirt river road that ultimately joined the recently built highway beyond. Although the official's coach was well away, Margaret continued to wave until it was out of sight.

Speaking in Dutch, a soft, feminine voice asked anxiously from behind. "Then is he gone?"

Margaret turned to address her maid, a tall, stocky, dark skinned woman in her mid-thirties wearing a grey linen dress appropriately covered by a muslin apron. The maid's feet were clad in fashionable three inch, wide-heeled, square-toed shoes that were similar to those worn by her mistress. "Yes, Mr. Kent has departed though I fear Brownie gave him a terrible farewell." Margaret smiled before adding, "No doubt Bess's hound continues his brash assault upon the carriage and I suspect he will follow them halfway to the Rye farm before he stops barking."

Stepping forward to the parlor window, Marie glanced out, reassuring herself of the departure. "Good, I will tell you that I have been unable to sleep these past nights. Did you know that Mr. Kent was down by the mill and all over the farm yesterday? He be just standin' round and watchin'—watchin' everybody, and everything they did. I profess I do wonder if Mr. Kent will go to and fro as he pleases like he did here, him just quiet and watchin', at every farm he invades, he uppity and all like he be, with his account ledger in hand."

Having seated herself comfortably in a high backed chair beneath the ornately framed scripture painting of Jesus healing the blind man, Margaret folded her hands casually in her lap. She studied the servant woman who lingered across the room beside the small panes of glass, thinking how much Marie resembled her father Zebulon, the African slave brought back decades ago from the Waldron farm at Harlem.

Margaret began softly, "Marie, please come sit by me and have a seed cake before they grow stale. I gave Mr. Kent my permission to go where he might please, and speak to whomever he had a mind to interview. Good manners demand our hospitality, and we have nothing to hide. It was best to give him liberty."

Obediently Marie sat down. The expression across her face was as if she had just bitten into a sour apple. "I can not understand your calm demeanor, Peg. That man even went so far as to be bothering Titus. What information can be gotten from your stableman? Yet, now you sit enjoyin' caraway cakes as though nothin' were amiss, and you seem not at all put out by the fuss of the goin's-on that have been put upon your household."

"Put out?"

"Yes, he insulted your generosity," Marie said fidgeting in her chair. "You were good enough to give him leave to go where he would, but still, did you not feel distressed when Mr. Kent questioned many of your people without you being present? What right does a census taker have to wander alone where he would?"

"Perhaps Mr. Kent has an eye for good horseflesh. Whatever he was doing, my person was not put out at all, and nay, I was not offended, as I mean to go by the law," Margaret answered indifferently.

Marie raised an eyebrow. "I would think that you might think Mr. Kent took too many liberties."

Margaret smiled pleasantly while passing the plate of bite size cookies, but her reply was resolute. "You are loyal and that has always pleased me. I confess that I too was surprised that the man stayed another two days, but now we have come by it all none the worse." Leaning forward, Margaret lowered her voice. "I, of course, produced all proper documentation on your behalf, though your freedom is common knowledge in this part of our country, and Mr. Kent was well aware of your position here before his arrival."

Marie shot her mistress a look of surprise. "Do you think I worry over my freedom? I do not. Since I was three years of age, you have been my beloved mistress. With or without my papers, you will always be the same. I do not worry myself over your good care, Peg. My concern is only over that little man's probing of private affairs, and I never knew you to take so kindly to being lorded over."

Margaret laughed and then patted Marie's hand. "Indeed, and though you be free, I shall always protect you. All is in order with the little man. In truth, I found much of my discourse with Mr. Kent most pleasant and did not feel put out at all. When we spoke of you he had naught to say but that which was complimentary of your good care of my house. He spoke most highly of your good cookery. You seem so worried, but believe me, you have nothing to fear."

Marie abruptly rose from her chair, folding her arms defensively. "Oh, say no more of this to me; he is a small, uppity man and I did not like him. He is not the sort to be trusted."

"You think worse of him than you should. The gentleman seemed to especially enjoy the trout that you and your mother prepared for mid-day meal. And I too was pleased to see that you had little Sally making herself useful with the serving."

Marie offered a tenuous smile. "Master Vandenberg, the Almighty bless him, was always happy with the fish, and I thank you for the compliment, though you will not turn my head about Mr. Kent."

"So I see." Margaret replied drolly.

Marie sighed. "I am glad to hear that you took note of Sally. She is a good girl and very careful."

"Yes, you train her well, and to be sure, your poor mother needs her help in the kitchen. Sally is eight now, is she not?"

"Yes."

"She is old enough then to work around the meal table."

"Oh, yes. She is plenty old enough."

Margaret nodded approvingly, "Now, I bid you do not worry over the census taker any longer. All was in order, and there was no further question posed to me with regard to your freedom, if that be what troubles you. I know you protest that it does not, but should this be a part of what troubles you, trust me and be at ease. I will speak no further about it. I am weary enough with all else that is at hand."

Marie, still looking doleful, nodded her reluctant acceptance.

"Come now let us forget about Mr. Kent who I doubt we will ever see again. I have happier news. As you were in and out of the room, perchance did you hear the census taker's talk of Tenbroeck the silversmith living at Albany? You will recall he is the craftsman who fashioned my new silver forks and the round handled spoons. Remember? I brought them back from Albany last spring after my visit with my cousin, Catharina, and her family."

"Yes, of course, I remember, Mistress Peg. It was a sad time for me. I stayed to home to tend my father who was so sick we all thought the Lord would take him."

Margaret softened. "Mr. Kent tells us that Coenradt and Gertie Tenbroeck have a new infant son, and it sounds as though he is a quite large and a most robust babe. It seems prior to his arrival here, Mr. Kent was about his doleful business upriver by Coeyman's trading post, and the infant's grandmother could not keep from boasting upon the size of the latest addition to the brood. Goodness, she must have more than a dozen grandchildren by now, but you know she will go on and on as if her newest grandchild were her only one."

Marie, her earlier fears seeming to dissipate, smiled and replied, "A grandmother will always sing the praises of a newborn. Mama did with every one of hers. I will be sure to pray for the Tenbroeck babe's continued good health."

"Indeed, I am pleased to hear that you will do so. Then be off with you. Put on your old wooden shoes and go out to the ridge and pick me a large bunch of wild flowers. And mix them with the ferns as you do. They are so pretty that way. I will have them in the house should the Reverend Thomas Barclay stop to call on his way to visit his son as he said he might in his last letter." Margaret sighed adding pensively, "To be sure, a large bouquet would chase away his melancholia."

Marie turned to leave the room as Margaret added, "And do endeavor to find Mr. Lapett, as we are far behind in this other business we are about."

"I will see him," Marie replied offhandedly. "I recall the painter saying that he would have a long stroll after the morning meal."

"A stroll indeed!" Margaret expelled exasperatedly. "Well enough. If you come upon him, send him forth."

Picking up two empty beer glasses from the table, Marie hesitated by the door. "I will do as you say, Mistress Peg, and try not to feel ill will toward Mr. Kent." She added with a twinkle in her eye, "I will also include in my prayers that the Lord keep him in good health, but keep him far away from here."

Alone, Margaret again glanced at the clock and sighed, speaking softly to herself as she often had these past weeks. *Dear God, where is Benjamin? Why did I allow myself this foolishness, and now the world will know of my vanity having had such a loudmouth as Kent underfoot. Surely, I will be the talk at his next host's supper table. Oh, I am a foolish woman.* Reaching for a pearl-backed looking glass left behind after Marie had touched up her austere braided coiffure, she brought the mirror closer to her face and began examining the dark circles surrounding tiny pillowed sacks under each eye. *Oh Peggy, you truly are too old to be put upon canvas.* She pinched her cheeks as severely as could be endured, wincing while at the same time succumbing to the realization that self inflicting this sort of pain was a useless pursuit. No pink would be coaxed from these cheeks without the direct intervention of heaven's angels, but what could be expected? The blush of youth was long gone. She had fallen passionately in love when most women her age awaited the blessing of grandchildren, not the tantalizing caress of a zealous suitor. *What a dismal subject I will make for the artist this afternoon.* Wistfully, Margaret looked around the room. *Perhaps the light will not be of his taste, and he will not avail himself today.*

Not a woman easily discouraged, an idea brewed within, soon boiling over like a pot set too long over fire. There must be something that can be done that might enhance her countenance, though certainly Lapett's strokes would be forgiving. She would send Sally to the hut of the Tuscaroran Indian, saying that the tenant farmer should bring hither his mother, Mamma Shasa, up to the house at first light tomorrow, making sure she had along her herbal pouch. Spotted Bird's mother would prepare her a good strong tonic from her herb garden as a remedy. She must not, would not, look this way when David returned to her from Albany, or he would think her a corpse in the making rather than a bride awaiting. Mamma Shasa had never failed her. Surely, this was the closest she would come to any sort of Godly miracle.

Putting aside her mirror, Margaret struggled to regain her decorum in time for Lapett's arrival, recalling the words her native Lenape grandmother had often whispered to her in the past...a simple Indian prayer that spoke to her Christian heart.

Give praise for this day.
Honor the great Creator
who gives to you all things:
life, strength, and joy.
Hear the bluebird call at dawn:
Each day another gift

Margaret thought, *If only I could hear the bluebird's call during these trying times. Of course, my grandmother's struggles were not mine, and so perhaps her bluebird has become shy.*

Marie appeared at the door. "I am sorry to startle you, but the artist bids me tell you he will come forthwith. He was down yonder by the mill watchin' the men-folk."

"He stands by the mill? I pray he comes before the light is overshadowed, yet I fear the day may already be a loss."

"Would you have a tankard for offering to Lapett?"

"I would have two when you see him come in. And Marie, please try to remember to speak the English even when we are alone. It is good practice."

As Marie left, Margaret reflected upon the census taker's visit and the various conversations that had transpired between them since Mr. Kent's arrival. His examination of everyone he had interviewed had seemingly gone well enough, praises to God, yet his observations in general of the status of the populace, as well as those of his counterparts fanned all across the province, was beginning to reveal disturbing, unexpected news. Mr. Kent perceived that once the census was completed the summation of the slaves living within the New York colony would number more than six thousand, the vast majority, of course, being Negroes living in and around New York City. This head count meant that fifteen percent of those living in the colony were slaves. Margaret had noticed that Mr. Kent had seemed especially concerned when he had spoken of the current counts in comparison to those of the last census taken twenty years before. In 1703, the slaves then living within both the city and the province had numbered only two thousand four hundred, Mr. Kent had noted. This new census was showing a marked increase that he believed was cause for sounding the alarm. He had sighed loudly before pointing out that with the brisk slave market, weekly auctions in the city, and the traders profiting one hundred percent on each slave sold, soon slaves would outnumber all free men in the colony. Expressing fears of another slave insurrection such as had occurred a decade before, Mr. Kent had concluded the discourse with a sobering supplication to the Almighty Father asking for preservation of all property owners.

Although concerned by his unsettling report, Margaret thought the paunchy little man an exaggerator who enjoyed the sound of his own voice. She had smiled to herself thinking of the official's unsettled demeanor when the following evening she had asked him to consider the words of the revered John Calvin, who once wrote, *"Faith is not a distant view, but a warm embrace of Christ."*

Her young sister-in-law, Bess, had been seated beside Mr. Kent at the table, and despite her blush, Margaret had pressed further, suggesting if Christianity, as Calvin proclaimed, were embraced in the same manner as the Lord Jesus had instructed, to be sure no quarter would be given to those who laid claim to salvation yet bred treachery by a lack of tolerance for all of God's created beings. Mr. Lapett had shifted uncomfortably in his chair, prompting her to go still further, flatly stating that she had inherited the responsibility of her Negroes from her departed father, but would purchase no more. All could rest easy in their beds knowing that she had not, nor would she be, adding to slave tallies. The census taker, suddenly at a loss for words, had given no reply, and all had retired early that evening.

Margaret thought again of her mother, who had grown into her maidenhood without benefit of Christian instruction, yet believing that human beings, trees, berries—everything in the world—came from the hands of the Creator. Among the Indians there was no slavery. Captives were either adopted into a tribe with full rights or killed, death being considered a blessing. Bondage was not an alternative. Though a terrible thought, Margaret had long believed that death upon the slave ship was far more merciful than life under a bad owner.

She began pacing the parlor as she continued to review the visit and the official's close interrogation of nearly every person on her plantation. Had her outspoken nature given him cause for any further investigation? Had someone spoken to him of Lizbeth? What was he thinking as he journeyed to his next stop? The assured front she had put forth for Marie's sake began to dissipate. Worry though, did her countenance no good. She forced her thoughts to return to Lapett who had been staying with them for several weeks while he painted what would be her bridal portrait.

Normally she looked forward to Benjamin's visits. Lapett's wife and girls had always been a delight to her heart, but today, even where her dear friend was concerned, additional fortitude was required. In the middle of dire concerns, she considered this particular pre-nuptial endeavor nothing more than foolish vanity and his presence had begun to add to her tension.

Never a practiced coquette like some of her New York acquaintances, several of whom were members of Peter Schuyler's powerful inner circle, Margaret disliked adhering to society's recommendations for ladies of her position. The insistence on a bridal portrait was only one of many such requirements. Yet, despite her household worries and as preposterous as the ordeal of posing seemed, she had vowed that the woman drawn by Mr. Lapett would be one who inspired nothing less than complete admiration and respect. It was the persona expected by all, and she meant to accommodate that expectation with the truest spirit of love for David's sake. John need not worry: her soon-to-be new husband would never regret his proposal of marriage. Whatever the cost, she would do her best to see that her portrait would grandly dispel any lingering question of status.

Studying the half finished canvas lying against the easel, Margaret envisioned the portrait hanging majestically in the great entrance hall of her house; at the same time thinking how much life had changed upon this land since her Indian mother and Dutch father had spoken their vows amidst the River Nation peoples. For that matter, how her own priorities had changed with the arrival of the western frontiersman David Karski. How the world had shaken when his strong arms had encompassed her. Much of the rituals of her Northern plantation life that previously had commanded her attention season after season now hung suspended amid distant clouds. There was no doubt that the order of her universe had been rearranged when nearly a year ago her brother had brought David home. The blatant testimony to that stared back at her from the canvas.

As she examined the full portrait she had to admit that thus far she was quite pleased with Mr. Lapett's work. She was happy that she had not engaged Nehemiah Partridge as had her Albany cousin, Catharina Waldron, who had contracted the well respected Partridge to paint the portrait of her husband,

Peter, which, according to Peter, had concluded with an unfavorable likeness. It had been a year, and from what she understood, Partridge had still not been compensated with the beaver furs promised. Hence, the artist would not sign the work, and Catharina was reduced to tears by her husband's stubbornness. Margaret did not know who was right or wrong, yet thought it far better that she had chosen the French Huguenot than a Bay Colony man for the task. She had known Lapett for many years, and of course, outsiders, as her cousin had experienced, were not always reliable. *Yes, perhaps, after all, there was some value in all of this nonsense of idly sitting for one's likeness.* She conceded that the woman elegantly dressed in an imported, French embroidered stomacher and a finely stitched, green brocaded gown had not evolved easily, yet she believed that in the end she would be satisfied. A smile began to form upon her lips. Well, at the very least Benjamin Lapett would sign the portrait as she, unlike Peter Waldron, had paid in advance for the artist's work. There had been no need of a contract between friends. Honor did not require signed witnesses.

She smoothed her skirt once again as she had repeatedly done over the last half hour, searching the room for a suitable means of productivity. Her gristmill account book lay on the walnut, drop-leaf trestle table near the window, but she reached past the closed ledger for a letter that Marie had brought in over an hour before. The handwriting was that of Anna Stoudt. Margaret was surprised to receive the dispatch, knowing that Anna and her husband were scheduled to arrive within a short time, Anna having sent a prior post that she would gladly help with the arrangements for the wedding. Anxiously, Margaret broke the wax seal and began to read the correspondence dated 1 July 1723, immediately noting that there were few of Anna's customary beginning pleasantries. Her good friend was quick to come to the point of her discourse.

Margaret's agitation with Lapett dulled when, after a sentence about a change of travel plans, Anna related news of an incident involving an African man: a slave owned by a Manhattan neighbor.

The Negro was discovered in a surprisingly clever plan to kill Mr. Dugan, who resides near Captain Waldron on Beaver Street, and had it not been for the goodness of the Captain's loyal cook, surely his murderous task would have been accomplished. The desiring to commit this murder was by one of those who had been brought over last year on the "Elizabeth".

Her heart skipped a beat as she read the name of the ship. Every colonist living between the Bay and Virginia colonies knew of last year's slave uprising aboard the vessel.

The captain of the ship, wishing to keep his credibility with his colonial customers and impart a sense of calm near every auction block, had taken immediate action upon his ship. The execution of the leader of that rebellion had been carried out swiftly on deck. It is said that all one hundred ten shackled Africans had been brought up from below to witness the justice of the punishment. The instigator had been beheaded in front of all his fellow countrymen before the ship came into harbor. The leader's head had then been mounted upon the bowsprit. There it had hung for several days serving as food for the gulls and a constant reminder of what would not be tolerated by the captain or any other future master. These actions, Margaret surmised, surely were thought at the time to be an especially potent warning for all the Negroes because many of the Africans religiously believe that a man's spirit can never return home to Africa without all his body parts.

Margaret wondered why Mr. Kent had mentioned none of this. Her hands shook as she continued reading: *Oh, Peggy, did we not feel that all troubles with our Negroes were long ago settled? It saddens me to think that after all our diligent work, so many remain unsaved, and their hearts are filled with a terrible resolve for vengeance.*

I can tell you that with regard to this most recent tragedy the African was quickly tried and executed, yet I am fearful for I now believe the whole shipment aboard that cursed vessel, many of whom walk among us, are possessed of a rebellious spirit. I am afraid that they will infect all the others and we will face another insurrection. Poor souls, they cannot know that, for them, there is no way back across the seas. Our minister implores that we look to the Scriptures for our answers. To be sure, we seek divine guidance since we are all in the hands of the Almighty.

Pausing to reflect upon the troubles to which dear Anna referred, Margaret realized that they were both well acquainted with the web of discontent found in the slaves' circle of suffering. They had often seen among their own neighbors the terrible conditions that were inflicted upon these poor souls. Yet, there was little that any woman could do to help ease the pain brought by unscrupulous owners in the name of justice.

She contemplated the possibility that she and Anna shared a common branding of their own, a stigma burned into their souls through inheritance. By way of rights, they had been forced into the position of Master, and as slave owners must witness this "ring of tears" as the Africans referred to a slave's life. Anna, an only child, came by her title of Mistress upon the death of her father and then once again with the death of her husband. Margaret herself had also become Mistress through her own father. How often have they shared their sentiments, finding their responsibilities a thorn laced legacy.

What defense could be presented before God, knowing the misery of so many was a scourge instigated by her own Dutch ancestors, and that had been embraced by fathers, brothers and husbands? All of her life, Margaret had pondered the question. Come judgment day, would kindness and good stewardship of her slaves be considered a worthy atonement?

Or was it true, as her father had insisted when she sought his wisdom, that the Almighty himself never forbade slavery, and that she was concerning herself without reason over the trading of property. As proof of his opinions he would read from Exodus: "*Thou shalt not covet thy neighbor's house, thou shalt not covet thy neighbor's wife, nor his man-servant, nor his maid servant, nor his ox, nor his ass, nor anything that is thy neighbor's.*"

All of these things, Gerrit pointed out, were written about a man's property as proclaimed by God. Slavery had long been a part of the civilized world.

Though she was satisfied that her slaves were well-cared for and treated with kindness, the overall New World institution of slavery initiated by the Spanish nearly two hundred years before she had been born, personally validated by her father, was an anchor pulling at her heart. Most lately there had been incidents, behavior among her mill workers she had thought odd, whispering in the garden, and yet she justified such notions as womanish flutters that come naturally as prelude to vows.

Her mother once commented that she held within her breast her father's staunch, hard heart. This heart, said her mother, would help her walk tall. Margaret recalled that at the time she had not understood her meaning.

Still, despite all her efforts for those entrusted to her, what prayer could be offered that would ascend high enough to reach the throne of the Almighty? She was ashamed to think that while falling in love she had ignored responsibilities. What amends could be made if, through her lack of a diligent proper stewardship over her servants during these last months, her people came to harm as had others in the past?

The stench of terror filled the spaces between Anna's written lines. Anna, who had once trusted and loved, now feared. What a dreadful state to be in. Margaret couldn't imagine fearing Marie, or any of her servants. Indeed, since childhood Marie had been her beloved companion, a servant who was never looked upon as a slave. They had played together as children and argued just as hard. When her own mother had died, it was Marie who had held her hand, while Marie's mother, Eva, wiped away her tears. Together they had all cried for Lizbeth.

For decades she and Marie planted and harvested the same garden beside one another. As women they had carried the fieldstone from afar alongside the workmen who built this dwelling place; when she moved into her fine house, calling it her own, Marie had accompanied her—but not as a slave. No, she could not conceive of fearing Marie anymore than she would entertain the thought that Marie, though a freed woman, would abandon her.

Quakers of Pennsylvania had called for the freedom of all their slaves, but the Pennsylvania Assembly had quickly quieted such cries. The Quakers in Pennsylvania and the Jerseys had, for a number of years, discouraged further importation of Negroes or Indians, even going so far as to impose a duty, but the English Lords of Trade in mother England insisted that no colony had the right to interfere with British commerce. Obviously, interference in the business of slave trading had been all but eliminated as was evidenced by Mr. Kent who spoke of a demand in New York for the importation of more than a thousand slaves a year. It was all too much to think upon. All she could do was to do her best as she stepped forward toward her marriage. She and her people would do as they had always done. They would care for one another.

Hearing Mr. Lapett's approach she quickly wiped away a tear as she re-read Anna's last lines: *These are trying times, for you know not which of your own servants or those of your neighbors you can trust. How sad is a world without trust.*

Folding Anna's letter she placed it into the desk drawer and rose to greet the artist.

"Ah, Benjamin, at last you are here, and look, the sunlight has accompanied you."

Chapter 2

In every way possible Margaret Vandenberg believes that she is an independent woman. She prides herself as stubborn, if not downright formidable, and despite the scowl of her up-country Dominie, tells anyone who will give her audience that she senses her resolve to be the most valuable gift The Almighty has bestowed upon her. As testimony to this self observation she'll often resurrect her departed father, Gerrit Vandenberg, citing how often he praised her tenacious good care. As the Dutch minister sighs, Margaret is quick to point out that she accepts her esteemed father's praise as the highest of compliments.

Yet, who is prepared to argue with today's beguiling mistress of the manor, especially those who might have heard past rumors of the lady's enthusiasm for life after the headstone was placed above her father's earthly remains in the Dutch churchyard. Who is there who will dispute this woman's word? The only other witnesses to Gerrit's care, those allowed into the old master's bedchamber toward the end, and who may have been present to observe Vandenberg's last breath, were his Hessian manservant and the Negro woman, Mae; both their souls now long departed. Some had said that the old man cheated the Hessian his wages and severe grievances were held. Some said the big German had helped his master see the face of God. Had old Mae seen any wrong doing, the woman could not testify since she was mute since birth and could neither read nor write.

Margaret dismissed the gossiping whispers of such possibilities. Although she harbors earlier regrets, the care given to her father is not one of them. She was the dutiful daughter who remains respectful to his memory. With her tender nursing she had honored him. She had kept the fourth commandment of God. If judgment be based solely upon the attributes of a faithful daughter, she is not afraid to stand before the Almighty on the last day. As for the Hessian, he was a faithful servant and her father an honorable Master who placed great stock in him. If the German held a grievance, she would have known about it.

All the same, Margaret silently laments that she could not recall a time in her adult life when her father had kissed her or for that matter offered any sign of tender affection toward her person. As the anniversary of his death draws near, she gives little thought these days to the dead Hessian, but does wonder if indeed her father had ever loved her. Possibly in the end she had gained his respect; the sort that the schoolmaster holds for the ardent student who excels. But, beyond her childhood, had her father felt as a loving father should feel toward a devoted daughter who had given up all for the sustenance of a parent? Had he loved her? She had no answer and she supposed that she never would.

Taking stock of all that has transpired during the last number of years in her country, Margaret reasons that although her life has been difficult, indeed some might say quite unmerciful, she notes that personally the last decade had also been one of remarkable productivity on her large farm. The stewardship, which had fallen upon her and her elder brother's shoulders after the death of her father, and the disappearance of her younger brother, had been challenging, but she had held the reins steady. The mantle of competency warmly cloaks her shoulders, and though pride be a sin, she takes pleasure in this private thought. She believes that her father would have been astonished to see how his original patch of thick woods had flourished.

The *farm*, as Margaret refers to her holdings, encompasses field, glen and forest of a three thousand acre parcel; a section of the New York colony that defines a good portion of the seemingly endless banks of the rich bottom land of the upper North River valley. The Vandenberg property supports an active grand manor house, bake and brew house, smoke house, several barns, as well as an eight-stalled horse stable, lumber mill, and grist mill. From the fields of wheat and the waters of the river, a dark beer is brewed. The vegetable and herb garden to the rear of the manor house extends more than two hundred yards, abutting several slave cabins, and not far past is the vast apple orchard giving up fruit from trees planted fifteen years prior. For the better part, the apples are grown to be drunk. The cider produced is consumed not only on the farm, but also sold to merchants in New York City and Albany, and in recent years exported to England where the drink has received glowing reviews.

To the new visitor, one solely familiar with the history of the founding Dutchman and not having had the opportunity to be personally acquainted with his daughter, all that first confronts one's senses when arriving at the compound's river wharf is the connective testimony to the man whose reputation, even after all these years, still remains large beyond the grave. Neighbors from the outer big woods who have come to call might reminisce with their hostess and her guests over a bowl of warmed cider or a good glass of beer about by-gone days, and when they do they will often speak of Gerrit Vandenberg passing by their farms on a summer's morn while on his way to Sam Waldron's Horne Hook farm at Harlem. Those who are old enough to do so are obviously fond of remembering Gerrit, his eyes shaded by his broad-brimmed leather hat—he in those days surely near his eightieth year—riding his favorite stallion, Brown Buck; the old man still tall and straight upon his mount with only a colorful blanket between him and Buck. Gerrit would call out a *how do*, they say, but would rarely stop though he had been mounted for hours. It was a hard ride in those times before the laying out of the public highway.

Usually there is a respectful pause, a smile comes to the lips of many a neighbor in the kinship of the memory, but to anyone seated in the company of Mistress Margaret, the image of the horseman soon fades and the truth of what is beheld is generally understood. Vandenberg Manor and the Mistress are now one and the same. What is not apparent is that it has been this way for a very long time.

Few would know for example that it was Margaret, and not her older brother, who quite often saw that their house as well as the farm was in good order during the Master's absence. She gave the same particular attention to the physical and spiritual needs of house wenches as she did to the estate's slaves, both Negro and Indian, the majority of which had been born on her land. From an early age she understood the importance of the estate's servants; astutely conscious of her responsibilities, most especially her responsibilities toward her Negroes. It is the African men who turn the mighty grindstone of her mill, thus forwarding the never ceasing wheels of the productivity she has come to so dearly cherish.

Yet the success of her northern frontier farm depends not only upon her slaves. Exercising ancient European feudal-like authority, as the health of her father declined, Margaret likewise gave direction as Landlord to multiple tenant farmers, among them several Germans who along with their wives and children had fled their turbulent European homeland along the Rhine River. Through many harvests she has relied upon the Germans as well as her plantation slaves, and although her brother has disagreed with what he terms too soft a hand, Margaret feels she has established what she considers a sensible relationship with them.

She had made a similar tenant arrangement with a Tuscaroran Indian slave called Spotted Bird who was purchased by her brother years before at the Carolina country market. Despite his fondness for the Tuscaroran, John reminds his sister that he has found fault with this arrangement from the beginning. He argues that she puts too much stock in their Tuscaroran, and it does the man no good to be treated as though he be free when he is not. He reminds her that though Spotted Bird and his family are all baptized, and are good practicing Christians, it was important that they take care not to lead them to wade in murky waters.

Unlike their Hessian tenants, John would stress, the Tuscaroran was a slave and as an Indian slave, governed by the newer English laws of New York by which they must abide. Whether Margaret like it or not, the old provincial law under the former Governor Dongan setting Christian Indians capable of speaking the Lord's Prayer free had been set aside in 1706. Granting freedom, as she had done with others, was costly and difficult. A deed of manumission surely was of no benefit to the slave owner, and in her brother, John's opinion, freedom did not benefit their Indian either. What would happen to Spotted Bird should he be granted his freedom and then decide to go off on his own, since a freed Indian slave could never own any property? John knew well his sister's heart and he feared that her lenient arrangements with their Indian slave would eventually cause problems with the Hessians as well as with their Negroes. Yet despite such criticism from her brother and others, the covenants she had made with the Tuscaroran and his family and those made with the Hessians stood firm.

Regional dominion was based on several valuable connections. She is the daughter of a union between her Dutch father and a Manhattan Island born Lenape Indian, and as such is ranked as esteemed kin by the small band of Lenape who live, in these times, on the north patch of her holdings below Kinderhook village. The few remaining Lenape living along wild Munsie Creek that cuts through her properties to the west affectionately call her their friend, as do the Mohawk and Schoharie Indians. In fact, during recent years, with a heavy heart, she had become a tolerant Mistress to many invited displaced natives of various lesser tribes who have scattered across her New York soil.

Striving to be an effective manager through difficult times immediately following her father's death, Margaret held fast to the belief that, overall, he would have been happy with her decisions as she put to rest the finality of his affairs. While missing a father's counsel, such thoughts warmed her heart, but as it is with all children who accept the reins of responsibility from a powerful parent, ultimately a time came when there were choices to be made that only a Heavenly Father could understand. Margaret had felt compelled to follow an obstacle strewn path knowing full well that her decisions would alter the course of her life, but never could have conceived of all the other lives that would also be altered. Not long after her father's passing she had a dream, a vision of freedom for two of her most precious slaves and closest companions, the thought of which had stirred the deepest part of her soul. Gerrit the patriarch would not have praised her subsequent actions. Of this she had no doubt, but it was her choice to make and so she made it. The consequences were hers to hold forever.

Chapter 3

Although Marie was years younger than she, Margaret could never recall a time when she had not looked up into Zebulon and Eva's firstborn's face. Without a doubt, Marie had inherited her stature from her African Dinka father. But, her broad smile and open-hearted concern for those who were broken inside or out were all Mama Eva's doing.

The morning had begun with a gentle rain that soon had given way to blue skies. As Marie placed the ornately embossed, silver chocolate pot on the pedestal table, Margaret crossed the room to the spoon rack hanging on the wall. She began to collect several of the spoons the Albany silversmith had recently fashioned for her. "It smells delicious." Turning toward her server she asked, "Did you have a cup yourself?"

"I did, and it is as you suggest…delicious," Marie replied while carefully pouring the steamy liquid into a small, white English porcelain cup decorated with tiny rosebuds. Speaking in Dutch, Marie asked, "Are you feeling well, Mistress Peg?"

"Yes, well enough. Why do you ask? I do weary of my obligation to this portrait painting, yet this morn I find that I am tolerable."

" 'Tis good to hear."

Margaret lifted the cup to her lips and sipped the chocolate. "Oh, indeed it is so good to taste, and Mr. Lapett will be pleased for we all know how he loves the chocolate."

"Indeed, he does," Marie replied softly.

"Yes, as I say, I am well enough," Margaret sighed. "My concern is that I do not know what prevails outside these walls. I feel as if I have been closed away from all but Lapett's scrutinizing eye for years, rather than weeks." Sipping the last drop of chocolate, Margaret added, "And I tell you, I have felt that mischief may brew while I stand foolishly idle awaiting the painter. Duties sing out to me from every corner."

Marie observed her mistress curiously. "The mischief is long gone, and Monsieur Lapett asks if you are ready to receive him?"

"Yes, I am ready. Where is he? Bid him to come to me whenever he wishes to do so. Indeed, bid him come in all haste, for I pray that he brings with him the last of this ordeal!"

Glancing at the large painted canvass supported against the easel, Marie whispered her approval. "It is a true likeness of you, Mistress Peg. You stand as grand as any queen. You will make a good marriage with this man and be much blessed, of this I am certain, for a true heart is worth a crown of gold."

Margaret burst into laughter, adding sheepishly, "You think you see a queen? Oh, kindest of friends, I do thank you for your sweet words, yet I think you are blinded by your loyalties. Now then, go find Lapett before I grow too old for the bride's bedchamber."

Embarrassed that she had said too much, Marie scurried away like a mouse from under a broom.

By the window Margaret warmed her face in the morning sun. Closing her eyes, she thought of David and how he had kissed the palms of her hands when she had accepted his proposal of marriage. Holding her close against himself the man she longed to marry had looked straight into her eyes before placing his mouth upon her own, kissing her deeply. Her thoughts skipped along pleasantly, recalling their time in the garden the evening before he had departed for Albany. He had kissed her again, and again, in the same fashion, but this time as they embraced she had allowed his hand to cup her breast. She felt then and now as if she would swoon. Lost in her thoughts, she stared out the window wondering if David and John would return tomorrow.

"Have I startled you?" Benjamin Lapett called in a soft, tentative voice from the doorway. Seeing the usually steadfast Margaret leaning against the wall, pensively rubbing her temples, the artist had stopped short before entering the parlor. Quietly, he had stood beside the door to study the interesting persona before him. In recent days Lapett had begun to discover curiosities about Margaret that he had never before noticed. He had observed that the opulence of the attire she had chosen for her portrait presented an interesting paradox to the woman underneath. Hands scarred by decades of hard work yet bordered by lace intrigued him. He noted in particular the absence of a single glittering jewel. No golden adornment signifying her position as a member of the old and established affluent Dutch was visible. Instead, her slender neck was garnished merely with a necklace of hand-strung kernels of corn. Undoubtedly it was worn symbolically in proud remembrance of her mother's kinsmen, the people who had planted corn in New York soil for more than a thousand years, and was probably made from the Indian corn that she ground in her mill. Again, Lapett cleared his throat. "Might I enter?"

Startled, Margaret whirled around. "Yes, come in," she encouraged. Flush faced, she lowered her arms away from her head, waving him forward. "I am unaccustomed to this pretentious, braided arrangement that Marie has fashioned so tightly for me," she replied, telling a half-truth.

Mr. Lapett remained at the door. Until now, it hadn't occurred to him that Margaret's coiffure was a grand concoction endured solely for the benefit of her bridal portrait.

After a moment, Margaret collected herself enough to advance toward the spot in the room where she had grown accustomed to standing these last few weeks while posing. Her heavy, formal shoes made a clump-clump sound as she walked across the hard, wooden floor planks. She was far more accustomed to, and desirous of, wearing her moccasins or even her wooden Dutch shoes. She hoped that this would be the last day she must put up with such nonsense, and the last that her hair would be bound so tight. Still, she doubted that the completion of her likeness and subsequent letting down of her tresses would completely remedy her true ailment.

Lapett had not budged from the entrance. "Come in, please" she repeated, making a renewed effort to offer a gracious smile. "Forgive me. I fear that I've been so lost in womanish thought that I had completely forgotten the time. But, do come in Benjamin. The sight of you is most welcome."

The short, slender, man with the meticulously trimmed, gray beard wore bright blue, woolen breeches and a full leather apron over his white silk shirt. He proceeded toward his client's portrait which was braced against a large, handmade easel that stood at the opposite side of the room. As he passed her, Margaret noted the subtle, yet distinctive fragrance of rose water that accompanied him.

"My deepest apology for having kept you waiting, Peggy." Then he added quickly before Margaret could offer her forgiveness, "I went for a walk earlier and wandered much further than I had intended. The morn is so magnificent. I must confess that I myself was lost in thought along the river. When I returned, your Negro woman, Eva, offered me a bit of her honeycomb pudding, and how could I refuse? You know, Peggy, I am the weakest of creatures when it comes to such a dish; I cannot resist a bowl. I am so partial to the cinnamon. Scold, if you wish. I will not hold the least bit of grievance if you have a mind to do so, for I know that you must have had your fill of this tiresome schedule. I should have been more attentive to the hour."

Margaret held up one hand. "Your apology is not required, Benjamin. Truly, I long to release this mane, that is all," she said, absently pointing one finger toward the area of her discomfort. "But, I also had much to do at my desk. Come have a taste of chocolate."

"I am relieved to be forgiven," he replied as Margaret poured. "To be honest, I had hoped that my tardiness would be soon forgotten as I give you the good news." Margaret handed him his cup. After a sip, he sighed, "Ah, thank you—this is excellent."

"I would embrace good news," Margaret interjected, carefully placing the pot back onto the table.

"Earlier today, before my walk, I came into the parlor to assess the progress of your portrait. I believe now is the time to make my proclamation."

Margaret smiled. "And what is your esteemed judgment?"

"Stay the course, Mistress, and I promise that we will soon come to port."

Margaret's smile faded. The artist gave out a long deep sigh in response to her obvious disappointment.

"Do you still ask forgiveness?" she asked, matching his sigh with one of her own.

Lapett answered pensively. "Of course, I can see you are anxious to be done with all of this, and, of course, I can understand your feelings. Who could blame you for wishing a conclusion to all of this disruption, yet, as for me, this port of which I speak will be a sorrowful place. Once we arrive at our destination our artistic journey will have come to an end, and you will be done with me. The completion of your portrait offers me a mixed blessing of joy and regret. I sorely miss my family in the city, yet it is so beautiful and peaceful here, and I have enjoyed the work."

Stunned by what appeared to her to be his genuine sadness, Margaret replied, "Dear Benjamin, you have no idea how soothing your kind words come upon my ears. But you will not take your leave so soon I hope, and you will return with your wife and daughters for my wedding, will you not?"

"Of course we will be here. My ladies will see you wed, or I should be put to the rack."

"I am so pleased to hear you say so."

"Will your sister-in-law join us for the mid-day meal today?" Lapett asked, resuming a light-hearted tone.

"I do not believe that she will," Margaret returned, "I fear the squirrel and chestnut stew I brought up to her last night did not sit well with my sister-in-law, and of course—" Margaret paused to sigh. "Bess says the child within complains. She will keep herself apart from our company today, I should think."

"Oh," Lapett said, seeming disappointed.

"I can see that you have taken to her as have I. I have been happy having her here to keep me company whilst David and John are in Albany."

Lapett nodded his understanding. After a few more pleasantries, he cleared his throat. "Please do not misunderstand me or think me bold, but I sense something more troubles you than your coiffure or Bess."

Margaret replied. "Old friend, you have always been good at lifting the mask. I would speak with you in confidence. Shall we sit for awhile before we begin today?"

Seating herself, Lapett did the same.

Haltingly, Margaret began. "A letter...a letter came from our friend Anna Stoudt two days ago, and I had just finished re-reading her correspondence before you came. She writes of renewed troubles in the city, telling of a frightful ordeal that occurred within a household situated only a few streets away from her own house. And then yesterday morning, I received another dispatch, this one from Mary Beekman, which has left me quite bewildered. She and Colonel Beekman will be unable to come to the wedding. As you know, I am fond of the Colonel and Mary, and her regrets leave me distressed."

"I am truly sorry to hear this, but I am sure that if it were at all possible Henry would see to it that they would attend. What of her sister, Susanna?"

"She will not attend either, says Mary; she offers the excuse that they must all go to their cousin's in Kinderhook. I must say, Benjamin, this is so unlike Mary. She gives no explanation except to say that they regret this unavoidable conflict."

"Well, I am sure they are all as disheartened as you are, and I am equally certain that soon you will have a complete explanation. Try not to be too disappointed. It would be foolish to let the Beekman's absence overshadow your happiness, and I can not imagine Mary wishing such. But what of Anna's correspondence; tell me about this ordeal in New York that obviously has also given you great concern."

Margaret began to relate portions of the letter as she recalled them. "There was awful trouble with several Africans. Another near insurrection has taken place, I am afraid. One of those brought over on the *Elizabeth* attempted to kill his owner."

The artist sat straight in his chair, visibly shaken. "An insurrection?"

"Yes, but praises to heaven, the treachery was avoided when another servant overheard the murderous plot and did her duty," Margaret quickly replied.

"Odd that while in the city I did not hear anything about this," Lapett pondered. "The rebellion could not have been too severe or widespread. I would not think that it was as bad as what happened ten years ago. The troublemakers must have been swiftly caught. When did this occur?"

"Anna's letter was unclear, but I have in mind it must have been only a fortnight ago."

Lapett's face registered both confusion and concern. "Was Anna acquainted with the family?"

"No...alas I can not say," Margaret replied tentatively, believing she knew the root of this line of Lapett's question. "As I mention, Anna wrote that those involved had arrived on the *Elizabeth* which docked a year ago.

"The *Elizabeth*," Lapett repeated his tone full of disgust.

Margaret continued. "But she refers to a neighbor, a Mr. Dugan, as the slave's owner who was spared the African's wrath."

Lapett was contemplative. "I do not think that I am acquainted with any Dugan in the city."

"Benjamin, I have known Anna for many years and visited her before she was married, when her dear mother owned the house, so I know her street and yet throughout all of these years I have never heard of a Mr. Dugan. However, it was Captain Waldron's cook who bravely stepped forward. I pray that God blesses her for her courage. You know, of course, Will Waldron has long been a friend to Anna and to our family, yet he is also a man of few words. I can not think that the Captain would divulge the news of such a disturbance to Anna or to I. I should think he would feel it far too upsetting, he knowing the suffering we all had over Lizbeth."

Lapett smiled, replying, "The old Captain is a quiet man these days. I saw him at his brother's house last year."

"I have always liked him," Margaret replied softly.

"I think that you should take heart, Peggy, for it can not be as bad as you think. Yet, I am not shocked that such an occurrence would take place."

"Why would you say such a thing?"

"After the deadly trouble on the *Elizabeth*, the talk in the city was that her cargo was viewed as cursed by many who would normally have gone to the market seeking a fresh African. From all accounts, the captain had washed his hands of all wishing only to distance himself. I heard that the auctioneer was having a difficult time selling the lot of them. Only the roughest sort of a man, one seeking a bargain, would have been interested in bidding upon any of those aboard the *Elizabeth*."

"How pitiful," Margaret whispered.

"Lord knows what became of them all, but most assuredly most of the Elizabeth's cargo found a place in the fields of a Virginia planter."

Margaret sighed. "We have had this sort of discourse before, Benjamin, of slave ships captained by Christians, many renowned for their valor upon the seas. I have aught to wonder the prayers that they offer after the deliverance of such a shipment as the *Elizabeth* carried. I have been told that the Africans are always terrified as they disembark at the harbor."

Lapett's reply was terse. "The *Elizabeth* had a cargo doomed before the vessel left port."

Margaret added anxiously, "Anna is fearful that more trouble will come."

"Let us hope not, but if this bitter trade blustered by the English is to continue there must be a change of heart among those conducting such business. Still, after listening to the census taker I feel our country is seeded amidst a bed of corruption. I ask myself what captain has a Christian heart beating within his chest."

"I would not know."

"I have long valued our friendship Peggy, and would offer you peace of heart if I could do so."

Margaret's sadness edged toward frustration, her voice quivering as she spoke. "What hatred must swell up within the beaten man's heart that would press him to murder? Though I know others would think my feelings unsuitable business for a woman, should I speak truthfully I would still be glad to see the last of such ships reach our shores and the market itself burned to the ground. What is the sense of a bondage that turns a servant into a dangerous, godless beast, fit for nothing but vengeance?"

Lapett sighed, shaking his head. "Do not be deceived by what others may say. Your thoughts are shared by many men who would oppose this curse of slavery. Yet, you must know, my dear, that there are not enough of them to go against all of those who profit in the disposition of the Africans. In this colony the seasoned West Indian slave is worth his weight in gold on the block. The privateers these days are doing far better business than the Royal African Company who import directly from Africa. Though we may not think it so, the slave trader is highly respected in his business. Those who would protest for change could number a thousand voices, and yet I fear the clamor would fall upon deaf ears. We have done our part before, Peggy, and now we can do nothing but pray. We have no right to interfere with the British laws on trade. I caution you to keep such notions as the burning of the block to yourself."

Margaret whispered, "I understand."

Lapett leaned back into his chair, and the pair remained silent. Finally, he spoke. "I tell you true, I did sense something amiss as I departed the city. It was small chatter...broken lines of conversation that I overheard whispered by a few drunken sailors down by the wharf. I had assumed their talk to be just a bit of normal mischief. I had my family along seeing me off, and so, not wanting them to be abused by vulgar talk, we moved away from the rabble.

"It would be interesting to know how Anna knew of the murder attempt as I suspect the authorities would wish to keep the trouble a secret. It is better that the public is not aware of every evil deed that is committed, especially those of our Negroes, lest the whole city and the province be in panic. We had enough of that kind of madness a decade ago."

"Yes," Margaret agreed. "Madness is a proper description of those by-gone times."

Lapett continued. "There was talk six months ago of a conspiracy by poor whites and Africans to burn down the city, but of course the authorities must have had all of that well in hand, and no more was heard about it. 'Tis good I didn't know of this recent treachery or I would not have left my family alone these past weeks. Now I am considering whether those who were a nuisance six months ago were part of those from that same ship."

Margaret was obviously surprised by Lapett's comment. "Anna said nothing of burning the city, Benjamin. I thought the situation of which she spoke was an isolated incident. Now I am more concerned. The man who had conspired to kill his Master—the African to whom I refer now—was caught and swiftly dealt a righteous punishment. Anna said he was taken by the authorities and then executed, though I know not how or where. She didn't mention anything about the city being threatened by fire!"

Lapett shook his head in disbelief. A few moments ago he was wishing to linger an additional day or two, but now he longed to see his wife and children.

He noticed that Margaret suddenly seemed remote, and he imagined that his account of conspiracy in the city, although the insurrection had been quickly put down, had brought back severe and regretful memories.

"I should not have mentioned the plot for I have only made you more uncomfortable," he said. "I also share the old memories of the madness to which you often refer."

"Yes, Benjamin I know you do."

"I've been an insensitive fool," he said. "Please forgive me."

"Thank the Almighty that now it is all in the past, Benjamin. Yet, I find myself thinking of Lizbeth, and I often wonder if her death was not mine for the blame."

Lapett bolted to his feet. "How can you imagine such a thing?"

"I can because it was I who gave her her freedom and then arranged for her to go to the city. Had she not been there she would never have become a party to the scheme. Had she stayed at home she would be with us now and not laying within her grave."

Lapett was now beset with worry, as well as genuine regret, as he patted Margaret's hand reassuringly. "I understand better now what troubles you so deeply. But we must both keep our faith and trust in God that all of these recent troublemakers will be apprehended. Forgive me, Peggy, I should have been more careful in choosing my words when I spoke. I know these incidents draw your heart to the past, but you must give yourself some peace, my dear. You must resist the darkness of what has gone before; do not cause yourself to become ill. The girl's death was not your fault. You must believe that."

"I only wish that I could believe what you say, yet after all of this time I can still see her bright face, her sweet fingers stitching..."

"It is understandable that Anna's letter upset you so," Lapett consoled.

"I cannot forget our Lizbeth. I do not want to forget..." Margaret said softly, feeling herself glide toward tears.

"Margaret, consider this," Lapett said, anxious to pull her from the state of melancholy into which she was slipping. "You honor Lizbeth's memory by wearing this beautiful dress that she sewed for you with much love. Her excellent skills will be treasured for generations to come, for I have taken great care to combine every detail of your attire with your fine features."

Embarrassed by her unseemly display of emotion, Margaret attempted to recover. But it wasn't just the memory of that terrible time in her life which Anna's letter had resurrected. There was something more. The loss of Lizbeth had left deep scars, and as much as she fought it she was filled with the dread that something ominous was brewing for the future.

"Keep to your faith, Margaret. To be sure, she is with Our Lord." After a respectful moment of silence he added, "Shall we continue today? Perhaps you would prefer that I withdraw and we proceed on the morrow."

"No, let us continue," Margaret urged with a sigh. "I cannot dawdle further. I must have my portrait complete and hanging prior to the wedding. David has suggested that it would please him to have the likeness where it may be viewed by our guests."

"Are you most certain?"

"Pray continue," Margaret urged again, and Lapett began to mix his paints.

He would not admit as much, but Anna's letter had filled him with concern, as well as resurrecting a few regrets of his own with regard to Lizbeth. He had encouraged Margaret in her desire to free Lizbeth. It had been his good wife who had been supportive, suggesting possible positions for the girl within the city.

He recalled an opinion Margaret's father had once shared with him. An elderly Gerrit had insisted that to cast out one's Negro into the darkness of freedom was an injustice to the servant who had no knowledge of the outside world, and no means to care for himself. Peggy had always disagreed with her father's viewpoint with regard to their slaves, and how dear the cost had been to her.

Lapett recalled how, many years prior, they had worked together in the city to bring the newly arrived Africans to Christ. Sponsored by the Venerable Society, in a Manhattan building within sight of both Trinity Church as well as the slave block, several of them had ministered to the poor whites and Negroes of the community. For a good number of years there were no insurrections. Life amidst the colony proceeded in an orderly fashion. The Africans, both slave and freed, moved among the Colonists and about the city at will. Alongside immigrant Elias Neau, a Huguenot refugee turned Anglican catechist—who at one time had been scheduled to die on the gallows in France—they had all given their hearts and lent their hands to the teachings of Christ. They were the first to work with Elias whose own life was spared, as Elias would later jokingly remark, "through the grace of God and banishment from France by King Louis XIV."

As he painted, Lapett thought that in some ways Margaret and the woman of twenty years ago differed very little. The wide-eyed, impressionable country girl who his neighbor, Mrs. Reed, had introduced to his then equally wide-eyed and impressionable young wife had become a hardy businesswoman whose sympathies toward those who suffered had not been diluted by time. Over two hundred were baptized.

But then came the terrible uprising within the city and poor Lizbeth's untimely death. Later Margaret had used the modest church at Claverack as a classroom for teaching a small group of Indian children the Christian Gospel. Renewing her promise that not one soul would be left behind without benefit of baptism, she had reunited with some of the original group, and they were able to rescue a few more from the streets of the city. But the classes had lasted only a short time before their cherished Elias was laid to rest in Trinity churchyard.

Obviously overwrought and tired, Margaret stood nobly for her portrait, and Lapett found himself wishing that her marriage to David Karski would be a happy one. If any woman was entitled to happiness it was she whose life, by many accounts, had passed from childhood into maidenhood and beyond under Gerrit Vandenberg's cold and indifferent parental roof.

Chapter 4

John Vandenberg met Evert Wendell at Lansing's tavern. Situated along the King's Highway, the inn was only a stone's throw from Albany's west gate blockhouse. At forty two, John felt that Wendell's appearance hadn't changed much at all during the years since they had last met, although Wendell's profession and circumstances were remarkably different. When last they had dealings together, Evert was unmarried, and meandering in the fur trade business far to the west in Onondaga country. In those days he made his largest profits from selling liquor that he advertised as the strongest drink to be had in all the colonies. Having past sampled Wendell's product on one or two occasions, John could attest to the validity of the claim.

Wendell had long since given up selling hard liquor. Now a highly respected Albany attorney, in addition to having made a small fortune in the lucrative Albany fur trade, Evert Wendell exclusively handled the grievances of Dutch speaking clients such as Margaret Vandenberg. Though fluent in English as well as the Dutch, Margaret spoke highly of Wendell. She had engaged him several times over the last decade on various matters, and had suggested that John meet with the attorney while he and David were in Albany. Margaret had thought it was a good idea that John discuss with Wendell what they had in mind to do concerning the division of a piece of land that he and Margaret owned jointly.

John had barely dismounted when he heard Wendell's familiar robust voice call out to him from the tavern door. "John, John! What a sight you are to see! How long has it been?"

Stepping forward, John returned the salute with equal enthusiasm, "Good to see you, *Lawyer Wendell.*"

The tall, wide-shouldered man grinned broadly, "Ah, yes, I hear the joviality in your greeting and I can see, Vandenberg, that you restrain your mirth when addressing me thus. Understandable to be sure, but a man must change his life when he marries and makes a family, so I will not hold it against you."

Laughter escaped as John tied his mount to the post and entered the tavern. "Well said," John replied slapping the lawyer on the back. "I suspect my sister wrote to you that I also have a wife. She is large with child and at home with my sister."

"God's blessings, and so you begin with your first. I have six of my own, but like you, John, I was an older groom and slow to the march. Twenty years ago, I was the most wicked of adventurers of the westward wilds and would never have seen myself as a domesticated man who dries the tears of babes. But God's will be done. Come, let us sit. The rum in this place must be tolerated as barely palatable, but they do have good beer. They get it from old Brew master Ryckman down near the river…"

"Captain Ryckman is still brewing? He must be eighty years old or more. Will Waldron of Manhattan, to whom I was apprenticed, crafted barrels that I delivered."

Searching the dimly lit room for a serving wench, Wendell added, "Ah there she be." He yelled across the boisterous din, "Two tankards, Jennie, and say to my friend the proprietor over yonder that I bid he draw the brew from the freshly arrived barrels from Ryckman."

The young black girl juggling several plates of hot food at a table on the far side of the room nodded in Wendell's direction.

John observed his companion whose thick, long brown hair worn fashionably tied behind had not a strand of silver. He said, "You look none the worse for the wear of a family."

"I have no complaints. My wife is a genteel, handsome woman, and she is as strong minded as she is beautiful. It is to my wife that I give all the credit for my success, for she was the one who insisted that I lay monies aside for the purchase of real estate to our betterment."

Jennie appeared with two large pewter tankards, placing one before each customer. John lifted his first, "A toast then to marriage and our wives."

"To the women and a serene house," Wendell replied emphatically lifting his tankard, swiftly drinking down half the serving. "Ah...yes, satisfying like none other."

As they finished their toasts, the door was thrown open, and several more travelers piled into the already crowded room, including the coach driver who flung an assortment of mail onto a side table. The coachman stood in the middle of the room and bellowed out, "Here ye, Here ye—Post!" Proprietor Lansing, muttering insults directed at the driver, rushed to the table to collect the correspondence for safe keeping.

Wendell sighed. "Poor Lansing must be constable as well as tavern master or I fear none would see a written word."

Smiling, John nodded his agreement. "How is your brother Ephraim?"

"He prospers and has his health, thanks be to God."

In a quieter tone John said. "I thank you for meeting me. I understand you are a man with many burning fires."

Wendell said, "No need. I was pleasantly surprised to receive your sister's communication, and our arrangement offered me occasion to come up here. I was delighted, of course, to hear of your sister's impending marriage, although I do not believe that I know of the gentleman who is to be the groom."

"There is no reason that you should know him. He is an outsider who I have had the good fortune to come to know over the last years."

"I had hoped that he would accompany you today, and that I should be able to make his acquaintance."

"I left David across the river at our cousin, Cornelius Vandenberg's farm. My cousin has a contract with the city of Albany to provide several eleven foot tall oak beams made round by eight inches or more that are to replenish those gone bad along the stockade fencing."

"I am happy that Mayor Myndert Schuyler has finally opened the city's purse for the matter. Many years ago when Johannes Bleecker was mayor of Albany, he pushed for repairs to the city's wall and it was done, but much of the wood has deteriorated. 'Tis best we repair it and do so in all haste that we be secure should the French have a mind to attack." Wendell took another swallow of beer and then added thoughtfully, "I am acquainted with Vandenberg, and I have been to his farm. He has a fine looking bull at his place."

"So he has," John agreed. "I would have stayed at the farm for longer to help with the work, but for the invitation of Indian friends whose sachem bid me come to him. The chief, who I would not wish to offend, had heard that I was married, and wished to present me with a few beaver skins that I should take home to my new wife with his good wishes. After his squaws filled my sack with the furs, he then insisted that I stay the night that we might make merry with all the brethren and dance."

Wendell nodded his understanding. "One can not go against fair custom between those we consider brothers. It was well enough that you went. Will not your wife be pleased to have the extra pocket monies those pelts will bring to her!"

John nodded. "She is in want of nothing, yet desirous of a kas of her own for the house. The skins will provide the money for the cupboard and more."

"I could take a look at them and make you a fair offer?"

"Thank you, but I would take the furs home to my wife first before I trade them. I am anxious to return before my child is born. I have been away more than at home these past months, spending much time sitting by Mohawk counsel fires in the capacity of interpreter for Colonel Greenwood. "

"I understand completely," Wendell replied.

The two sat quietly for a moment, drinking their beer and listening to a conversation at the adjacent table. Two men were in a heated discussion regarding the great number of New York Palatines living by the rivers; who had in recent months flocked to Pennsylvania. It seemed that the Hessians were taking up the invitation from Pennsylvania Deputy Governor, Sir William Keith, to relocate to a more opportune and perhaps hospitable area. Obviously land owners themselves, the two travelers were irate that their tenant farmers had up and left them holding an empty sack just before harvest season. John wondered what this would mean to Margaret's Hessians.

Wendell turned, spotting the serving wench a few tables away. "Two more, Jennie!" Growing more sober he asked, "Well, John, I know that you are here on other matters; how can I assist you?"

John began to describe the property that Margaret had suggested that he use for his own. She and he had talked about it a short time after he had returned to their northern plantation last summer. He explained further that he had cleared the lot, building a small house for he and his wife. "With being a married man and my sister soon to be the wife of David Karski, it is better that we make the proper changes to the deeds. My sister has employed Phillip Verplauck, a land surveyor from near Kingstown, who will come to do the work after Mr. Karski and my sister are wed. We would have you come down to witness the proceedings and write the documents for us at the same time, if you are willing."

"Send word to me when the time comes, and I will accommodate you and Mistress Vandenberg, or should I say Mrs. Karski?"

John retorted, "She can not turn back now. She has already declared her engagement, publicly signing the engagement contract papers before three witnesses, and her bridal portrait is nearly completed. The artist is a man she met in New York. His name is Lapett. Do you know of him?"

"No, I do not believe that I do."

"Well, no matter. My sister says that other than the freedom papers she signed years ago for her Lizbeth and Marie, this contract is the most important of all documents she has ever lifted her quill to sign."

"'Tis true. For any woman it is the most precious document to bear her name. No turning about the cart and bolting can be considered after signing," Wendell offered half jesting.

John became serious. "I wish only to do what is right by her," he said. "Peggy has been a loving sister to me, and she has done far better than might be expected for someone standing with one foot in the Christian world of the whites, whilst the other lingered behind with the heart of an Indian. Much was forbidden her that as a man was left to my pleasure. I have begged her forgiveness for my neglect these many years whilst I was away from home, knowing how she has endured a great weight upon her shoulders. I was successful in my dealings out west. Mr. Karski and myself found copper and mined it for three years before selling it."

"Ah, I see. Have you heard of Arent Schuyler? He did the same, and the copper mine, along with the boards he ships to Manhattan, has made him a wealthy man."

John nodded his understanding. "I have always believed that my father's properties are filled with untapped riches. I have pressed upon my sister that I would explore these possibilities, but she balks at the idea. I fear that she is not altogether happy that I have come home to stay."

Wendell interjected anxiously, "I have it from her own hand John that she is delighted that you have returned. Of course, your sister thought you a dead man, and I doubt not that seeing you much alive and in good health filled her with immense happiness. I would assume too that presenting an agreeable husband for her has sweetened your reconciliation. I have always found your sister a generous woman who responds to honesty in kind. Still, let me give you a bit of advice that I offer at no charge. Women do not take well to changing the landscape of their properties, anymore than they welcome change within their house."

Obviously perplexed, John answered flatly. "I am doing all that can be done."

Having discussed a few more of the particulars of contract possibilities as well as Margaret's wedding, the two finished their drinks, bidding each other farewell. At the door Lawyer Wendell explained that unfortunately he would not be able to attend the joyous celebration, he having another commitment. He had already sent his regrets.

As John departed the tavern and rode back toward his cousin's farm he thought about the troubling discourse that had transpired between he and his sister in recent weeks, the root of which was the division of duties now that he had returned. He meant what he had said to their lawyer, but how could he pick up the shepherd's staff and make a right of things when it seemed that Peggy resented every one of his suggestions? He was accustomed to dancing in the company of men, but dancing around the changing whims of a woman, especially one with such a stubborn nature, was another matter.

He would think upon Wendell's advice. When he returned he would say that he begged forgiveness for acting like an ungrateful brother. He would remind Peggy that they were children of the Clan of the Turtle, bound together as such, and that he loved her the same as when they were children. Were not all the riches of the earth a gift from the Creator? He would approach her with a straight eye. Yes, she would come around to the possibilities of his proposals. He had only to make her understand that he was a renewed man. With his friend and partner's help it would be done. The Prodigal Son had returned.

Chapter 5

In the dimly lit bedchamber of early morning, Margaret lay in her bed propped up against feather pillows. Mama Shasa massaged her feet with a buttery ointment that the Indian servant woman had made from ground sage and wild spearmint picked the day before from the leaf-covered floor of the grove of white wood trees near her cabin. Shasa's eleven year old daughter, Betty, barefooted, diligently attended to her assigned task of turning the bedchamber's ceiling fan.

"The heat is already dreadful today, is it not?"

"Yes, Mistress."

"Ah, Shasa," Margaret purred, "your hands are a blessing. Though I can not think why it should be so, both my legs and feet ache to the depth of my core this morning."

"Shasa will make the pain run away to the hills," the Tuscaroran said, moving her hands to the leg calf as she continued with the deep massage.

"Ah, yes, good. The ointment is cooling to the skin. Oh, my poor feet. Whatever must I do to get them into my shoes again. It burns me that I am put upon by these hurts and can not accomplish the work that must be done."

Marie, who had been busy with her needlework by the window, looked up. "Peter and Sally are fast at work in the garden pickin' beans, but soon they will be finished with the pickin'. I will tie this off now and go down and have the young ones go to the creek to fetch a bucket of cool water. You might at least soak your feet and be cooled."

"What a delightful thought. A bucket of water would be most welcome."

Closing her wicker sewing basket, Marie rose. "Mamma is cooking the partridge with the beans for midday meal."

Examining a sore, swollen toe, Margaret said, "I can not think of eating partridge with my feet afire, Marie, but perhaps by and by I will be more tolerable. Have Peter bring up two buckets of cool water." Glancing at the elder servant woman she said, "How say you, Shasa? Would you and Betty not welcome dipping your toes in a bucket? Would that not be to your liking, Betty?"

The child smiled, "Yes, Mistress."

Departing the bedchamber, obviously annoyed by Margaret's special attention toward the others, Marie's reply was laced with sarcasm. "I will have Sally bring up the large majolica basin for you, Mistress Peg. Peter will bring up a full bucket and fill your washbasin. I should think that enough water will be left over for the servants to dip their toes. "

After Marie left the room Margaret observed Betty. "You please me with your work, child, and I have a mind to keep you here at the house and to put you alongside of Sally to be trained by Marie in other duties."

Betty, her eyes pleading for her mother's support, was obviously frightened by the prospect of moving into the big house and being under Marie's tutorage.

"You would miss her sorely not being by you in the beginning, Shasa, yet it would be far better for the girl. And we will need the extra hands when Bess gives birth."

"Yes, Mistress," Shasa replied.

Addressing Betty, who continued at her duty teary eyed, Margaret cajoled "Come, come now. Do not weep, child. I know the heart of a young girl separated from her mother. We shall wait until after I am wed, but it is good that you know my desires on this matter."

Shasa nodded, sealing the covenant. "Thankin' you Mistress for your kindness to us," she croaked.

"Then it be settled. Betty, your Mistress is not so different from you though our home countries are far apart. My mother was of the River Nations, her people being Mohicans and Munsee who had lived here along the North River since Almighty God created this valley. In those times the Great Creator was known by the Lenape as Kishelemukong." Betty stared back at Margaret wide-eyed, bewildered that her Mistress would speak to her so plainly.

"Do you understand me child?"

Although she did not, Betty nodded.

"As our friends who live by the Munsee creek tell us, the ground upon which this fine house and all the other buildings stand was always a special place of trading for our people. It is believed that the stars of the heavens tell the olden story of the hunt of the great black bear. Have you been told the story of the great black bear?"

Betty glanced anxiously at her mother and back to Margaret. "Nay, Mistress," she stammered.

"Surely you have heard the story, Shasa?"

"Nay, I hear no such tale, Mistress."

"It pleases me to tell you of it as my mother told me, so be done with your duties and sit by me. It makes no sense to put on more ointment if I am to cool my poor feet in the basin."

Shasa did as she was bid and wiped her hands on her apron, after which Betty helped her mother as she struggled to sit down on the bare, wide planked floor.

Margaret began, "The ancestral chase is begun in springtime as the big, sleepy beast comes forth from his slumber. If it be God's will, he survives. If soon killed, the heat of summer melts the fat. Thus, sap runs down the bark of the trees. In the fall when the bear is wounded his blood turns the leaves of the trees red, but when in winter they have killed it, the snow is made of the bear's fat. And so it is not only with the bear, but also with all living things. To each season and creature there is a purpose. They are all connected. It is not so different between men and the bear. As each new human being comes into the world, he or she begins a new journey. Soon, we pray God, a new babe will be born here on the farm and begin a journey. All the people, the animals, and the birds of the sky are a part of the circle of life. Like the bear, each of us has a purpose—even you, young Betty. Each of us affects the world around us just as the world around us affects us." Addressing Shasa, "You have been given the gift of healing. I wonder, will your girl inherit the skill of the mother?"

"She be learnin' Mistress," Shasa replied quickly.

"It is my desire that you teach her everything you know about the plants of the forest and show her how to use her hands that they may give comfort to those afflicted."

"I teach her."

"I think too, when it comes Bess's time, Betty should accompany you for the birthing. We shall think of it as a part of her training."

Margaret's lesson and queries were interrupted by the clamor of Peter bringing in the heavy bucket. Marie, close on his heels gave stern direction. "Careful now, boy: do not spill a drop when you fill up the Mistress' basin or you will hear my displeasure." Tipping the bucket, Peter carefully directed the fresh water into the majolica. Margaret quickly followed with first one foot and then the other. "Yes, yes, oh that is good."

"I would have both to you," Marie said apologetically, "but the other bucket was far too heavy for Sally to carry. I put her to work in the kitchen snapping the beans. Go now, Peter, off with you, and fetch the other in all haste."

Margaret chuckled. "Marie, you are on the boy like a hound on a fox."

Frowning as she followed the slave boy out of the room, Marie called over her shoulder. "You might laugh all you like, but I know how that one chases the squirrels. He be as absentminded as he is lazy and be assured, Peg, if you do not poke him often he would be off sleepin' in the reeds. Henry says so himself."

"I hear your words, woman, but I think you and Henry fret too much," Margaret whispered half to herself, recalling that Zebulon had nearly gone into a fit when John had suggested that Zeb's grandson Peter be made new keeper of the cows.

In the silence that followed Marie and Peter's departure, Margaret again thought about how grateful she was for the steadfastness of Shasa's quiet presence. Once again the Indian woman had brought in her goodness. As she thought back about her brothers' purchasing the Tuscaroran and her son,

Spotted Bird, from the Carolina block all those years ago she again realized that it had been a right decision, although well she remembered how Teunis had fought with John over the purchase. Now she wished that Teunis were alive and with them today so that he could see the value of this fine family that he would have denied entry to Vandenberg lands.

Soon Peter lumbered in with the second filled bucket. Margaret ordered him to divide the water between the two wooden containers. "You boy, return to Mistress Marie and await her bidding."

Peter bowed, quickly disappearing out of sight.

Shortly thereafter, squeals of delight echoed through the house as Shasa and her daughter both dipped their toes. "Now dry your feet and be off with the two of you. Before you return to your cabin look in on James down at the mill. Sally told Eva this morning that her uncle is in a sore way, as he has what looks to be a spider bite and his arm is red and swollen. The girl says he is feverish."

As her servants left the room, with Shasa sure that she had a proper remedy for the bite, Margaret was already making a mental note to speak with John about the white trees in the grove near Shasa's cabin that soon must be cut down. They could use another canoe or two, and this type was the best to hollow out for that purpose. She would tell John to have Henry put one of the men to this task. She and her brother also needed to discuss the number of oak and elm that should be harvested from a small section of the forest. With peaceful times upon them, Manhattan city's streets boomed with carpenters and bricklayers building new dwellings. Though not on such a grand scale, the city of Albany had also become a busy hub. The lumber in the Manhattan and Albany market places would bring them a very good price right now. She would talk to John about meeting with the building merchants in the cities. She also thought about the game within those groves. Although she suspected that John would argue that their forests were not over-hunted, it had been many years since she had seen the deer run together thirty or more at a time. There were still Munsee living along the creek; the wildlife and fruits of the forest must be considered.

As Margaret hobbled around the room searching for her moccasins, Sally suddenly appeared at the door.

"Mistress I have been sent to give you sad tidings."

Margaret froze, preparing herself for the worst.

"Mistress Bess' bad hound has eaten your prize peacock!"

Chapter 6

Prosperity hasn't excluded the affluent Margaret Vandenberg from life's struggles. The offspring of a common yet highly ambitious Colonial Dutchman and a Lenape Indian woman, she was born to hard work. From childhood she knew the taste of her own salty perspiration dripping down her face, and how it felt to fall into her bed numb with exhaustion that came after chores done sunup till sundown.

Before Margaret was seven she knew how to tend a fire and her lessons in cookery had begun, learning early the intricacies of putting together a meal that would stick to the ribs on a cold day. Along with her young cousins, the girls were taught how to prepare a good stew of Samp, including soaking the hard corn kernels and ashes from burned tree stumps overnight in water. During much of the autumn harvest season, her mother's Samp porridge recipe, a concoction of venison, corn, and beans, was eaten daily at the midday eleven o'clock meal. It tasted the best though (her father always said) after the stew had simmered in the pot for a week or more. Strawberries, blueberries, and blackberries picked in early summer were dried on racks placed high over the fire. Berry picking was a time of praise and celebration among the native peoples of all New York, a custom that her Indian mother had incorporated into her Dutch husband's home. Margaret could not remember when she had not fished the waters of her country. Next to her horses, fishing was always her greatest passion. From her mother's cousin, One Who Stands Tall, as small children still living with her mother's people, she and John learned how to effectively stake a shad; springtime shad bakes on the farm were favorite meals of her father's when her mother was alive. Her memories of those times were good, but they were also tinged with the realities of frontier life. Margaret also knew the look and feel of hands cracked bloody raw from work, the bite of a snake in the grassy fields, and the threat and misery of smallpox.

With honey-bronzed skin and perceptive, flashing dark eyes set above high cheekbones, the whole of Margaret's being provides a rather troubling visible reminder of so many who have been expunged or evicted by the white Europeans. She is fully aware that she sits upon a confusing piece of center ground for many of her prosperous white neighbors living up and down the banks of the North River highway. She is, after all, a half-breed, a flesh and blood living monument lodged amid them, a constant reminder of their own inability to either properly corral or to accept the native inhabitants of the land which they now call their country. The feelings of the whites, her mother had explained, would never change, and for the most part Margaret had found her mother's words to be true. Colonial Christian New Yorkers did not ignore the baptized Indian woman who carries her Dutchman father's name, but neither did they look upon her with genuine love as scripture instructed. Despite close, lifelong, personal relationships between her Vandenberg kinsman and the Van Rensselaer family, as well as with other prominent families in the American Colonies, and in spite of her acres of holdings, to many she knew that she was known only as the "high-brow Indian woman". Affluence, Margaret understood early on, was never, nor would it ever be, an effective shield against the hurtful stigma of prejudice.

* * * *

Margaret's father, Gerrit Vandenberg, was a tall, slender, serious-minded widower approaching the mid portion of his life, when in the year 1676 he wed the sixteen-year-old maiden then called Gentle Heart Born Under A Full Moon. The story that Gerrit had liked to tell his children as they sat around their hearth on cold winter nights began with the fact that his old friend Mathais Thomas had introduced him to their Indian mother. It was a tale told often in the old days, and yet Margaret would remember that the words to the familiar family narrative never seemed to grow stale. Those memories remained vivid, even the way their father held his long stem clay pipe. The second line of the introduction to the remembrance would come as he glanced in the direction of their mother. He would add reflectively that if Matty had not been a shoemaker in New England in the old days, then most likely he would not have a story to tell. He would jest that it was his big Dutch feet that had given him a second wife, another son, and a daughter. Margaret remembered that her mother would not look away from her beading, but would always smile as her husband began in depth.

Mathias Thomas came from England across the ocean by himself when he was not much more than a boy. An orphan whose passage had been paid by his uncle back in England, he landed in the Crown Colony at Boston in September of 1653, soon afterwards traveling to Wethersfield where he made his home along the Connecticut River on the farm of immigrant Englishman, Luke Hitchcock, an old friend of his uncle's, and his wife Elizabeth. On the Hitchcock farm he labored alongside of Luke and his young son, John, and he learned the shoemaking trade. A number of years later Matty took the Freeman's oath, announcing to all that he was now to be acknowledged as a man free of debt owing nothing to any other mortal. Matty would most likely have stayed a New England man for life, Gerrit emphasized, but for God calling Luke Hitchcock. When Luke Hitchcock died and his wife remarried, deciding to move with her new husband William Warriner and her children to Springfield, Matty decided he'd move on too, but in a bold new direction.

In 1664 the English took New Netherland from the Dutch. While Dutchmen within the newly named New York struggled to keep their wits during those trying days, it seems that the word around Wethersfield was that there were renewed opportunities to be had for an Englishman on Manhattan Island, especially a free tradesman. Though Luke Hitchcock's widow did her best to dissuade him, warning that the conquered Dutch peoples of the former New Netherland might not look kindly upon an Englishman, Matty said his goodbyes, and with his few belongings placed into a sack thrown over his shoulder, he headed to New York.

The Englishman would often make it plain that he was greatly surprised by the variety of immigrants he met at the city that many still called "the Dutch town". The settlers of New York bewildered him at first. They were far more of a mixture of displaced citizens from every part of the world than the clusters of Englishmen found throughout New England to which he had been accustomed. What astonished the Englishman all the more was how amicable the people were amongst themselves—and to him. Despite past differences and differing backgrounds, they, for the most part, got along well, and Matty got along with everyone.

However, he wasn't to stay in the city for long after hearing of an opportunity to join another shoemaker as his assistant. He soon moved beyond the planked wall to live at Harlem with the family of Cornelius Jensen. It was here that Gerrit Vandenberg, then a young farm hand on the neighboring Waldron farm, made his acquaintance. A few years later Matty said his goodbyes once again and relocated himself further north into the territory of the Sinanoy Indians.

Nobody knew exactly why Matty had suddenly left Harlem. He had done well with his craft and seemed to get on well with Jensen. Perhaps it was his inherent wanderlust. Gerrit would say that Matty's rambling heart wasn't satisfied until he moved to the wilderness of the big woods beside the Walkill River. It was here, many miles north of New York near the village of Esopus that he and his pioneering friend were to rekindle their friendship.

Gerrit knew of the lucrative fur trade flourishing along the North River between New York and Albany because it was often a topic of conversation. In the early years of his first marriage he had tried to convince his Dutch wife to make the move northward, but she would have none of it. She said she would never move far from her mother. She would not suffer the pain of loneliness as her own poor mother had done when her mother had emigrated from Holland to New Amsterdam.

After his first wife's death Gerrit still had a mind to try his luck elsewhere. Perhaps a change would quell his and his boy's grief. Midway north, he and Teunis stopped at the inn at Esopus, and there he rediscovered his old friend. Gerrit, tired and hungry, from his day's journey, nearly bumped into him at the inn door. They quickly renewed there friendship over a couple of pints. It was as if it had never been interrupted.

As it came to pass it was Matty who would lead Gerrit to a new life and a new wife. It was Matty, Gerrit said, who had told him about the value of a set of good snow shoes and discouraged him from making his own, saying that during the harsh winters of the thick wooded North Country a man could not gather firewood or hunt small game without benefit of decent snowshoes. Matty bragged that he knew the best place to trade for such a set of snowshoes. It was not a secret. Everyone knew that the Indian village women of whom he spoke were the best crafters. Besides good snow shoes, they made strong, beautifully beaded moccasins tanned from the hides of moose, as well as excellent buckskin leather leggings. In the past year the women of that village had made two hundred pairs of moccasins, many of which were of outstanding quality, catching the eye of wealthy womenfolk in the city, so one had to act quickly to make a trade himself before the merchants sent their traders.   Matty spoke to Vandenberg of the harsh winters in a place so far from Harlem, adding this warning: if a man and his young boy were to survive in this wilderness, it was of utmost importance to find a wife as soon as possible. An Indian woman would be best. With such a woman beside him, he and his son would stay alive, because an Indian woman knew the land and how to endure it.   Choosing a squaw over another Dutch woman was the best way to ensure success, and he knew this to be the truth because he had found such a woman himself among the Sinanoy tribe. Though in his estimation the women of the Sinanoy did not have as natural a gift for beading as others, his squaw woman was as strong as any ox.

Gerrit had listened and taken the advice to heart. He soon accompanied his friend to the small, native village deep within the woods where the women were esteemed for their hand work. It was not all that long thereafter, once again, that the widower found himself no longer a man alone.

Dominie Hendrickson of the Dutch Calvinist faith married Gerrit and his second wife under the low-slung, thatched roof of Matty Thomas' humble log cabin, situated on Muskrat Island, a stone's throw from Esopus. The only witnesses to the binding ceremony that the Dominie had been gently encouraged to perform on that cold, rainy April day, were old Baron Resolved Waldron, who came from New Harlem with his son, Barent, and son-in-law, John Nagel. Also present were Gerrit's ten-year-old son, Teunis, and, of course, his good friend, Matty, who along with his three little barefoot boys stood sober-faced beside Matty's own Indian wife as she held their sleeping infant son.

As far as Vandenberg was concerned, no church roof need be over his head, nor were recordings of the marriage necessary. A Christian minister of the Lord, accompanied by a proper witness, had wed him and Gentle Heart (who henceforth would be known to her white Christian neighbors as Ruth Vandenberg). That was all that was necessary. But he also understood that there in the wilderness, to make a good peace with his wife's people, he would have to bow to her relatives' traditional Indian spiritual beliefs. If he was to achieve the lofty goals he had painstakingly set out for himself, he would be wise to marry according to her customs.

Prior to their marriage, at Gerrit's insistence, Gentle Heart's mother had consented to Christian instruction for herself and her daughter, and the two had traveled southward along with Gerrit toward Manhattan Island where the Indian women received the holy waters. As the story went, after the wedding, through an interpreter, the bride's mother made herself clearly understood. The marriage made by the white holy man between her beautiful young daughter and the skinny Dutchman was all well and good, yet she would not sanction the union until her daughter was married according to tribal rite. Gerrit conceded that it served no purpose to alienate his new wife's mother, aunts and grandmother, since the possibility of any transfer of land to his holdings was finalized only upon the approval of these Indian women. Three days later, Gerrit and Gentle Heart were united again according to the traditions of the Lenape people.

Margaret could recall several of the old stories that her father had recounted when she was only a child. The one she seemed to enjoy telling the most began with her parents Lenape wedding day. The sun had shown brightly, a good sign of things to come, said the elders of her mother's tribe. Gentle Heart walked beside her own mother, the two of them accompanied in a happy procession of female cousins and aunts toward her new husband to whom Gentle Heart had offered a gift of corn bread, a symbol of her labor. The bread, which would normally have been presented to the bride's future mother-in-law, was given to the groom since Gerrit's mother was not present, having long since passed to her heavenly reward.

Gerrit respectfully exchanged Gentle Heart's gift of the bread for his gift of freshly killed deer meat, which he gave to his new bride. The meat represented the labor that he would provide. In short, the lives of husband and wife would be a partnership of labor, each with expected tasks. The simple ceremonial words were spoken in Munsee, a dialect of the Algonquin language, and were followed by sumptuous feasting. Later, as was customary, Gerrit and Gentle Heart began their married lives together, along with Teunis, in the palisade village of Gentle Heart's mother.

Raven black ringlets wetly plastered to her tiny head, Margaret was born the following spring, announcing herself to everyone in her grandmother's elm-barked longhouse with a fierce cry. The elder Lenape said that the child's wail reminded her of the big cats that sometimes roamed the cliffs near the edge of the river. She was named Margaret by her father in honor of his maternal grandmother.

Eleven months later, baby brother Johannes, always called John, came quickly and easily during the stillness of the night, his head covered with curious fuzzes nearly the color of the snow dusting the ground. For some years thereafter, Gentle Heart and Gerrit Vandenberg's young children, as well as the boy by his previous marriage, all thrived within the Indian community, the family lovingly nurtured by relatives, all of them members of the enormous Clan of the Turtle.

A shy, golden-haired boy who had spent most of his early childhood within the rigid confines of the Old Dutch Calvinist village of Harlem a half day walking distance from New Amsterdam, Teunis grew independent and strong among the free-spirited natives who taught him to hunt and fish. Within a short time he spoke the local Indian dialect. As he listened by the campfire to the ancient legends of his adopted Indian family who called themselves the *Human Beings*, he eagerly awakened to the deep cultural roots of his stepmother's people.

Gerrit's new wife also learned the customs of the Dutch from her husband's firstborn. Teunis taught her to speak Dutch quite well, and soon she clung to his renditions of favorite Biblical stories. As his Dutch mother had taught him, Teunis also trained his new mother Ruth to play quite proficiently at cards.

Vandenberg was not the only white man arriving in New Amsterdam with little else of his own except the shirt on his back, but he was one of the few who, through an Indian union coupled with resolute perseverance, ultimately become a wealthy land baron. A Native American connection allowed many, by way of the clan mark, or a simple "x" placed upon a penned deed of their own language, to acquire vast stretches of rich river valley land.

He told his children that, prior to his first marriage, as a seventeen-year-old soldier attached to the service of the Dutch West India Company; he had scorned what he believed then to be a "sore mix of the flesh". When they winced, he would, on occasion add that he was ashamed of the foolish words of his youth. Sometimes he would add that he may well have been one of the few newcomers to marry an Indian woman who was completely satisfied with his decision. Their time together was good, and he was much pleased.

Generally this was how her father would conclude the evening's stories.

In a few years, Heart was called by God. Thereafter, her family spent many nights sitting before the burning embers in silence. Gerrit would never completely recover. He never told the stories again. Margaret's recollections of the early years of her life were often her only source of peace.

Chapter 7

Land speculation was in the minds and hearts of nearly all colonists, and young Gerrit Vandenberg was no different. For the seventeenth century common man arriving on American shores the prospect of owning property in the old country had been only a dream. His cousin, Arent, a corporal with the West India Company serving at Fort Orange, sent letter upon letter home to his relatives in Holland encouraging them all to come over, yet Gerrit's father urged him to stay away from the wilderness of Fort Orange and the grip of the Van Rensselaers' serfdom. When an opportunity for service at the New Amsterdam post arose, though he was barely seventeen, his father encouraged him to depart for America. From the time Gerrit boarded the *King Solomon* at Amsterdam bound for the new world to weeks later disembarking onto a busy New Amsterdam wharf, he had done nary else but to think of how to elevate his life through property acquisition.

He was not yet twenty when he partnered with another young soldier stationed at New Haarlem which consisted of approximately twenty families at that time. The two young men pooled their limited resources to purchase a lot. They had thought that they would like to grow tobacco, but that plan was never to materialize. Instead of growers, the two had become traders in the Dutch West India Company, twice traveling home to Amsterdam as agents for Isaac De Forest, a wealthy entrepreneur. In Amsterdam they would sell tobacco grown by other planters and purchase merchandise to be sold or traded in the colony on return. Later, when the English Commander, Colonel Nichols, took control of the Dutch Colony, the two young Dutchmen applied for a patent from the English King. After the death of his first wife, Gerrit had lost heart for all of it and sold to his partner his share of his Harlem lot, house, and the two domestic slaves that his wife had inherited from her father. He made a good profit on the bundle which gave him the seed money he needed for his expedition to the North Country. It was on this first journey north that he reconnected with his old friend Matty Thomas, and shortly thereafter met his future wife, Gentle Heart.

The first few years after leaving Harlem he and his new family lived with his native wife's family, yet all the time Gerrit worked toward establishing his family within a dwelling place of their own. Though he and his family fit in well enough with Heart's people, Gerrit thought it not a natural way for a Christian man to properly raise his children.

With the help of his friend, John Nagel, who had come up from Harlem after the snow melted the first year, and Matty, the three men had labored hard to make a clearing. By late summer they had built a modest two-room thatched roofed house, and attached to the house, an excellent barn triple the size of his dwelling, as was customary. Shortly thereafter Gerrit returned to Manhattan Island along with Nagel with a specific purpose in mind. He would shop the slave block near the planked wall of the city for a healthy, well seasoned African male, preferably one who had worked the Caribbean sugar plantations. John owned several such workers who labored along with himself and his sons in the fields of his and his father-in-law, Resolved Waldron. John would advise him in the purchase process before returning home to his Rebecca.

These additional laborers were necessary to make it possible to push forward with his original dream of a northern plantation. He found and purchased two strong African males off the slave block. With Matty's help, and now with his newly acquired Negro slaves, the virgin, thickly wooded lots surrounding the barn were well cleared by autumn. The logs of the felled trees were split and stacked high for Gentle Heart to keep the hearth ablaze during the long, brutal winter season. During this period Gerrit and Matty left the side of the Lenape to trade with the Algonquin-speaking Mohicans, a branch of the Lenape, allowing the experienced hunters to provide them with many deer, otter and beaver furs. The following springtime Gerrit and Matty traded those pelts for necessary supplies at Albany. Afterwards they parted company at Bear Creek Run, and Matty returned to his home.

Gerrit, his young son, and his Negroes then planted the first acre of his new northern plantation. The rich, fertile land he had acquired through Heart soon blossomed into the proficient farm that within the following decades grew into a vast estate.

After the second harvest, and the sale of the cut timbers, Vandenberg bought back the woman known as Madagascar Eva, the slave woman that his first wife's father had purchased as a young girl from an agent of the Royal African Company. Branded as a child, like hundreds of other women, Eva bore the scar of the English trade above her right breast-RAC. Eva was well trained in the Dutch culinary skills to which Gerrit had become well accustomed while living in New Haarlem, and he had great hope in the beginning that ultimately she would pass these attributes on to his native-born wife.

A year later, he had an opportunity to purchase an African Dinka man. Gerrit hadn't planned on acquiring another slave, but his old friend, Resolved Waldron, then the constable at Harlem village, had written that the Negro's owners were giving up their farm and returning to Holland. Everything was to be sold, Waldron had been told, because they had no plans to return to the colony. The Constable wrote with a tinge of humor that the owners no longer had good use for a near seven-foot black man who was an expert in handling cattle, a trade as natural to the African Dinka tribesmen as breathing. The asking price was fair, and he should act quickly, or be the unhappy loser of such a bargain. Waldron had assured him that the Dinka would be no trouble to take into his own household and would suffer no remorse in leaving Harlem. The slave had no other kin. He knew this to be a truth because the Dinka's young wife and infant had caught the fever and died the previous summer. Waldron had devoted a few more lines of his correspondence regarding the Negroes of his own who, they being closely related to the deceased woman, had been given permission to attend the funeral of the mother and her infant, adding that the two had been buried together within the same grave at the Negro burying grounds. Waldron had concluded that he would have purchased the man himself, but was more in mind of dividing properties these days than buying.

Remembering the towering African quite well, not only for the oddity of his stature, but also his obvious good nature, Gerrit had agreed and went immediately to fetch the one the man's owner called Zebulon. Once back on his farm, he put Zebulon (soon to be called Zeb) in charge of his infant herd which consisted of a bull, six cows and his prized fat hens. Thinking him impressive and having fine blood, within weeks he arranged for the Dinka and his cook, the comely Eva, to be married and recorded their marriage in his account book.

During those times Matty often scoffed at Gerrit for the care he paid to his Negroes, saying that he served them more than he was served. But Master Vandenberg was resolute that fair treatment of a man, be he slave or free, produced satisfied workers, and a contented worker made a good farm. When Zeb and Eva's first child was born, a daughter called Marie, Gerrit heard from Gentle Heart that Eva grieved that she might be sold away again. After hearing of these concerns, Gerrit summoned the local magistrate and swore an oath that he would not sell her, the Dinka, or this child, or any other children who were born. His people could take comfort in the knowledge that they were firmly planted in Vandenberg soil. He considered them an extension of his plantation family.

As time progressed Matty sired seven robust sons as well as eight sturdy girls. He would boast that, unlike the Dutchman, he had no need of Africans, nor did he want any and the troubles that came with bought foreigners, dark skinned or white. He, along with others, mused that Gerrit's oath was merely a gesture, rather than something that could be held up in a court of English law. But Gerrit's sworn word was a promise that he kept until his death, and an unspoken rule that came to build both bridges and walls within his children's future lives.

Margaret was five, and John four, before they and their mother came to live in the small house nestled within the valley of the mighty North River at that place which would come to be known as Vandenberg Estates. Teunis was nearly a young man when his father decided that he could spare his eldest to continue his education within the framework of established Colonial society. He was apprenticed to a well-established miller at Harlem, a full day's travel from the estate.

During the following decade Gerrit grew his holdings to a second barn and a gristmill that also served as an Indian trading post. He had planted crops of corn, wheat, hops as well as tobacco, but after a few years time he gave up on the tobacco plantings, as had other settlers, feeling the harsh climate simply not suitable. Instead he turned toward lumber, the abundant crop the Lord himself had sewn generations prior to his arrival, and began operating a saw mill. Within the first years he had also set about plantings for an apple orchard. His apple cider was served not only in the Colonies, but also at the finest tables in London. His livestock flourished. Under Zeb's stewardship no calf was ever lost, and his herd had increased to more than one hundred cows.

But as the first dozen years of plantation life drew to a close, a terrible blow was dealt when smallpox took his beloved wife along with half the residents of the valley. Upon Gentle Heart's death, Gerrit spoke not a word to anyone for many weeks, refusing to see the Dominie. Her people grieved, the Indians who had refused baptism saying she had received the white man's curse along with the holy waters. Although he said he was not, Vandenberg grew bitter. Matty once suggested to his family that he believed his old friend had lost his faith. From Gerrit's own lips he had heard the sharp words spoken, "If there is an Almighty God, to be sure I have been cursed by Him."

The native people of the woodlands, family and friends watched as over the next year the man who had once offered the most amicable of discourse, a fair master and loving father shrank away into the darkness. To many, it seemed as though the devil had put his hand upon Gerrit Vandenberg's soul. What other explanation could there be for a man turning his face away from God? What could one say of a man who closes his heart to the psalms following the death of an Indian woman? Was it not a sign that he would no longer sing as he had done in the past while splitting logs beside his Africans? He was no longer telling the old stories to his children or reading scripture from the Bible. Though Matty and his family stayed with him at the farm through that summer, his neighbors began to avoid his person. His children feared for their father's immortal soul.

What Gerrit did in response to his grief was absorb himself in his work. Soon he had acquired another two thousand acres by coaxing the signatures of local chiefs (who later claimed they were tricked) out of their property after Vandenberg had made them drunk on rum. The deeds were determined legitimate in the courts, but his long-standing friendship with the local natives suffered severe injury. Fearing him damned, though innocent of wrong doing on paper, many of his neighbors who had once counted him a principled man lost their respect for Gerrit.

The following year, in a subsequent purchase from Mahicans near Pachwack Falls, Gerrit attempted to quell unsavory rumblings of disreputable dealings on his part by setting aside a portion of his land for continued native habitation. He restricted colonial settlement and farm development upon this section, believing that his action would ensure a healthy supply of furs and regular trade with the local Indians. The forest was thick with whitewood, trees that later Peter Schuyler purchased for constructing a flotilla of canoes. As time would tell, Vandenberg's decisions would pay off handsomely.

Chapter 8

The sickness that had killed Margaret's mother also claimed the lives of many tribal peoples living within the North River valley; those dead included several of her aunts and cousins at Muskrat Island. Of those natives who had survived, many soon joined with other Lenape and Nanticoke living far to the southwest of the Vandenberg farm. Most of Margaret's remaining kinfolk eventually scattered themselves amid the villages along the South River (which in time would be called the Delaware). The Lenape continued to be allies of the great covenant with the powerful Iroquois, although their Iroquois protectors did not always treat them with respect; the Iroquois at times speaking down to them at council meetings. Some of the ill feeling on the part of the Iroquois came about because the Lenape would not join with the Iroquois or the English in providing warriors against the French. For some colonists these actions on the part of the Lenape suggested that the Lenape were consorting with the French and therefore not to be trusted. Young Margaret was no longer allowed to visit those few of her mother's relatives who had chosen to remain fairly close and whose village in those times was for her less than a half day walk. After the death of her mother, her kinswoman who had come to her and her father meaning to comfort them in a time of great sorrow were not made to feel welcome by the plantation master. Her bereaved father could barely look at her mother's kin. Shortly after one such visit he had determined it was better that all old ties be severed with those relations calling themselves the *Human Beings.* He told her and John it was a part of her past, and while acknowledging that her mother had been a good woman who had taught her many necessary skills, he instructed her that it was in her best interest that she should not look back. Lessons in cookery, planting, harvesting and stringing wampum would surely serve her well in the future, but for now, Gerrit insisted, they had all come into another time.

After completing his apprenticeship in Harlem, Teunis had sailed to Holland where he spent a year learning every aspect of his uncle's gristmill in Rotterdam. The following year was devoted to assisting the overseer on his cousin's plantation in the Indies. But before returning to his home country to take his place at his father's side he would go to Holland where he would seek a proper Dutch wife. He was living in the Fatherland when his Indian stepmother died. Nearly a year had passed when a letter arrived from his father imploring his return to the colony. His father had need of him as he was considering a partnership in a new business that would keep him away from the plantation for long stretches at a time.

Gerrit was determined that his younger children be clear about his meaning of what was to be the new part of their lives. Their Indian mother had taught them everything that she knew to be useful within the world of her people, and he was grateful for the skills she had imparted, but he had come to the realization that the wilderness of the big woods was disappearing. He could see that it was time John and Margaret were educated properly in the ever changing English dominated world. A new, and as he saw it, cruel civilization was dawning in their country, and he would have them well positioned to take their rightful place beside their elder brother when the time came. His children should not think of him as a hard-hearted father, but one who understood the ground that lay beyond the farm. In truth, Gerrit said, baptism sets free the soul, but not the body. Since the death of their mother he had come more to witness a danger that awaited them. It was plain that the path upon which they must walk was not easily tread for the half-breed, for it would be strewn with serpents, many of whom called themselves good Christians. Vandenberg assured them that though the changes he imposed might be difficult, the lessons learned would make their journey a better one as they grew.

Having spoken his mind, Gerrit placed Margaret and John, as well as his house Negroes, under the supervision of Widow Reed, a strict, Rotterdam-born housekeeper. Raising the eyebrows of every Dutch Reform church member in the valley, he also arranged for an Anglican tutor while on a visit to New York City, who was the first of what would become a succession of Anglican tutors. It was decided that John would spend another year or two at home perfecting his command of the English language as well as his mathematic abilities before being apprenticed out for a term in Manhattan, as had his elder brother. Resolved Waldron's eldest son, William, a cooper living on the Broadway road of the city with his wife and family, had already made a bid for John to join him where he would learn the trade.

The day after Margaret's fourteenth birthday, barely a month after the arrival of the new governess, Mistress Reed, Gerrit set sail on the *Maria* for Europe, leaving Teunis to oversee the operation of the manor as well as his two younger siblings.

Many more years would pass before Margaret saw Muskrat Island again, embraced her aged Indian grandmother, and sought the elder's wise counsel. But, upon greeting her mother's mother, she immediately realized that she was too late. The woman she so often recalled was no longer the same person. Her grandmother, being feeble of mind, could not respond to her questions about the strange ceremonial visions she saw in her head. Margaret was sure that her thoughts were an omen sent from the Great Creator, but she dared not mention such dreams to anyone within her household, most especially to dear Mrs. Reed whose strict yet caring ways she had grown to love.

She was no longer part Indian she told herself. The Indian half of her heart lay silent beside the gentle spirit woman of the Lenape who bore and loved her. Until she was twenty Margaret caught rare glimpses of her father, the powerful landowner and merchant, in his brief stays at home amidst his many travels between the American Colonies and Europe. In those times, to the dismay of Mrs. Reed, her family and servants often referred to her as, "the orphan girl."

But the memories of the old days and the old ways of her Indian family were not so easily dismissed as Margaret struggled to keep her thoughts that of a pure, Christian woman. She remembered Mrs. Reed's warnings, and for the most part, kept to her father's rule of silence on religious matters. Munsie, the language of her native ancestors, came to her and her younger brother's lips only when certain that they would not be overheard.

As the years passed, Margaret became a capable young mistress, and Mrs. Reed, her services no longer required, decided to move to New York City where her affluent, recently widowed sister had want of her company. As the two bid each other an emotional farewell, little did Margaret know that Mrs. Reed's decision to relocate would become a means for yet another change that would affect her way of thinking for the rest of her life.

Chapter 9

The year following Mrs. Reed's departure, as the aroma of the apple blossoms filled New York's North River Valley, Margaret celebrated her eighteenth birthday, and that week an unexpected invitation arrived at the manor house. Mrs. Reed wrote that since she and her sister had decided not to go to their brother's country house at Kinderhook, they would be delighted to have Peggy take lodging with them in New York City for the upcoming summer season. She explained that she had taken the liberty to write to her father, presently in Holland, some months prior regarding the idea of a visit. Recently she had received his return communication giving his approval of the arrangement along with certain instructions. As per Master Vandenberg's suggestion, it was determined that Peggy, along with her maid, would be accompanied by her brother, John. The widows were most eager to receive all three of them at their home in the city sometime in early June after May's Pinkster week celebrations had concluded. Surely by early June they would all be recovered from the festivities surrounding Pinkster, as well as their indigestion caused by the eating of so many colored eggs. Margaret smiled, recalling how she and Mrs. Reed had enjoyed coloring dozens of eggs, arranging each egg into a colorful mound piled high in the large Dutch majolica bowl that her father had brought back from one of his voyages to Holland, and the hilarious sight the housekeeper made after a few glasses of spiced wine prompted her to lead the "Guinea Dance."

Mrs. Reed concluded her letter saying that John would, of course, stay a few days and then proceed on to the home of William Waldron to resume his last year of apprenticeship. Should the young mistress think it agreeable, she would be welcome to keep company with the ladies through August, returning home to her plantation in time for the harvest season.

Margaret was ecstatic when she received Mrs. Reed's letter. She had led a rather cloistered life, her only travel of consequence the prior year having been the annual trip to Harlem where she had visited with Teunis' mother's relatives. Although she had reservations, she was so excited that she had sent Marie upstairs to her bedchamber to start packing her trunk even before she wrote her acceptance.

The following weeks passed slowly in anticipation of the trip, but finally the departure day arrived. Mrs. Reed had been right in urging that she not be fearful to make the journey down river. All had passed peacefully during the day of the journey. And she soon discovered that the city people living in lower Manhattan embraced her warmly, seeming to find her mix of Indian and Dutch cultures intriguing. In response to this warm welcome, Margaret quickly overcame her natural reserve, opening her heart to everyone she met.

This first visit to New York City initiated a parade of similar visits in subsequent years, each filled with plays, concerts, and shared dinners with some of the most prominent families of New York.

She also attended several lavish parties at the grand Wall Street house of Sarah Rouseby, who had been the wife of Captain Kidd. Young Margaret found the stories about the Scottish born Captain quite dashing, and in her innocence she could not understand why he had come to such terrible ruin. How could all of this have happened to a man such as Kidd, welcome in the best houses, and the holder of the King's license to capture French and other disreputable vessels? Was he not a hero?

Mrs. Reed's deceased brother-in-law had been a staunch Anglican, and a pew-holding member of Trinity Church. Mrs. Reed's sister, formally a Dutch Calvinist, had been unwillingly collected, Mrs. Reed implied, into the Anglican Church during her marriage. It appeared to Margaret that Mrs. Reed had also been assimilated as the three of them regularly attended services. More than once as they took tea after services they discussed the goodness of a man undoubtedly unjustly accused, for how could a man who gave so generously to his church be a convicted pirate?

Captain Kidd, hung on the gibbet at England's Newgate Prison for murder and piracy, had lent a runner and tackle for hoisting stones to build the first Trinity Church, a good deed later recalled by a few parishioners in defense of his widow struggling to keep her church pew (as well as her dignity and good standing). Margaret would never understand how such a grand man came to such terrible ruin, anymore than she could comprehend the strength of his surviving widow. What could a mother say to her children of their father's chained, tarred body that reportedly continued to hang, the flesh rotting away from the bones, over the Thames River? After a time, Sarah remarried, becoming Mrs. Christopher Rouseby, and she and her two small daughters resumed life, but Sarah did so with a noticeable absence of her prior flair. Sarah and her family were able to remain members of Trinity Church, as well as becoming devoted friends to Margaret. As the years passed the upriver manor became an occasional refuge for Mrs. Rouseby. Margaret had heard that the Captain had hid a great fortune, but it was of no consequence to Sarah, who had regained all her properties and remained a wealthy woman in her own right. When she visited they never again spoke of Captain Kidd.

* * * *

The third year that Margaret summered with the widows, the trio along with their servants departed New York City for Philadelphia to visit kinfolk of the Evans (two brothers who were silver merchants residing two doors away from the widows). It was a trip that was to make a profound mark upon her life.

Arriving at the impressive brick home of a cousin of the Evans brothers, Margaret was told that their hosts were also related to His Honor the Governor of the Colony of Pennsylvania, William Penn, on Penn's mother's Dutch side. On that day, while visiting the Evans, she became acquainted with another visitor as well, a vivacious Quaker girl, Letitia Penn, the daughter of the esteemed William Penn. From Letitia Margaret learned that Letitia's father was a beloved friend to her own Lenape peoples who were the majority of the natives inhabiting his "Holy Experiment."

Margaret had responded to her new friend that she believed this to be truly spoken because many of her deceased mother's Indian family had left New York to go to live near the South River. She had heard, not long ago, that those Indians living along the river banks were now called the Delaware Indians. Margaret told the Quaker girl that she had also heard of the great man, Penn, before this day. He was the man the Lenape called Onas, meaning quill, or put another way, *one who signs with honor.*

Letitia smiled at this and went on to relate a portion of her family's history and her London born father's accomplishments, explaining that years before, King Charles II had given the lands of the big forest that had become the colony to her father as payment for a debt owed to her grandfather.

Here is the place, said Letitia excitedly, where my father dreams all men and all women of every religious sect can be free. When Tishe, as Letitia preferred to be called, learned of Peggy's native heritage and of her being a distant kin to their Delawares, Margaret found herself in receipt of yet another invitation. Tishe insisted that she be allowed to introduce her to her father, to her beautiful, young stepmother, Hannah, and to her baby brother John, at their country retreat. The great house was situated on the banks of the "Lenape Wihittuck" the same river which the English called the Delaware River. The Penn's country estate was called Pennsbury Manor.

Margaret doubted that she would ever forget the exciting five-hour, twenty-six mile voyage to the Manor, which they made upon the Penn's slave-manned barge. That was the year that Letitia's little dog sprang from her arms into the wild waters of the river. Much commotion had ensued while two of the African rowers were immediately ordered overboard in pursuit, leaving the remaining oarsmen struggling to keep control of the vessel. It wasn't long, however, before one of the slaves had caught hold of Tishe's dear beloved pet, and soon the soggy, furry mop was brought back on board. As Letitia comforted her shaking little dog, the second slave, not being such a strong swimmer as the hero of the ordeal, nearly drowned and would have had the captain not thrown him a rope.

The subsequent visit lasted more than two weeks and was, in Margaret's eyes, as equally notable as meeting the great Proprietor himself, because it was at Pennsbury where she met a gregarious, broad shouldered young man by the name of Harry Stocker. He seemed to proffer tangible sparks of romance that could have been encouraged to burn as brightly as the stars of the heavens, had time and circumstances allowed. But a great love followed by fruitful marriage to Mr. Stocker was never to become a reality. All too soon her duties at home would separate them. Another disappointment was that late that August Letitia's aunt took ill, and she was compelled to return to London (or this was the explanation given for her quick departure).

Back in New York after Letitia had sailed, the widows discussed another possibility for her speedy departure. The talk was that Letitia's father, the Honorable William Penn, was a remarkable, yet somewhat unique Quaker, who may dance with the natives, but had the devout heart of a cautious, well-meaning father. As such he was not pleased with the attentions paid to his daughter by one William Masters of Philadelphia. His Honor would set another path for his favorite daughter.

Her brief romance with Harry Stocker had made Margaret fully expect that her own father would also act prudently and provide her with a good suitable match, a husband who would bring her blessings. But when Gerrit finally returned to his grand estate his health was broken, and Margaret had no other option but to devote the next decade caring for the needs of her aged parent. Suitors were rare. Her escapes to colorful New York became fewer and fewer before they evaporated all together. Thoughts of matrimony were seldom entertained after she passed her thirtieth birthday. To think of herself lying within the folds of a husband's arms as once she had done now seemed foolishness. Approaching forty, she had become comfortable within the billowy folds of the plantation's work.

Margaret reconciled herself to her spinsterhood and occasionally consoled herself that although she knew many happily married couples, it was better to be content alone than miserably entwined. When she weakened, she thought of Tishe with whom she had retained a long distance friendship.

Poor Tishe, now Mrs. William Aubrey, who years prior had put aside the proposal of a true lover, the handsome William Masters, only to become a barren, drawn woman captured within the loveless marriage arranged by her father. Each time Margaret received a letter from London, she hoped that Tishe fondly remembered their happy days spent together and perhaps sometimes recalled a few, sweet stolen moments with her one true love, William.

Though Margaret's own would-be suitor had married another the following summer, the memory of the warmth of his mouth upon her own as she stood on that moonlit evening under the white poplar trees on her Quaker friend's lawn had sustained her through many a cold and lonely night. Their fathers might have dismissed the yearnings of two young maidens for what they considered the better good, but such sweet girlhood memories were hidden treasures, a golden dream only relinquished upon the death of the dreamer.

After Harry Stocker she had believed that a young man's passionate kiss and accompanying promise made by moonlight, and the holy union that his sweet, warm touch had hinted upon, had escaped her forever, and that a loving marriage like that long shared by some of her dearest friends was to be denied her. Until recently she had come to accept that her journey was to be one of rigorous obligation, punctuated on occasion by personal success. This was enough to give her purpose. It seemed that it was the Lord's will that she walk tenaciously without the support of a mate, and she could not complain; certainly she would not question His will. God knew that there were many poor souls who were looking to her for hope, and she was duty bound to give them that—at the very least. Despite the consequences, for the moment, she had found a certain peace. This, and all the daily-orchestrated needs of her demanding northern plantation, had been enough to fill her life…until now.

Chapter 10

Rubbing her eyes, Margaret put down her quill. For over an hour she had been attempting to write a response to an unsettling letter that she had received from her North Country cousin, Catharina Waldron, residing in Albany. Her mind was exhausted. It had been a long time since she had thought of the Manhattan slave insurrections that had led to the death of her sweet Lizbeth, Zeb and Eva's second daughter. Her cousin's disturbing post, relating the hanging of two runaway Negro boys near the Half Moon village who had been caught with their master's quilt, had reopened many layers of old wounds that she had believed long healed. Catharina's letter also brought to the surface more imminent dangers that she would rather not face.

There was absolutely no doubt in Margaret's mind that had her father been able to call down from the heavens to her, he would have bellowed his admonishment over many of the decisions that she had made over the past decade. Without question he would have thought it far worse than merely unwise that she had posted a four hundred pound bond while obtaining freedom papers for two servant women whom he had left bound to her for life. Had he wished freedom for Marie, Lizbeth, or any of his slaves, he would have written so into his last will and testament. But freedom for the women was a promise she had made, and so with all goodness of the heart her stubborn nature had overridden her father's will. Ironically, the freedom she had meant for Lizbeth as a precious gift had most assuredly led to her death. It was an act of kindness for which she would never be able to forgive herself.

Although many years had passed, the relentless memories attached to those dark, harrowing days surrounding the slave insurrections of 1712 had left her questioning the purpose that the Almighty intended in giving her such strong resolve. Many times when reexamining her conscience one question above all others persisted and that was whether or not God had accepted her confession. Was she forgiven?

She could well imagine what her father would think of her closing her eyes to the comings and goings of those in her charge on her own plantation. After poor Lizbeth, he would think that she had lost all her senses. She had strong suspicions that under the cover of darkness her trusted Negroes might have given asylum to runaways as they made their way northward along the river toward the French territory. If this were true and it were to come out, there would indeed be harsh consequences to herself, as well as to all those to whom she had sworn protection.

Margaret's eyes focused upon one paragraph in particular. She shuttered as she read what Catherina reported. There had been accusations made against a Scot tradesman living a few houses away. The Scot had been loose with the law in the past; a few weeks prior allowing his Negro to drive his cart within the city, and he had been arrested and fined for the offense. Not long before this, one of his Negroes, a boy of fifteen, was caught on city streets after sunset without the Scot's written permission. The boy was severely whipped before being returned, but his owner claimed innocence, saying he had merely forgotten to write out his permission. Now the Scot was suspected of harboring runaways and was interrogated by the authorities, but then released. Some say he was in collaboration with the French. Catherina further wrote that her husband thought the Scot would soon be a dead man.

Flushed, Margaret dabbed with her handkerchief at the beads of perspiration brewing about her neck. She had overheard the whispering within her own house and feared that by remaining silent she had entered into an illicit partnership. Perhaps the whip now would save slaves of her own from the rope later, for surely this, or worse, would be their fate should they be discovered. On the other hand, as had been suggested by her neighbors who had used such punishment for a servant's wrongdoings, a number of lashes would be an act of kindness. Yet, the thought of such punishment sickened her stomach. Hating the impudence of the rebellious slave, yet yearning to understand, she felt like the biblical camel attempting to pass through the eye of a needle.

Looking out the window, her gaze followed Eva, now bent with age, as she with her young grandson drew water from their well. Her heart rested for a moment as she recalled how as a young boy, Teunis would often help the slave woman with this chore. But the sweet memory lingered briefly, replaced by another of all of them surrounding her elder brother's tombstone. For a number of years she had struggled to put aside her anxiety over how she might be judged in the afterlife for encouraging her older brother to partake of the smallpox vaccination. She had meant only to block the dreaded disease from coming upon them all, but perhaps she had stepped, as her embittered widowed sister-in-law, Rachel, once said, where only the Lord Himself was meant to walk. The sacredness of living and dying was not something to be decided by mortals. Had her stubbornness killed dear Teunis? Margaret sighed. One must accept God's will. Perhaps the generous God of the universe might understand her heart and take pity.

The question of the Lord's justice came more often than not during quiet days such as this as she sat by herself. If, as scripture taught, no thought or word could be professed except for what God allowed, then would she be held accountable for decisions she made? Had it not been God who had given voice to Dr. Van Ness?

It was Van Ness who had told her of the Massachusetts Bay Colony's minister, Cotton Mather, who practiced the inserting of infected puss into the blood of a cut wound of a healthy person to prevent the spread of the terrible smallpox illness. Word had come to her that three Indian villages along the Mohawk River had lost more than half their inhabitants, and the sickness had reached a village not thirty miles from Vandenberg manor. Panic had consumed her, and although she was at first appalled at Mather's technique, her own Negro, Tom, like many other Africans, recalled a similar practice in his homeland. Tom, who had been one of the first to come to them, had been inoculated as a child in Africa, and although half those captured slaves, as well as half the crew on the slave ship carrying them, died from an outbreak of the pox, he had survived the voyage. The African slave's testimony, Margaret assured Tunis, provided good evidence that, should they be inoculated, their lives would be spared. Their own African's salvation could be none other than a good sign.

Teunis had remained stubbornly unconvinced and had voiced his feelings loudly. He always thought her belief in their Negro's superstitions a sin, and the utilization of such barbaric procedures practiced by heathen tribal peoples of Africa ridiculous to consider. Knowing that Mather had learned of the proposed pox remedy from his personal African slave—a man called Onesimus—he was particularly incensed. Teunis had cursed the minister as a lover of Negroes. He went further, denouncing Onesimus as the devil who would lead all good Christians on a path of destruction by brewing a poison for their Masters rather than a remedy. After this he had gone to the aged Tom and rebuked him severely.

But as angels throughout antiquity had spoken to the faithful, so it happened that her elder brother was to receive such a message. Teunis had said that in his dream he had heard an angel speak to him, saying that he and his family should all partake of the treatment and not to be afraid. Deciding that his dream was not the work of the devil, a fortnight later the physician from the city came and inoculated the family; Margaret too was inoculated. Why Teunis had been struck down and not the rest of them Margaret could not understand. All she knew was that this was another death that in some way or another she had called down upon them.

Above all though, this morning her thoughts were of her brother John who had returned after an absence of many years. He had come home with a soft-spoken, golden haired young woman who was large with child. It was obvious from the glances exchanged between Bess and John that the two held great affection for one another. John had immediately set to work on building a modest dwelling for his family upon acreage he and his sister jointly owned. It was clear to Margaret that this time he planned to stay put.

Margaret was suddenly awakened from her musings, mesmerized by an unusual show of light coming through the parlor's colored windowpane. She sat motionless. The morning's bright luminosity was near blinding as the sunbeams played a spirited game of tag across the smooth, wide-planked floor of her parlor, the streams of light seeming to snake along toward the hemline of her dress before encircling her slender, silk-gowned figure. Soon the stark white of the plastered walls was ablaze with color, the light dancing across her Turkey-work tapestry unleashing a wild spectrum of indigo blue, crimson, and violet hues, a collage of wonder that lifted her spirit. Breathlessly she felt the warmth of the sun enfold her entire being as she listened to the soft, sweetly fluted voice of her maid, Marie, singing a familiar Dutch hymn.

Startled, yet unafraid, all of this she thought must be a sign from her Precious Redeemer for which she had so fervently prayed. What she was experiencing surely was meant as an encouragement while she navigated these difficult, uncharted waters leading to another chapter in her life. *Dear Lord, let this be so,* she whispered as she reached for her pen and began to write *…yes, Catharina, you have heard correctly. I will soon be married. My future husband's name is David Karski. And yes, he is the gentleman who came back with my brother, John, some months ago, and the one whom your Peter met whilst he visited us a month ago. Mr. Karski asked John for my hand and I have accepted his proposal of marriage. I am quite sure that many in New York will be turned upside down when they hear the news.*

I will tell you that I have already heard indiscreet gossip. I suppose that such talk must be expected; undoubtedly a union between a woman my age with a much younger man will raise a few eyebrows. I know many think my intended an opportunist, he being a man of lesser means than myself, and, of course, a frontiersman from the west, as yet unknown to all here about. Yet John places great stock in him. I've heard that some say Mr. Karski has carried away one of the richest women in the colonies. They speak as though I were blindfolded, as if I were a twig of wood floating aimlessly in the creek. I will share with you, dear cousin that nothing could be further from the truth. As I write to you now, my heart beats louder than summer thunder. I know Mr. Karski's affection to be equal to my own happiness.

After a few more lines referencing Catharina's queries and suggesting prayers for the departed souls of the Negro boys, Margaret affectionately signed and then sealed the letter. Still, her thoughts reverted to her suspicions about her slaves, her concerns overshadowing her joy.

A supper conversation at Pennsbury Manor of bygone years came to mind. The discourse was between William Penn and her father. Her father thought his host's words were so impressive that he later wrote them into his journal as best as he could recall them. The celebrated Quaker's wisdom had stuck with her all of these years:

"There is hardly one frame of government in the world so ill designed by its first founders, that in good hands would not do well enough…Governments, like clocks, go from the motion men give them, and as governments are made and moved by men, so by them they are ruined too."

Margaret couldn't help but think that marriages were much like governments. At first, they cannot be envisioned to fail, yet somehow, many of them do. (She thought sadly about her dear friend Tishe in this regard.) And it is the two participants who bring that distressing result to the noble endeavor. Leaning back into her chair she reasoned that if her marriage to David was to be successful, she must summon courage from deep within her soul and be willing to submit herself completely to the sacredness of matrimony. There must be no secrets between them when they are wed, for she was determined that their house not be tainted by deceit. They must be together in *all* things. There was no question that she wanted David as her husband, but there was also no question that she must find a resolution to her domestic problems or face bitter consequences. There was also no question in her mind that she could not afford another scandal. Especially now.

Chapter 11

Finishing an impromptu polish of the silver funeral spoon collection, Margaret replaced the last of them into the wooden wall rack. She lingered briefly to admire the assortment hanging against the colorful, birded wallpaper that she had imported from England. She was fascinated by the detail of the design and found the partridges exquisite.

Marie looked up from her sewing. "They look to be as bright as stars. I would have done it for you, but it does no good to argue with you."

"I can use your service as you sit. Pray continue with the handkerchief. I must have two dozen embroidered in time for my wedding, and I have no time myself for sewing even one. I must finish what I have begun for the baby." Margaret glanced at the open woven wicker basket nestled in the corner of the room. It contained several pieces of small, colorful patches of fabric along with a tiny sleeping gown that she had been embroidering for her brother and sister-in-law's expected child. Her lips softened into a smile as she picked up the garment from the basket.

"'Tis good to work quietly," Margaret whispered. "We hardly can hear ourselves think these last weeks with the scurry of workmen to and fro, the surveyor, and then, of course, Mr. Lapett."

"I do not mind the company. I think the activities pleasing," Marie replied softly.

Margaret searched through the various colored threads in her basket. She longed to be with her betrothed, but with John and David away during these past weeks, their absence provided time for her to more easily consider the workings of her plantation.

"Oh, yes, you would," she replied knowingly. "I have seen you flirting with Van Rensselaer's carpenter. Beware of your conduct for you know that he will return to his master after the work is done."

"We have barely spoken," Marie replied nervously.

"I saw you earlier this morn. You were down yonder giving him to drink, and I think you spoke much."

Marie twisted in her chair. "It is a hot day, and a good man workin' hard at his trade becomes thirsty. Am I not to be hospitable?"

Margaret sighed, yet her words were tender. "I am always the first to praise good hospitality as you well know, Marie, but I would more have you keeping good sense. I would not wish you any hurt."

"I know why you are concerned, Peg. Do not worry. I will not lose my wits. I am not my sister." Laying her embroidery down on a side table she rose. "I have a mind for a glass of beer. Would you have one to drink yourself?"

"Nay, I think not, but thank you."

As Marie left the room Margaret threaded her needle and began to stitch. She thought of John who would soon be a father. It was a thought peculiar to her senses as it seemed to her that it had been only yesterday when they were children. It was difficult to think of John as a man, let alone a husband, and now almost a father.

She was sorry that they had quarreled so much of late. Quarreling with him had brought her a most sour stomach and her household nothing but tension. She had resolved to have done with it, if not for her own sake then for the sake of Bess and her child. God bless Bess; she was an ointment between them. How fortunate to have her as a sister-in-law, and John fortunate to be blessed with a gentle, caring wife who tolerated his volatile nature exceedingly well. Bess's sweet disposition had transposed a rough-edged, irresponsible young man into a tender, caring husband, and thoughts of an infant's gurgling delighted her soul. Her parlor's painted birds would make a pretty companion to a child's laughter.

Somehow she must learn to love John the man as she did John the child. In her minds eye she could still see them as children running beside their father and Matty Thomas as the men guided the oxen while the animals pulled away the heavy stone boulders to clear the fields. She could hear the boom of the gigantic ancient timbers as they fell to the ground. The fresh smell of the big pines had filled the air, a scent of balsam and pine, to her always more pleasing than the finest French rose water. Father gave them and their mother the task of carrying off the smaller rocks that would be used for a garden's edge. She remembered well the two of them complaining to their mother that the stones outnumbered all the birds of the sky and the earth's insects. Was it not only yesterday that they were picking up hundreds of pieces of red ore from their fields before the cleared virgin lots were seeded? She recalled the many cuts upon small hands, and the terrible sting of the orange ore's dust that seemingly no amount of washing would remove. In those sweet, childhood days, she and John were together in all things and never quarreled as they did now.

What an irony that John's childhood fascination with those rocks would become a man's quest that could possibly bring dramatic change into the lives of so many. Was it not a plan of Almighty God that John meet David who himself had worked such a mine? The chance of an iron ore forge had brought the three of them together, yet would her brother's dream drive all of them apart before the first shovel of dirt be dug? She could not allow this to happen since all of this must have been ordained within the heavens. Was this all not a part of some divine plan?

Marie returned to the room with a pitcher and two glasses. "It is water. I drew a fresh, cool bucket from the well. It is too warm for even a short beer today. Would you have a glass?"

Margaret indicated acceptance of the water. Sighing, she glanced toward the ceiling. "I hope Bess has been able to sleep some. The babe inside her has given her much discomfort these last days." Accepting the glass from the servant she said, "What do you think, Marie—should it be a boy or a girl?"

"Oh, I do not know so much about these things."

"I do not know so much myself, yet I think the child will be a male."

Marie smiled. "Why say you so?"

"Your mama says it shall be so, and she should know, having birthed six of her own."

After a swallow of water, Marie replied thoughtfully. "That be true, but mama said that Henry's Martha would have a boy and then came out Hannah. So, though she knows such things at times, she could not say about her own grandbaby."

Margaret laughed. "What do you think of this little nightgown?" she said showing the miniature garment to Marie.

"I think it fine work. I think Bess will hold it dear."

Margaret laid the tiny piece of clothing down on her lap. She closed her eyes, wishing that she could believe in John's ambitious plans for the future. After a moment she looked over at Marie. "Did you see the rainbow earlier?"

"No, Mistress Peg," Marie responded quietly. "I did not. Before I came to you today I was with my father in his cabin. He had asked Mama to bid me come. He had a desire to have discourse with me, and it was the first time in days that he was well enough to do so."

"Your father must have had great need of you to ask for you to come."

"He wanted to know about the census man's visit. He wanted to know what the census man might have said to me."

"And what did you reply?"

"I said that all was well. I told him too about what Mr. Kent had said about all the many slaves that live in our part of the country, and how you said that I am a freed woman. I told my father that you said not to worry as you have shown him my freedom papers."

Margaret said, "Later, after your father has rested proper, I will go to him myself so that he will be peaceable about all. But my heart is glad to hear that he seems improved."

"He will be happy to see you."

"Your father has always been a good and faithful servant. I should have him comfortable as he fights to regain his strength. When I see him I will tell him of the rainbow. It was your father who told me as a small child that the people of his fatherland believed the rainbow to be a sign of good things to come. Perhaps it came that I should see it so that I could tell him."

"My father will like to hear this."

The two women returned to their work, and Margaret's thoughts returned to her brother. She wanted all to be good between them, yet she would not approve of any venture forcing new Africans upon her. It was true that the fur trade that had brought her father his greatest wealth was not nearly as profitable as it had once been, and the ore or copper was a good idea for the replacement of revenues, however, much more discourse would be required before a plan could be projected. David had suggested that one alternative to acquiring new Negroes might be to arrange something with the Irish who had been coming over, since many of the Germans who have worked out well were leaving the North River Valley for free land being offered for colonization in Penn's woods. In Pennsylvania, settlers were offered freehold ownership of their lands. The Pennsylvania farmer did not bow to a landlord, and he paid no lease or dues for the land he cleared of trees or the rich black soil he plowed. The Irish were starving in their own disease-ridden country, and John had heard that they would give a hard days work in the colony for a crust of bread. There was no question though that, one way or another, they would have to hire five or more woodmen to begin their venture, since the wood had to be cut throughout the winter in order that they could start up in the spring. Some much-needed labor might be acquired from neighboring farmers while their fields lay sleeping, but those numbers that her neighbors could spare might be sparse and expensive. She could not possibly spare Henry or even one of the Negroes from her mills, which ran year round.

Still, if they did not hire the Irish, or establish some sort of tenant agreement with them, their only recourse would be to investigate the New York slave block. Margaret winced. At the same time, the thought of Irish Catholics working her land made her feel weak in the knees.

She had given her life over to her father, and then Teunis, and now John, rarely thinking of her own needs. With David, she would share a love with a partner; a husband sent by God with whom she intended to fully surrender herself heart and body. This time though it would be her decision to hand over the reigns, but before she surrendered her farm and those entrusted to her, all would be clearly acknowledged in a witnessed document. It was a dilemma that she must speak with John about as soon as he returned.

Marie folded away the handkerchief she had been working on. She pulled her chair closer to Margaret's. "I bid you put away your work for a time. I have a confession that I would make to you."

"A confession?"

Nervously, Marie replied, "Yes, if you please I would speak my mind."

Margaret's face registered concern. "You are smitten with the carpenter?"

Marie straightened in her chair. "Nay, but I fear what I have to say may be far worse for you to hear."

"Oh, Marie, speak that I do not give out my last breath upon this day."

"I have seen and heard somethin', Mistress Peg, and I have not confided in you. I have been afraid."

"What have you heard? Tell me so that I can make it right."

"I fear that my brother, Moses, has been hidin' runaways."

Something caught at Margaret's heart. Remembering her earlier suspicions, she asked, "Where does he keep a runaway that I would not know?"

"I think he hides people down by the river in the old stone cellar. You know—the place where in past we have kept our dead peoples during the winter before we can take them to be taken under in the buryin' place."

Margaret sighed. "Holy God, protect us!"

"I wanted to tell, but then the census taker came to the house. I have not rested, as I said, until the mornin' after he left, and that is true, but I did not tell you all of the truth. I beg of you, Mistress Peg, forgive Moses. He is a young man, hardly more than a boy, and does not understand how dangerous this can be to his person and for all of us."

Margaret interrupted sternly, "Does your father know of this?"

"Oh, no, he knows nothing' of this treachery. Moses does not know that we saw him either. I have not yet confronted my brother. But I lied to you before when I said that I hardly have spoken to the Van Rensselaer carpenter. One night we were down by the river together. It was the second time we were together and I swear to you that both meetin's were innocent. He held my hand and that was all, but we heard somethin' this last time, and saw a man wadin' away in the shallows. It was dark, but I know it was Moses who I saw in the moonlight along the shore. I said nothin' to the carpenter that I recognized him. I am ashamed that I did not come to you sooner." Marie became tearful.

"Be calm, Marie. Tell me what night was this?"

"It was the night before the census man came to the house."

Margaret sighed. "I do not think Mr. Kent discovered any improprieties," she whispered thoughtfully.

"This was why I have been talkin' to the carpenter. He is a good man and wants no trouble. He is most grateful for the work and swears that he will say nothin' of anythin' that he has seen, especially since he feels for the Negro that risks all to be away from a bad owner. I believe him when he says to me that he will bring us no hurt."

Margaret stood and put her arm around the weeping Marie. "You did right to tell me. I will keep a staunch eye, and for now I will say nothing to Moses or any other, and I wish for you to keep silent whilst I consider what is to be done. Now go to your room and freshen yourself. We approach the mid-day meal and you must see to Sally."

Marie left the room sobbing, wiping her eyes with her sleeve.

As her closest friend disappeared, Margaret reached for the pitcher and poured herself another glass of water, desperately trying to regain her composure. What if John were to discover the secret of their household? She shuddered to think of his reaction. Soon, regardless of her sympathies, she would have to put a stop to the harboring of runaways on her properties.

The mid-day meal came and went. Margaret and Mr. Lapett dined alone. Marie had sent Sally to serve them. Bess could not leave her bed. The weather being dismal, no work could be done by the artist, and so the afternoon passed quietly. Margaret went to Zebulon as she said that she would, but had all she could do to offer comfort to the elderly man by presenting herself the image of the calm mistress.

As she walked back from Zebulon and Eva's cabin Margaret remained deep in thought. She must have all of this resolved before David returned with her brother from the North Country for she could well imagine what recourse John would suggest that they take. He would probably favor an appropriate punishment for Moses rather than a warning.

That night as she said her evening prayers, she begged the Almighty for direction, thinking at the same time that John would argue that Jesus gave no spoken word to guide his people regarding the issue of slavery. Her brother insisted that there was nothing recorded by the Evangelists who wrote of Christ's life on earth of Our Lord's sentiments on slavery. There was no question in her mind that if John found out about this he would be stern in his punishment of Moses. Most assuredly he would admonish poor Marie severely for not coming forth right away with what she and the carpenter had witnessed. And would Van Rensselaer's carpenter seal his lips as Marie had said he would?

She could hardly sleep. She could not rest her mind, so tightly wrapped was it around Marie's fearful disclosure. What could she do before the return of David and her brother? She visualized the scene that might take place if John came back home to find all of this. He would raise the roof, insisting upon the lash for Moses that all know that this sort of disobedience would not be tolerated within the Vandenberg household. Lawlessness could not be ignored. Moses might well be made an example to all. With Lizbeth, she had no knowledge of the happenings, and so, as Lapett had said, she could not be held responsible. But now, with Moses, she had full knowledge of his wrong doing and must take control. She understood that he did pose a great danger to all of them, but at the same time how could any Christian condone cruelty to one's fellow man and still be following the principals of love taught by her Savior? She had already made a mental note of the rebuttal she would give to John, recalling that in Deuteronomy: 23:15,16 it is written, "*Thou shalt not deliver unto his master the servant which is escaped from his master unto thee, he shall dwell with thee, even among you, in that place which he shall choose.*"

Perhaps her father had been wrong in his interpretation of scripture. Did the Bible not suggest that a servant being treated without justice had the right to find refuge, and that assistance to one in need receives the Lord's blessing? After hours of tossing, exhausted, Margaret finally slept.

At dawn, awakened by the call of the rooster, Margaret thought her direction more clear. Alas, her wealth had granted her much, yet the English laws of trade were something over which she had no command. She must do as she must. Despite the written words of the gospel, she had no recourse but to uphold the property laws of her country. All the same, she would endeavor to protect Zeb and Eva's son from harm's way. At this point she decided that she would have stern words for young Moses and demand his solemn oath that he would never be a part of such mischief again. She must make him understand the terrible consequences of his actions should this become common knowledge, and she would swear to him that she would administer the lash herself should he disobey her.

Chapter 12

Margaret laid down her playing cards, triumphantly proclaiming, "Thirty-one! I have the set!"

Lapett groaned, "And so you have. You are the devious one. Once again you have beaten me. In this lifetime, Peggy, will you ever take pity upon me? Might I coup a victory once whilst at your table? Just one victory; that is all I beg of you."

"Oh come, Benjamin, do not wail so. The deal, as you well know, is in God's hands just as the fleas are upon the dog. Believe me, I have as much control over Bess's scratching hound or the cards as I do over anything else."

"Oh I would not go so far as to say that, my dear. I believe you understand the mathematics of the game, and I dare say no self respecting flea would enter your house."

"Mathematics! Mathematics has naught to do with games of chance. Perhaps I am just more the clever player."

"I will submit to that possibility," Lapett replied dolefully.

"Nay…I only jest. I should think that I have fair success because I so love a good game of Cribbage. I find it much more interesting that the old Nodde. Do you not agree?"

"Yes, I would agree."

Margaret replaced the playing cards into a small, white, gold trimmed box, suddenly becoming somber. "Teunis did so love to play at Nodde. He taught both John and I the sport of it, and later it was he who introduced us to Cribbage which has been my passion ever since. My father, of course, would not tolerate a game of cards whilst he was in the house."

"He did not sport?"

"Nay. He would race the horses up north at Schuyler's flats, but I can not recall my father playing at cards. On occasion my mother did much enjoy it. I remember that sometimes in the winter season we would play by candlelight on a Saturday night. That was a long time ago. I was just a child. But, my father, nay, my father did not like any of the English or the Dutch parlor games. He always thought them a waste of time."

As Margaret placed the ornate card box beside a gleaming, etched silver snuffbox on the walnut side table, Lapett glanced at the pearls that hugged her throat, reflecting upon the stark contrast that they made to the strung corn kernels that she had worn almost daily for the last number of weeks while he had painted her portrait. The lustrous pearls, he thought, did not seem to compliment her half as well as did the kernels. He supposed that Margaret had scarce time for fashion during the regimented days that had been her life, and he had heard her say that surely God intended women more as companion to the male species than as ornamental structures to be paraded. She would, he supposed, leave the strutting of pairs to the peacocks that roamed her front grasses at will.

"I have given up smoking my pipe in the parlor," Margaret said with a sigh.

"Oh?"

"Anna tells me that I am uncouth to enjoy the smoke, and that no proper English woman in New York would consider putting the long stem of a pipe to her lips. I told her that, as she well knows, I could care less what an English woman would or would not do, or would or would not fancy, but I would be sorry for anyone to consider me uncouth."

"If you are so course in nature, I dare say that most every good woman in the valley would also be so, for there is hardly a Dutchwoman who does not enjoy a pipe alongside her husband."

Margaret laughed. "That be so, and I would keep on with the smoke but for fear of soiling the new pretty wallpaper. So I have taken to keeping my pipe and tobacco down in the kitchen where I smoke it most of the time by Eva and she grieves me not. This inconvenience is all most difficult as I have enjoyed a good smoke since I was a very small child. What do you think Benjamin? I have never seen your good wife with a pipe, but should she take one up would you think her uncouth?"

Lapett stared back blankly, not quite sure what would be a proper response.

"What is it that distresses you today, Benjamin? It is true that I am a far better card player than you, but today you had difficulties concentrating upon all the plays. We have known one another a long time, friend. I can see that your heart is not into the playing of cards. Are you missing your family?"

"Yes, though your company be a delight, I have missed them all since the very moment I bid them farewell, but I have of late been thinking of others, too. I am, I suppose, sharing many of your own sentiments. So often I am thinking of the old times. I think of all those who I have known and who have already gone to our Savior."

Margaret nodded. "Yes," she sighed, "'tis true, so many are gone from us. Before John left for Albany we were talking of our dear mother and Teunis. John thought of others, too, who I had not thought about in many years. He was remembering the Indian one called Saga Yeath Qua Pieth Tow, the King of the Maqua's, who went with Schuyler and the four other chiefs to see Queen Anne in London. The English called them all kings, but other than the Indian chief known by his Christian name as Hendrick, the others were not so high.

"The King of the Maqua's was also called Old Smoke Brandt. This one had come to my father's house to see him around the time of the New Year whilst many Indians here about celebrated White Dog feast. Later that year he along with the others departed for England with Peter Schuyler. I remember now that John had known this Indian whilst he was with Schuyler at Fort Ingoldsby the year before. My father invited me to sit in with the men and to have smoke. I enjoyed the time immensely. All of us had lengthy discourse with the Maqua, who, of course, would not take a seat on any chair we offered, but sat on his knees. I also recall how taken I was with the beautiful designs tattooed over his face and chest. He was magnificent to look upon."

Lapett's attention had been recaptured. "I have heard of the portraits of these Iroquois done by the artist Verelst by request of the Queen. I would be quite enchanted to look upon them. Yet, my understanding is that there were only four Indians who made the voyage."

Margaret responded, "There were five Iroquois who went to England, yet there are only four who were painted. One did not survive the voyage going over. 'Tis good that the King of the Maqua's likeness was made by Verelst for he died shortly after his return from England. We were all deeply saddened to hear of the tragedy. It was said that he had caught the white man's sickness while in Europe."

Lapett sighed. "Now we hear that Schuyler is very ill and may not last the year." "I have been saying prayers for the Indian's beloved Quidor. He is a man who is brother to the Indian as well as the whites." Margaret paused and then added, "You know, of course, that the Indians call Colonel Schuyler 'Quidor' because it is difficult for them to pronounce."

After an appropriate moment of silence, Lapett said, "In truth, my thoughts today have been filled with one much closer to your family. I was recalling the last bride whose portrait I painted. Of course, I speak of Christina."

Margaret stiffened. "Yes, of course, I remember all the fuss."

Lapett seemed not to notice the change in the demeanor of his hostess. "Your former sister-in-law presented much to consider; she is a mother who knows what she wants, but being the father of a large brood of girls myself, I understood a mother's concern."

"Ah, concern is a polite word," Margaret whispered half to herself.

Lapett leaned forward adding, "Christina was a delight, and thankfully, we were able to finish well within the schedule insisted upon, despite her mother's clucking."

"My sister-in-law always meant well I suppose," Margaret replied, passing her hand across her stays that insisted upon a perfectly straight-backed position. She noticed that her head was beginning to ache again from her tight coiffure.

"Forgive me. You know, of course, I meant no disrespect to your former sister-in-law."

Margaret's dark, pensive eyes flashed. "Oh, please. I know Rachel well. No insult is taken. My brother was very impressed with Christina's portrait, Benjamin."

Nervously Lapett interjected, "I should think that the children miss their father dearly."

"Yes, as do I. For myself, I miss his brotherly affection. Teunis was one for hugging me with the strength of a bear."

Quietly Lapett replied, "I enjoyed his company more than not."

She studied Lapett steadily for a long moment and then remarked softly, "Teunis and I often disagreed, as do most brothers and their sisters, but our arguments never stood for long. I pray God that before my brother drew his last breath he came to believe that I wished only for his just rewards in heaven. I can only imagine what he thinks of the man who moved into his house and his bed within months of his passing." Lapett offered a thin smile and quickly changed the subject. "I had thought that John and David would have returned by now."

Margaret rose and walked to the side table where earlier Sally had placed a fresh pitcher of beer. "I expected them three days ago, but I do not suspect foul play," she said handing over a glass. "I know that John had business to attend to and that he had a mind to combine a visit with Mohawk friends whilst he was at Albany. He also meant to gain an audience with General Schuyler and to introduce David, but, since Quider is so very ill, he may have left David in the good hands of my cousin, Cornelius."

"I am most certain, dear Peggy, that there is no need of concern."

"I should expect them momentarily, but John would be right to stay there that he can learn all the news of trade. Changes are coming to our country, Benjamin, and we in the countryside must be vigilant. I have heard that Governor Burnet has made arrangements just this year for Indians as far away as a thousand miles northwest of Albany to bring their furs to that city to trade. Like me, those merchants up north who make their profits trading with the French trappers are not so happy, I should think. The Governor wishes trading with the French to cease."

"I should wonder what Peter Schuyler thinks of all of this."

"It was one of the reasons John would wish to speak with him."

"I see. By your leave I would stay awhile until the men return that I may pay my respects."

"Yes, of course. Margaret responded, wondering if he had heard the whispers of the rift between hers and Teunis' widow's family, or if now he guessed at her thoughts. She was sure that he had noticed the absence of her elder brother's widow and the absence of her nieces and nephews from her house during the artist's stay. Margaret still could not understand why Rachel would put aside the memory of such a man such as Teunis so quickly to remarry. But her feelings went deeper still, oscillating between tolerance and unabashed dislike for Rachel's new husband, Tom Kingman. *God forgive me for I have been the sore looser in the games with that one*, she thought.

"Well, God does his work in many ways, Peggy. Perhaps your sister-in-law was lonely, and the Bible does say that two are better than one. For yourself, He has sent Mr. Karski who is a fine man. All can see how he cherishes your company.

My wife and I are happy knowing that you have obviously made a match that will help you to shoulder life's burdens."

Margaret brightened. "If he is as good to me as your wife is to you, then I have no doubt I will be truly blessed. You must know that you and the presence of your family at my wedding will give me great joy."

"My wife and daughters speak of nothing else. Our house is filled with women's chatter of your upcoming wedding," Lapett extolled, gladly accepting a second glass of beer. Margaret lit a candle on the table and then went to the window where she stood looking out, muttering something about young Sally languishing yonder smoking her pipe.

As Lapett sipped his beer his thoughts were, as Margaret had suggested earlier, far way. It was true that there was little talk these days of anything but the Vandenberg wedding to come, but chatter was not quite an accurate description of the uproar that was taking place in New York City at his, and (he suspected) many of the homes of invited guests. All four of his daughters had begged to be excused, making a case that they were young ladies unaccustomed to the savages that would, undoubtedly, impose themselves upon the civilized guests. His eldest, who said she spoke for herself and her three sisters, wondered who could possibly want to be a witness to such an assembly—the marriage of a matronly Indian and a backwoodsman unknown to all. They had heard that the husband to be had roots in the Kingdom of Poland! Why, he might even be a Papist and neither bride nor groom had a drop of good English blood!

Replying to the haughty insolence, his astute wife had stung them all with a good sharp tree switch that she kept for such occasions...upon which, the four reconsidered. Lapett winced. He hated such harsh measures, yet he was grateful that their mother could hold them well in hand.

"The Moravian will be here as well," Margaret announced breaking the silence. "Phillip is such a dear, precious man. Did I tell you that he is composing music which he will perform at the ceremony?"

"Yes, I believe you did say so. I do look forward to hearing the piece."

Lapett stood to admire the dramatic life-size portrait. Yes, he thought, this is the Margaret who I will acquaint with generations to come. Let Duyckinck paint his women demurely with prayer book in hand.

Margaret half whispered, "I pray John and David return soon. I will be happy to have them safe at home."

"Do not fret over them. The two have survived far more than a short journey to Albany."

"Of course, you are right to say so."

Lapett chuckled. "They most likely make merry. A man who is about to marry is entitled to a small amount of merry-making before he speaks his vows."

"Be still, will you, Benjamin? You men make merry aplenty. I think my brother has it in his mind that he will have my future husband with him whenever he has the slightest desire for male companionship along the road."

Lapett felt a lump swell up in his throat, his humor dissipating. He couldn't help wondering how things would fare once she and David were wed, especially as it seemed that John wished to assert himself as an equal partner. He had been privy to a few of John's sentiments regarding the addition of slaves to their holdings, a plan that Lapett could see was already being met with great resistance on Margaret's part.

Suddenly Marie appeared breathlessly at the doorjamb, tears streaming down her face. Margaret hastened to her. "Why are you weeping, Marie? What is wrong, dear?"

"Henry's boy... Peter... is outside, Mistress. He implores you to come with him to the mill, saying there is terrible trouble down there. My brother, Moses... God help him... is near death! So says the boy!"

Marie paused, putting a hand on her chest. She drew in a deep breath before continuing. "Horsemen with their cloaks wrapped about their heads rode in near an hour ago. Heaven save us, Mistress! Peter says they cut poor Moses' ear from his head and then nailed it to a post in the mill house! Another ran his saber through his leg! They did these cruel acts saying that this must be so no one forgets!"

"Forgets! Forgets what, Marie?"

"I take not their meaning myself," Marie mumbled between her tears. "Peter saw that Seth was beside my brother when he fell. He says Seth begged them to be merciful and says one of the riders said to him before he rode off to tell his Mistress that they come as a warning to any slave or his owner who would take part in a conspiracy. Oh, Mistress, what foul play is this? What if they return?"

Lapett stepped toward the window. Looking out he saw a thin, dark-skinned boy of twelve or thirteen holding fast to the corner rail post of the front stoop steps. The lad was vomiting.

"Dear God, what about Henry and the others?" Margaret asked anxiously.

"Peter said that he and his father and the men were workin' in the field far out back of the hops house."

"Calm now, Marie, calm, sit yourself," Margaret said. Pulling over a chair, she gently guided the distressed Marie forward, soothingly patting her shoulder.

Marie tried to control her trembling hands. "He says they heard those horses approaching hard on them, but when I asked him who these men be, he could not say. All he knows was that Henry considered the riders be comin' from the east. I am thinkin' that Henry and the others paid the riders no mind, bein' they were riding so hard, like they be keepin' on their way."

Margaret's head was spinning. Who would dare come onto her plantation and attack her slaves in plain daylight? Who would be so insolent as to enter her mill to commit such crimes, risking a possible encounter with any number of neighbors who might be there having their grain ground into flour? The foulness of such treachery was unthinkable.

"Oh, Mistress Margaret, the boy told me he looked back once as he escaped to us. They have set fire to the stored wheat."

Lapett spoke firmly, "Calm yourself. You are safe within these walls. How many horsemen, say the boy?"

"Peter did not say. I think they were gone by the time Willie yelled up to Henry that he should come down; but the child out yonder is out of his mind with fear so I can make no headway when talkin' to him. When Peter first came to me I was in the bake house with Mama and Sally. He had but a little breath left, so I went out front to the dippin' well and fetched a ladle of water for him to drink. Finally, he tells me what has happened like I just was tellin' you... and that he fears his uncle will die from his wounds."

Margaret pulled her musket from the wall. Lapett quickly stepped in front of her. "Have you lost your wit? Margaret, let the Palatinate tend to this!"

"Leave me be, Benjamin. I cannot wait for the Palatinate." Her dark eyes glared toward the window where she could see smoke billowing high into the sky from the direction of her mills nearly a half mile away.

Tearfully, Marie interjected, "Oh, Mistress, remember that Mr. Altemouse took a wagon full of barrels with flour to the village at Slingerlands early this mornin'?"

"Yes, I remember. All the more reason I must go," she responded, glancing at Lapett. "Marie, run to the bake house and put Sally on the bell, and then fetch Martha. Have her come up here to the big house and instruct her to bolt the doors and windows once inside. Before she goes up to be by Bess, tell her to take up this pistol that I will leave for her here on the desk. My sister-in-law will know how to make proper use of this weapon if bloody violence should reach their door." Margaret opened the drawer to her desk, withdrawing the weapon along with a small ammunition pouch.

"When you have seen Martha on her way, go run quickly to Tom in the west field. Say to him that he must call everyone together who is there working beside him. Do you understand?" Having somewhat regained her composure Marie nodded.

"Good. And, do not dally in explaining the trouble to him. Only say that all of our people must drop whatever they are doing and go to the back shed to get buckets and pots. Tell them I have said that they should not be afraid, and I require that they all go in haste to Henry at the big mill. Henry will know what is to be done when they join him. Tell Tom to look where the smoke rises and to prepare for the bucket brigade. I will send Peter right away to my sister-in-law Rachel's plantation for help."

Lapett had listened nervously to these instructions. Once again he tried to dissuade what he feared was an irrational action that could very well be a prelude to terrible consequences. "How do you know that these violent men do not lay quietly hidden over yonder awaiting you? It could be that they wish to draw you forth. This is a dangerous business that might well end for you in the same way it ended for Lizbeth!"

Refusing to listen, Margaret reached for the leather ammunition pouch on the shelf in the cupboard beside the hearth and tied it around her waist. "Marie, you need not shed any more tears," she said tersely. "We have come through many hardships together long before the good strong arm of Mr. Altemouse was at our disposal, have we not?"

Marie took a deep breath and nodded. Standing, she went toward the gun rack on the wall. "Here, take the French musket, Peg. It is much lighter and is easier to handle than the English gun."

"Nay, I am well acquainted with this one. You keep the French gun and do not fret. Keep your wits and be strong."

Lapett continued to object. "Lord God, Peggy, you can not go out there!"

Ignoring his pleas, Margaret again turned to Marie. "After you have sent Tom and the others along, go quickly to the Tuscaroran's cabin and fetch him and Mama Shasa. Tell them of what Peter has seen. Bid they come in all haste, although…" Margaret's voice dropped to a murmur, "I would venture that if they have seen the smoke, they are surely on their way."

"Spotted Bird should also search the back side of the storehouse sheds for buckets as they pass on the road to the mills, and be sure to have Shasa bring her healing bag." Marie ran from the room, and Margaret removed her shoes and quickly slipped her feet into deerskin moccasins which she took from the cupboard holding the ammunition. Jumping up suddenly, as an after thought, she called out to Marie, "Remember your papers!"

Strangled by alarm, Lapett croaked his plea. "Margaret, please... I beg of you, hold off while I fetch my weapon. If you insist upon going down there..."

"I cannot wait, Benjamin. Do not worry. I am no goose running from the gander, I will not leave myself open to harm's way either. I will leave my horse stabled. I know my land and will keep to the side of the trees with my wits about me. Need be, I am an excellent markswoman, as well you know."

Lapett was angry. His face had taken on a purplish red color rarely seen. "You are a willful woman, Peggy, and I pray God to protect your stubborn heart!"

With the heavy English musket gripped hard over one shoulder, she pushed past him. At the door she paused. "I suspect they have done their hurt, and have all run away. Such brutes often be cowards. But, should they show themselves, they will not attack me. They dare not! But, be they so foolish, and come at me, I will not hesitate to put this lead shot into their worthless bodies!"

Exasperated, Lapett threw his hands upward into the air as Margaret ran down the steps of the front stoop. For a moment he stood in the doorway watching her as Margaret gave her two servants a few last words of instruction. Young Peter seemed reassured by his Mistress's determination, and soon the three parted company, each running off in a different direction.

Lapett rushed upstairs to the top landing where Bess met him in her nightdress. While ushering her back to the bedchamber where she had been resting before hearing the commotion, he explained in abbreviated form a version of what had happened down at the mill. He repeated Margaret's opinion that the worst dangers were over and reassured her that Martha would soon be there to keep her company.

As he approached an open window, he and Bess heard Marie scream something to Margaret as her mistress ran toward the mill. Bess lit a candle as Benjamin closed the richly paneled oak shutters. "God be with us all," she whispered.

Chapter 13

Stormy weather had hung over the Vandenberg farm the better part of August, the heavens regularly opening up for a pounding of hail and torrential downpours the likes of which had not been seen for years. Today's weather was the same. Dawn had produced another warm, muggy day of wild wind and foreboding clouds. Throughout the North River Valley, battered gardens and corn fields awaiting harvest had become swamps, and as September approached, roads more resembled creek beds than viable routes of transportation.

As planned, John and his future brother-in-law had joined up at the Rensslaerwyck farmhouse of Cornelius Vandenberg that lay across the river from Albany. There they were forced to hold up for days, accomplishing little of the work cousin Cornelius had scheduled for them. As the summer days dwindled away, even though Cornelius stressed his need for the extra help, neither John nor David could see his way clear to stay on till the weather was once again tolerable.

John was especially distraught knowing that Bess was due to have their child at any time. After promising to return as soon as could be arranged, the pair started out. Soon though, they found their route home nearly impassable, and so had to reroute via old Indian trails which had caused additional delays. They arrived two days after the attack at the mill to find their women folk running between wounded slaves and Bess in the throws of her time.

Their Negroes would survive, the barn had sustained little damage, the precious wheat gathered in July had not been burned, but both John and David swore to find the villains who had committed the atrocity. This year, like the last, planters had agreed that they would wait for a good hard freeze over the dirt roads before bringing their wheat into the Albany marketplace on sleigh. A coating of snow lying over the hard grounds would be a blessing. But as the storms persisted many wondered what crops would be decent for market, and if this was not a sign of God's displeasure and the beginning of the end to all mankind.

While just about every farmer in the valley prayed for clearing skies, as dawn shyly made entrance, not a soul in John Vandenberg's modest clapboard house was concerned with the possibility of another devastating storm. All thoughts and prayers in that household had been focused for three days and two nights on a far more imminent danger as Bess fought to give up a first born infant imprisoned within her frail, exhausted body. Just before the break of dawn, a girl had been born. The child was healthy enough, yet there had been no rejoicing as Bess lingered near death and their plantation struggled to recover from the attack the week prior.

In the adjoining room Mamma Shasa knelt in front of the enormous brick hearth. Hours before, gnarled arthritic hands had hung two large, black iron kettles: one filled with chunks of ripened pumpkin from an early harvest while in the other pot brewed an herbal tea. The tea was Shasa's own special recipe, a concoction she always made ready when she came to help birth a baby. As the tea simmered and the pumpkins stewed, a delicious aroma filled the room. Tired, yet capable, the elderly midwife gingerly stretched out to rake some of the burning wood chips from the hearth to make another fire on the floor in front of the big one and directly in front of her. It would keep the smaller kettle warm. Its contents were a hearty mixture of corn mash sweetened with molasses that she had specially prepared for the worn out Master and new father in the next room.

While maneuvering the heavy pots Shasa bent forward and as she did so her two waist-length graying braids swung dangerously close to the fire, one suddenly catching a flame. Frantically, Shasa stepped back, extinguishing her smoldering hair with her hands. Quickly she pulled at the folds of her skirt, nervously checking her garment for burn holes. Reassured that quick response had averted a possible disaster, she returned to building the new warming fire and laying the kettle of breakfast pottage onto the bed of hot coals on the floor. This accomplished, she returned to the ball of dough on the table, sprinkling a trace more of wheat flour on it. She quickly thrust and withdrew her bare arm from the wall oven after determining that the oven's temperature was just right for baking her loaves. After sliding the dough into the oven on a long-handled wood paddle, she turned her attention once again toward Bess.

Peeking through a series of strung blankets that served as a curtained wall between the two rooms, the midwife noted that for the moment her charge slept; her tiny, swaddled, newborn infant lay next to her, also at peace. Master John, bundled in an Indian blanket in a chair beside her bed, remained awake, the devoted sentinel. Satisfied that for now nothing more of her service was required for mother or child, Shasa retreated with a heavy heart to watch over her kettles.

Even though the Indian woman was confident that she had done all that she could for the new mother, she was concerned because her mistress had lost a grave amount of blood and was very weak. If Bess died most likely the infant would also since there was no other woman on their plantation who was still suckling one of her own. When Bess awoke she would encourage her to sip the herbal tea. After that, all she could do was to watch over her and wait to see if she improved or if it was the will of the Great Creator that she be called to Him.

Shasa had hardly laid eyes upon Master John until the previous summer when he came back from the wild frontiers, bringing that man, the big bull westerner, and his little Bess along with himself. After his long absence the first time she had seen him was when she had come to the big house one day last August to bring the Mistress her foot rub made from butter and wild mint. Shasa remembered that Master John was by the stables, and he paid her no mind. She was at the plantation because Mistress Margaret had called for her after learning that the Master's little wife was with child.

Most of Mistress Bess' laying-in time had been spent at the big house; Margaret fretting and fussing over her new young sister-in-law as if she had been beloved blood kin forever. Shasa suspected that the Mistress giving all that attention to the newcomer most likely put a thorn in the backside of Marie. Marie liked the Mistress' stroking as much as the horses in the stable.

Shasa remembered that sometimes when she came to see Bess while the baby grew her big, Master John had been home.

When he was there he seemed to watch everything that she did. He often had asked that she tell him every plant that was used for the tea and where he might come by it in the wild. Shasa thought him a strange man then and a strange man now. He just wanted to know too much.

As she watched him now beside his woman's bed she believed she was right. Master John was a different kind of man. What man would wish to know such things as how to brew a woman's tea? What man would stay by his woman in the birthing room? Master John was like none other she had ever known, and surely he was not the man she remembered picking her and her son from the slave block in Carolina.

Her thoughts were interrupted as John shifted in his chair and rearranged the blanket about his shoulders. It then came to her that the Master had not shut his eyes in all the time since she was fetched to the house, and she imagined that he had not been to bed the night before. She had no intention of allowing this unusual man with a big heart to become sick from worry and lack of sleep.

She rose from her stool and pulled the curtain aside. "Master, come sit for a cup of good tea," she whispered, speaking in a distinctive blend of Algonquian and New York Country-Dutch.

After what seemed to her a long wait for his reply, her anxiety increased. Forgetting all protocol she pressed further. "Will you not come to table, good Sir? If you not like my brew, how say you for the English tea? Mistress sent Sally back with this tea block for you. Your wife and the babe rest peaceably. You need not fret over their good keepin'. Come away now. You and your good wife will see many more babes."

John Vandenberg's eyes remained closed. He appeared not to hear a word of the Tuscaroran woman's pleading. He had not stirred or uttered a single word since Margaret had returned to the big house hours before. Although present physically, his mind was far, far away. His thoughts traveled from his wife's bed to years past when he first left his father's house and the side of his elder brother and his sister. Early in 1714, he had ventured into an area far to the west inhabited primarily by the Onondaga Indians, but where there were also scattered French, Dutch, Swede, Scottish and Polish pioneering families who had braved settlement on the frontier wild lands. There, among those known as the Hill People, he had taken an Indian wife who had given him a son. Just as his Indian grandfather had done, he had worn breech cloth, hunted, and fished. There for a time he had lived in peace and harmony for perhaps the first time in his life. There he had not been the second son of his father, but a whole man. The days rolled into weeks that became years. But a sickness had come upon the village and his wife and little son had died. He had pushed on further west past the great waters that roared to a settlement of English, Swede and Dutch. Two years later he successfully wooed his precious bride, Bess. She was barely twenty, a steady, gentle-spoken girl who was herself already a widow and thus knew his pain of loss for it was her own.

Finally opening his eyes, John stared across to Bess, her rich walnut colored hair tasseled loosely about her pale face, a face that he knew intimately to be as smooth as their tiny newborn child's. He understood now that the Almighty's will was done according to His divine sense of timing, yet this most recent wondrous event frightened him. He had a feeling of uneasiness about Bess and his beautiful new daughter. John knew his many sins, and he acknowledged that he did not deserve this miracle that slumbered before him. A good man and a good woman had died in order that the miracle of a marriage with this woman was made possible.

From all accounts Bess's first husband, William White, was an exceptional man, while he himself was an egotistical, selfish one. Most assuredly he was not the same kind of man as White, and it was still hard for him to believe that the Lord had taken that man so early so that he, John, might have a second chance. Why should he, a man so often so full of rum that he could not stand, be so blessed? He ought not be considered any better than a thief that came late in the night where Bess was concerned. Still, it made no sense to him that the Almighty would take her from him now. She had to survive.

He also pondered the many changes that had come into his and his sister's lives, and he wondered if Peg thought about all of this as did he? They had not spoken in depth since he had returned, and now that she was betrothed to David, it would be unseemly for them to discuss matters of a personal nature, but still, he wondered. It had never been his desire to grieve Peg, and he had never asked her pardon for every hurt that he may have caused her. He prayed that they could once again hold affection as brother and sister.

He had never intended to be away from home all these years. After the death of their father he had bid good-bye to his sister and Teunis. He had said he would journey among his Indian brethren and would live among them for a year or two that he might know his heart better. He thought that he would then return to his homeland a better man. Had he known of Teunis's death he would have come back straight away, but then, after two letters that were not answered, he communicated no further. When he had finally returned, determined to put all that separated him from his family aside, he learned from his sister that she had never received any of his letters and they had thought him dead.

Now as he looked upon his wife and child he had to believe that He Who Is Great had a purpose for John Vandenberg. Unlike his sister, he had not been a man of strong conviction about one matter or another, but his personal beliefs were changing as swiftly as all else in the world around them.

Thinking of all that had transpired, John recalled how he and Margaret had learned from their English tutor of the great waterfalls three hundred miles west. As a young man sitting by the campfire with fur traders at Albany, he had heard of the spectacular falling waters that roared so loudly that no other sound could be heard. It had taken him nearly two decades to make his way there. He now realized that, as wondrous as those falling waters and other adventures had been, he had been sinful in manipulating his way around and away from the wearisome duties of the properties his father had entrusted to his three children. He had been selfish and obstinate, and yet out of his sin came blessings. Would he be punished? Would Bess and this child be taken from him? Or had he, although unintentionally, truly made amends with Margaret through David. He prayed that was how the Almighty was seeing it now. As a sense of humility overcame him, he was sure of very little except that nothing was to be taken for granted.

Not one step of his life could be perceived as normal since the first day David Karski had made him acquainted with the enchanting widow, Bess White. Though he knew he ought not question the ways of the Lord, he couldn't help it. As Bess had suffered through her pain, John thought little of his unborn child, yet thought at great length about how much he cherished the woman he still hardly knew. He vowed that if she lived he would never touch another dram of rum as long as he lived.

Awakening from his dream's journey, as Shasa's voice penetrated his consciousness, John's eyes awkwardly met hers. His servant quickly glanced away but not before he had caught a glimpse of the compassion of her concern. Her kindness moved him. Straightening himself, he wiped the sweat from his brow, wondering if every man felt as he when a first-born thrust its tiny presence into this world. Most certainly the birth had made him a believer that there was nary a husband who could grow accustomed to the rigors of a wife's childbirth tribulation. He now understood why the Indians called it the *fearsome valley of death.* He acknowledged Shasa's concerned expression with a nod, whispering to her, "I will come soon to table and will be obliged for the tea my sister sent over." Shasa nodded back; a trace of a smile registered her satisfaction.

Rising wearily John paused, awaiting the rush of pride that he had been told to expect as a new father, but instead he felt only immeasurable admiration for Bess, and a strong surge of relief that her ordeal was over. And praise God, the child appeared healthy. The woman who gave reason to everything that was his life was alive, a thought that prompted him to awkwardly repeat his prayer of gratitude.

He listened to the steady, reassuring sound of his wife's breathing. He was still uncertain that he should take his eyes from her, still fearful that she might slip away from him at any moment. But she lay there in such a deep and peaceful repose that it was as if the terrible violence that had racked her tiny frame only hours before had never taken place. He was astonished. He glanced at Shasa who once again nodded reassuringly. He struggled to rekindle and embrace within his chest the old woman's words which echoed Bess's sentiments:

trust the Lord. If Bess and Shasa could trust the Lord Christ, he should be able to do the same.

Reaching over he pushed away a wisp of hair that had fallen across his wife's face. She had already gone through so much. Smiling, he thought of how Bess insisted that her grandmother, Sarah, had often told her that she had the heart of a bear. In his mind her grandmother's words were truly spoken, for at seventeen Bess had been married less than six months when her husband was murdered by the Shawnee while on a hunting trip. Two months later their child was stillborn.

Bess had concluded that since it was the Lord's will that she conceive by her second husband, she had no doubt that she would hold this babe—and each of her babies—and theirs would be a joyous life together. She had also announced that, should the child be a boy, he should be called John, and if a girl, the name would be Clare after her own mother. As he glanced toward the cradle where his robust daughter lay sleeping, he knew that whatever gave joy to his faithful Bess would also fill his being with happiness. He hoped that she had not thought him weak as tears had unexpectedly made their way into his eyes last night as the infant made her way into their world, but though he tried they could not be controlled. His senses were stirred by the dread that came upon him during that hour when the sound of her painful, pitiful cry cut through his heart. When his dearest had implored him to do so, he had remained with her until the women had dismissed him, grateful for the escape, yet hating himself for acting the part of a retreating coward.   In truth, he had no longer wished to remain. As his wife's screams had filled the room, hell, he imagined, could be no worse a dwelling place, and he was relieved to leave it all to the fortitude of the women.

Margaret had smiled broadly when she carried in the swaddled babe. As he looked into his sister's moist eyes he understood her unspoken sentiments. This new addition to their aging family was a blessed event that bore more than a subtle kinship to a miracle. The child called Clare would flourish. She was most assuredly a Vandenberg.

Despite Bess's faith, John had not believed that the hour would come when he would see his own living child. So, convinced that Bess and the struggling unborn child within her exhausted body courted death, the previous night he had done something that for him was very unusual. He had prayed. He had stood in front of their newly constructed modest home, faced the night sky, and begged mercy of the one true God. He asked that the Almighty pardon his fragile faith, forgive his sins, and preserve the lives of sweet Bess and their innocent unborn child. Within the hour his supplication had been answered. Once again he had been blessed.

After the birth, from a safe distance, John had curiously observed the Indian woman as she began to gently bathe his new daughter with a warm cloth. Soon Shasa whispered that she would wake Bess and return the child to her breast. As she spoke she seemed oblivious to the howl of a ferocious wind and the pelting rain that beat against the clapboards of the house.

A loud knocking beckoned Mama Shasa to the door. Opening it, she called over her shoulder, "My son has brought us fresh venison." Joining her, John saw a large buck hanging from a tree branch: the animal's belly had been gutted, and the blood drained into the ground turning the earth red. Shasa approached Spotted Bird, and John surmised that she was giving her son the good news of the child's birth.

"Feast!" Spotted Bird called out.

"Yes," John chuckled. "We will all feast greatly in celebration!"

Chapter 14

Just prior to his departure Lapett had strolled with David and Peggy along the shore of the river wharf, where Henry was waiting. He had been tasked to deliver Lapett by rowboat to Captain Waldron and his crew aboard the sloop *Rebecca* anchored fifty feet out. Sad goodbyes having been said, Margaret tearfully bid a final farewell knowing that she would not see her dear friend again until next he returned with his family for her wedding in early October.

As David and Peggy faded into the distance, Lapett stood at the front of the vessel, and although his prayers could not wash away the scenes of horror that had transpired over the past month, a sense of relief poured over him like a gentle spring rain. Finally he was on his way home.

* * * *

Smoke from one of the collapsed smaller barns billowed high into the sky as Lapett had, in full run, breathlessly arrived at the scene of the attack. Although there was no sign of Peggy, within a short time the artist had ascertained the scene was much as she had predicted: the perpetrators of the treachery had obviously retreated. The riders, Henry later said, had departed when hearing the sounding of the alarm bell. The wicked cowards had run away rather than face an armed opponent.

Running from building to building, Lapett had searched franticly, finally coming upon Margaret hunched over the barely conscious Moses. Henry knelt beside her, tears rolling down his face. Margaret held a blood-soaked piece of cloth in her hand while most tenderly examining Henry's younger brother's mutilated head. His right ear, as reported, had been severed. Lapett noted that Henry had already removed the fleshy ear cut away from Moses from where it had been nailed to a large oak beam. He had wrapped it in a small swatch of flower sacking for safekeeping, no doubt for burial later. Lapett also noticed that several other wounds had been inflicted upon Moses; most severe of all being a cruel gash across the calf of his right leg. Margaret struggled to bandage with strips of cloth apparently torn up from her apron.

Moses had survived his wounds thanks to Margaret's attention and the herbs Shasa had brought in her medicine pouch.

By the following day, however, his skin was on fire, and he was slipping in an out of a delirious fever. The leg wound was getting worse. The Indian women tending him had come up from Munsie Creek after hearing the Vandenberg distress bell. They told Margaret that Muxumsa Wehenjiopingw or the *Spirit of the East* was calling to him. Moses, they feared, was on the trail of death.

On the fourth day after the attack, David rode for the physician at Kinderhook village. The physician had arrived, and, after a brief examination, was obliged to cut away the Negro's foul smelling limb just below the knee in order to save his life.

Days later when Moses' fever had broken and the stump began to heal, he was moved to a fresh, straw-filled pallet in the herbal cellar kitchen of the big house where potions were brewed and remedies were ground. It was the place Mamma Shasa and Eva could best tend to their patient.

One evening after a late supper, Lapett overheard Margaret give Marie encouragement regarding Moses' condition. After her brother had healed, all would go well with him. Moses' new responsibilities would include tending the kitchen fire and keeping the hearth ablaze every day. He would never again be able to work in the mill, but she was not to worry over him, as they would find him suitable duties that would keep him useful.

In hindsight, Lapett thought Moses' hardships were minor considerations. He would endure. Another frightening development had occurred that was potentially far worse.

In the confusion of fire and choking smoke so thick that the mill's thirty-foot water wheel was made indiscernible, the boy, Peter, had vanished. At least that was when most observers thought that he went absent. Some believed him dead, although Henry feared that the boy might have been captured by the assailants.

Lapett had put up an optimistic front for Henry, telling him and the boy's mother that he would pray for Peter's swift return, but, after the many searches made resulting in no sign of their son, his sinking heart told him that their child was lost forever. Peter was, he prayed, in the arms of the angels; God willing, his kin would have the grace to endure the pain they suffered.

It was possible that the assailants had secretly shipped him to the Indies where he would be sold for a healthy price. John had ridden to Albany for help and an extensive sweep of the property was conducted by both Provincials and several English soldiers from the Albany garrison. Not a trace of young Peter was found. All concurred that the youngster had never arrived at the Kingman's neighboring manor house where Marie had bid him run for help.

Someone had suggested that, within the confusion of the smoke, Peter had possibly slipped and fallen into the river. Margaret would not believe that the fourteen year old was so confused that that could have happened. It was clear to Lapett that in her mind young Peter had been kidnapped. She was as much beside herself as was Peter's mother.

The uneasy silence that followed attempts to locate the boy, alive or dead, had provided the investigators more despair than comfort. No word or action indicated a clue. Weeks had passed and still there were no answers to Peter's whereabouts, or a single discovery as to who was responsible for the attack.

The mystery of Peter's disappearance had continued to press upon him to the last moment of his departure as Sam and Joshua ran alongside the riverbank, waving goodbye. As the ballooning sails of the sloop, *Rebecca*, filled with chilly, late September air, he waved back to the youngsters, immensely glad that he would soon be encircled within the loving arms of his wife. At last, within a few hours he would finally embrace the comforts of home. He glanced up at the full pillows of white clouds floating through the bluest of a blue sky, relieved that there was no sign of foul weather and a pleasant journey could be anticipated.

Lapett surveyed the deck and found a sturdy seat on a flour barrel, enabling him to keep his distance from two scraggly dressed young men who he had noted reeked of rum when they passed by him earlier. He thought from their attire and accompanying bundles, as well as the fairly new purplish-red bruises on the forehead of the one, that they might be the Meyndert brothers; sailors who John had mentioned had been visiting his cousin upriver. Whomever they be, he suspected that they were returning to duty upon one of the vessels moored at New York harbor. If they were indeed the troublesome brothers, he concluded that few in this valley would be sorry to see them go after the shambles he heard they had made of Tinner's Inn near Van Wie Point the week he had first arrived at Margaret's. There had been a terrible fight. Mr. Tinner and his wife no doubt would be the happiest of all to see these Meyndert's away to sea, and happier still if they did not return home for another seven years.

As Lapett settled himself, and the *Rebecca* pushed its long wooden hulk through the choppy, North River waters, away from Vandenberg's landing and all that had left him so utterly bone weary, he began to think of his girls. Surprisingly, he had laughed this morning for the first time in ever so long. He had confessed to David that he would actually welcome his eldest daughter's moodiness as well as the incessant questions of his youngest. He had laughed. How remarkable, he thought. A simple smile had been something difficult to achieve since the afternoon he had beheld the misery inflicted upon Margaret's slaves.

The vessel had been under way for a brief time when one of his fellow companions, a thin, sallow faced lad, began to sing. He gave Lapett a start as the meekly countenanced lad's voice was deeply melodious and rang out strongly with a sad lament. He instantly recognized the lyrics to the *Ballad of Captain Kidd's Execution*, a favorite of seamen for more than twenty years.

"*Come all ye young and old*
See me die
And see me die.
Come all ye young and old
You're welcome to my gold
For by it I've lost my soul
And must die
And must die."

Lapett took up his long stem clay pipe. He opened his deerskin tobacco pouch hanging around his waist, trying to ignore the remaining dismal stanzas. He wondered how often Kidd's family had been subjected to the humiliation of this woeful composition.

Standing, he put the small leather case containing his brushes and paint knives under his arm, walking to the other end of the vessel where his thoughts returned to the bustling New York block where he had resided with his wife and children for the past twenty years. This was a day for rejoicing not to be marred by past sorrows.

To cheer himself he thought of how good it would be to have a tankard at Janz Tavern once he was back home and had suitable time to reacquaint himself with the softness of his wife. Oh, the sweet gentleness of his dearest. He promised himself that he would hold his wife close for a very long time. He visualized awakening before dawn with his most precious sleeping beside him. He would rise, and from his upstairs bedroom window see their servant girl, Abby, sweeping down his front stoop steps. Next door, her sister would be similarly engaged at Mrs. Heaton's once her boarders were off to work. Already the aroma of the double sweet cakes baking in the ovens at Susana Bell's Bakery two doors away filled his nostrils.

He eagerly awaited the noise and capricious scenes of the street where he lived. He had been desirous of a game of billiards for some time, and there was always a friendly game at Janz Tavern. Although he had enjoyed playing cards with Peg, he had sorely missed Janz's. He smiled to himself, remembering that Janz's was not wholly approved of, but was patiently tolerated, by his dearest.

As usual, the North River highway was filled with many sloops, as well as life along the shores, prompting Lapett to take out his sketchbook. The *Rebecca* rounded the cove at Fox Hook where several Indian women were wading waist deep not far from the shoreline, washing their infants in the cold, pre-Autumn waters of the river. Astonishingly, only one of the infants was violently objecting, the others were placid as though the cold river waters had no affect upon them at all. The bare breasted squaws smiled and waved to passengers. Lapett laughed, watching the tranquil picture for a moment, knowing the bathing of the little ones was a first step in the children's ability to grow accustomed, and ultimately indifferent, to the bitter months that would soon follow. Margaret, too, had been cared for and strengthened in the same way by her own mother. Perhaps it was this endurance cultivated by a loving mother that helped Margaret go on after so many hardships—and then the attack.

The moody verses of *Captain Kidd's Ballad* had at last trailed off. When the boisterous, young singer attempted the start of a new tune, a quick end was put to his energetic performance of *Sweet Molly* when a voice roared down from the ship's mast above, "Quiet, will you, we have all had enough!"

Lapett chuckled, comparing the sailor's choice of merriment to the calming pleasantness of Mr. Lansing's own arrangement of *Love Sings Bright* as only Mary Strickland could sing the special composition. While visiting Peggy throughout the years, Mary had captivated all of them with her remarkable, angelic voice.

As the voyage continued Lapett was once again pulled back to events of the past weeks, wondering this time about Tom Kingman who until recently he had counted as more villain than valiant. Of course, his assumptions were purely unfounded, as he knew little about the man personally, and they had had few encounters through the years. He had never given him much thought in the past, but now he did. What sort of man *was* Tom Kingman? Within what seemed no more than an hour after he had arrived at the scene of the attack, Kingman and Rachael had come along with a wagon full of their Negroes; the Negroes armed with buckets, and Kingman and his wife as well as two of her eldest sons, armed with musket and shot.

When the fires had been quenched and all had calmed, Tom Kingman was questioned as to where young Peter might be since he was sent to alert him and bring him hither. Mr. Kingman had appeared genuinely confused and claimed that neither he, nor any of his people, had seen or spoken with any of the Vandenberg Negroes along Pontoon Road that connected their places. Like all others he had heard the bell and seen the smoke. Kingman also insisted, before being asked, that he had not seen any riders who would have been considered suspicious. Lapett thought him too anxious to offer this information, yet all the same, he had been of great assistance in putting down the fires.

Later it was determined that Peter had never been seen among those at the site, either when Margaret first arrived or later when Henry and the others were frantically working the bucket brigade from the creek. Nor did the Tuscaroran see the youngster beside the road as he and his mother rushed to aid their Mistress, having been beckoned by the bell and the black cloud that had mushroomed into the sky, alerting them to trouble.

In retrospect, Lapett thanked God for making those wicked men cowards. He dare not think what more malicious wounds they might have inflicted had they remained. When he had given his account of what he could recall from the confusion of that brutal day to the English sergeant conducting the investigation, Lapett had offered his opinion that whoever had done the deed had prior news of the status of the manor's household. Those men must have known that, other than he, armed men would be absent and that Margaret was at home alone with women and slaves. He had told the officer that if the riders suspected that he was there in the house, he was sure that the culprits would have considered one portrait painter no threat.

As the *Rebecca* continued her journey, Captain Waldron stopped at various locations along the river picking up additional passengers. Passing one of the Wendell estates, the vessel approached Bear Landing, the last place where passengers would be boarded before reaching the final destination at Manhattan Island. At Bear Landing a party of three loud, English speaking men boarded. Once on deck each man took a turn greeting Lapett before seating themselves comfortably only a few feet away from him and continuing what had obviously been an interrupted salty discussion on discipline.

"My Negro boy, George, waters his pallet nightly. Yet, I have found a remedy."

"What is that?" his companion asked.

"Before I left my house two days ago, I made him drink a pint of his own piss water. I told my wife to give him naught to drink but piss until I return and to give him fair warning, that he will feel my lash if the pint does no good."

Lapett noted the shock in the eyes of the other two travelers. Apparently, the disciplinarian also recognized their disapproval. The farmer added indignantly, "It's only right to break him of such a foul habit. The boy is seven or eight years of age, far too old for such behavior. I know what I am about. It was the cure for one of mine own."

Lapett gagged, rose and moved, but finding another seat brought him to another unpleasant discussion of the recent execution of a woman convicted of Petit Treason. With the help of her lover she had killed her husband. English law demanded that she be drawn and then burned at the stake. Her lover was hung.

"I heard that when the executioner tied her to the stake," the passenger reported, "he tightened it securely about her neck thinking he had strangled her before the first torch was put to the straw."

A white-haired man across from Lapett replied quietly, "She was fortunate he took pity upon her. No woman, whatever be her crime, should die like that."

"His pity was a sorry waste," the other replied. "When the fire leapt up, the flames went straight to her throat and burned the binding away and she fell forward still alive. Witnesses say she cried out and struggled against the stake, before the smoke overcame her and she was finally blessed with her death."

Needless to say the account had a sobering effect upon all, and for a moment there was stillness aboard while they contemplated the dead woman's anguish. The severity of English law and penal system justice these days was not easily swallowed by those who knew that anyone could find themselves incurring the wrath of a superior.

One of the young sailors mentioned, "Fredrick's Negro wench, the one they always call Princess, because she makes claims saying her African people are royals, is gone missing. Never ran before, and nobody could understand her running now. They got a notice up in Kent's tavern. Saw it there last week."

A tall lanky man who had introduced himself earlier as Jim Hill from Red Hook, replied to the sailor, "What think you of the weddin' plans up at the castle?"

Sobriety was quickly replaced with animated participation. "A woman her age grasps at whatever she can, and we all know that what this groom is seeking is nothing more than her fortune."

Several laughed, while another spoke up in a sullen voice, "He's nothing more than a puppet to the queen of the court. She will operate her properties in his name." Lapett sat rigidly, realizing that without question the woman who was being discussed with such vulgarity was none other than Margaret. The men smelled of strong rum. *If they are not intoxicated,* Lapett thought, *then they are complete fools having such discourse upon a vessel piloted by the Dutch Captain who is bound in friendship to all Vandenberg's.*

As if a mind reader, the younger man chastised his companion, "You had better not talk that way, Robbie."

"I speak the truth," the other slurred belligerently.

"These days truth is worthless. Authorities would knock at your door and drag you like a dog into the street to be disemboweled for speaking your sort of truths about one of the richest women in all the colony. The lady of whom you speak has powerful friends who have ears everywhere. Beware: it is wiser to keep your tongue in your mouth. That Mistress could have it sent to the Governor's house on a silver platter."

"I think you be right. I have no desire to call down the dogs."

"Nay, Sam, your wife will keep them out," the stout man jested snidely. He grinned cautiously in Lapett's direction. It appeared that he sought to provoke him into conversation, but Lapett turned his back, refusing to give rebuttal. It was futile to stand up justly for Margaret in the middle of men like these.

Once again he tried to absorb the calming essence of the leaning birch, hemlock, and the long, gracefully waving cattails, which dressed the shore. But, his attempt at peace of mind was not to be had for long. An Englishman, who he had met on the journey to Margaret's nearly a month before, and who had said he was fresh over from London where he had worked as a bricklayer, recognized him and began to engage in casual conversation. He told Lapett that he had found employment in New York City where the houses were now required to be fronted with bricks, but his employer, himself an Englishman, had granted him two days leave to make the trip to Albany for his sister's wedding. Now he was returning, still full of the spirits.

Finally aware that Lapett preferred to occupy himself quietly, the newcomer joined with the others in their conversation. Before long he was as loud as they, even becoming more vulgar than the farmers in extolling the intimate yearnings of Dutch maids.

Another traveler abruptly moved his wife to the opposite end of the deck, giving the group a disgusted look as they passed.

Lapett couldn't listen to them any further either. He imagined that the young man wished to gain favor in sharing the details of his supposed conquests, yet an opposite effect seemed to result. The farmers accused him of insulting all Dutch women. Within moments, fists were tightly clenched, and Lapett wondered who would keep these kinsmen of the maids from killing this stupid Englishman?

Someone had fetched Captain Waldron, who along with two of his shipmates were forced to lock the young man below in the Captain's cabin. When Captain Waldron returned, he warned the others that they too should keep a civil tongue or they would make the remainder of the journey below; his intention to turn them over to the authorities at New York. They took him at his word and peace was restored.

Later, the Captain, whose father had come over from Holland when he was a boy, strolled the deck to make sure all had settled down to good order. He paused in front of Lapett. "Small minds make smaller men," he whispered.

Lapett nodded. He had been thinking much the same.

Before Captain Waldron returned to his duties, he passed Lapett again and this time he added disgustedly, "My grandfather, God keeps him in His care, would have called those ugly mouths, 'Dutch low men'."

Whether or not his companions had heard the Captain's remark, one could not say, but the chatter had quieted.

Twenty minutes later a sudden upsurge in the passengers' voices indicated their sloop would soon dock at New York's busy wharf. Lapett's heart sang out. He was certain that his wife had sent a carriage to fetch him and soon the excited chatter of his daughter's questions and requests would flood him. No doubt his exuberant girls would exhaust him, but for now, he would be patient—happy to embrace each one of them. The journey had been long and wearisome. He would be glad to sit down on his favorite leather upholstered armchair at long last.

Chapter 15

As John stood in the doorway, he saw what he judged to be two riders approaching through the humid, dense morning fog.

"Colonel Beekman comes yonder!" Spotted Bird called back.

Narrowing his eyes, John saw clearly that one of the riders had the mounted six-foot frame of Henry Beekman. *What on God's good earth brought him out on such an unpleasant morning? He must have been riding half the night.*

As the riders drew near, John noted that Henry's Negro rode the pinto beside his master. The soaked pair dismounted, and the newly arrived servant along with the tenant farmer Indian led the horses away to care for them.

"By the heavens, Henry, come into the house. You be looking as though you could use a spot of rum."

"I'll be thanking you for your generous kindness," Henry Beekman responded, shaking the water from his wide brimmed, beaver-skinned hat.

As John closed the door behind them, Shasa followed the men in and scurried to close the curtains to the bedchamber where Bess remained sleeping despite the clamor. Returning quickly, the servant woman bowed her head and curtsied to Colonel Beekman before taking his hat and cloak and walking toward the side cupboard of the hearth where the two jugs of rum were kept.

John took his neighbor's garments from the Indian and laid them over the barrel chair near the fire. "From whence do you come, friend?" he asked.

"I come out of Kingstown yesterday morning, on my way to Albany. I had thought as the inclement weather approached that we would take our rest at Hoffman's Inn before coming to your manor, but the place was abandoned, so we forged on." Beekman was astonished to discover newborn Clare asleep in the cradle at the side of the hearth.

"God be praised, John, who is this?"

John smiled. "This be Clare, newly arrived before the dawn."

"And your good wife?"

"Bess is well."

Henry Beekman slapped John on the back. "Well done, well done!" he said hardily.

John shrugged his shoulders. "The Almighty has been generous," he replied softly.

Beekman nodded, soberly, lowering his voice. After another glance toward the baby he added politely, "She is a comely child. Favors your wife, I see."

John chuckled, nodding. Then, remembering his guest's words regarding his difficult overnight journey, he remarked, "Tavern owner Claus Hoffman, whose inn you mentioned, has sold out and gone to Housatonic River land to live with his eldest daughter and her husband. The new owners, I have been told, do not arrive for another fortnight."

"I wish I had known. Well, let us hope that the new man is as merry and hospitable as Hoffman."

As John invited his guest to be seated Mamma Shasa returned with two pewter tankards and half-filled them with rum. She quietly picked up the child, pausing for a moment; she cuddled the infant close before disappearing with the new born into the bedchamber. John's face registered tenderness and then confusion as she departed.

Henry winked. "Ah, trust this father of seven," the Militia Colonel said jovially. "You will see little of your child until after she has received the holy waters. Your servant woman does what is right. Leave everything to her good judgment. You know, do you not, that it is not healthy for the father to handle the little one too often?"

"I may not see my own child?" John queried.

"Nay, you will see her, but from a distance is best. Take heart though, for soon she will be consistently upon your heels and you will be wishing her away."

John laughed at the disparaging remark knowing how Henry Beekman doted upon his own children.

"What brings you to us this morning?" John asked.

"Sorry to say but 'tis troublesome news that I bear. Two Negroes have run from Seth Chandler's place over near Rhinebeck," Beekman responded quietly.

"The planter and shoemaker, Seth Chandler?"

"He is the same man. My wife urged me to come," Beekman went on. "You know, of course, the high esteem in which she holds your sister...as do I. We are concerned because Chandler has gathered several men from neighboring farms to come looking for his runaways. My man, yonder in your barn, tells me that there is talk that they plan to come to Vandenberg Estates to look for the runaways. There is talk, John...."

John interrupted. "Nay, nay, too much vile talk."

"Of course, of course, but Chandler is a crude brute, John"

John wrinkled his brow, not wishing to disclose the knowledge of the attack he had learned about when he had returned from Albany. "I did not know Seth Chandler owned any slaves. I have not seen him in many years."

Beekman replied, sipping the warm rum, "He has done well for himself, but I fear that he is a terrible master. I say to you, who can blame the beaten man who runs, or a kindness that is extended to the oppressed?"

Abruptly, John jumped to his feet, suddenly understanding what his old friend was trying to say. "Vandenberg's give no quarter to runaways!"

Beekman smiled nervously. "I said as much to my wife, that she should not be so concerned; but I thought I should come, that you be forewarned and prepared. I do not mean to give offense, but I would not wish to see you or your sister hurt. My wife has complained that she herself witnessed Chandler's harsh treatment while visiting with his wife, Mary. His wife confided to mine that he has burned her servant woman with a hot iron as punishment."

"Henry, though it is true that we cannot see everything, I give you my word: none of Chandler's Negroes have found refuge on Vandenberg soil."

Henry eyed John levelly for a moment. He slapped the table in front of him. "Ah, then that is settled. Your word is good enough for me, John." Beekman moved to get up.

"Nay, Henry, stay," John urged, seeing his friend's embarrassment and intent for quick departure. "Have something to eat. My servant woman has made fresh mush. I will have her fill a bowl."

Henry stood staring at the wood planked floor. "I am red-faced to come before you, John. But, to speak as an honest man must, Margaret is fond of keeping close friends such as Mrs. Rouseby, former wife of Captain Kidd, and her daughter, Elizabeth. And of course, after what happened all those years ago in Manhattan with your slave woman...well, it is understandable that it is difficult for some to believe—"

"I hear the words you speak, Henry. What came to Lizbeth was a tragedy that came upon us through no fault of anyone's but a poor misguided young woman who thought herself loved. My sister still grieves for her company though those days are long by-gone times. Speak kindly please, though, of Mrs. Rouseby and her children. Sarah is a Godly woman, and my sister does call her and her children friends. They have paid long and dear for the wrongs committed by Kidd."

"I do not doubt that Margaret is of staunch spirit in keeping to our laws; and she is devout in her love of God. But, all the same, I am glad that you are home and that she is finally to have a husband's good guidance.

"I thank you for the offer of a plate, but I will be off."

"So be it and God go with you on your journey. I bid you goodbye."

As John closed the door, Bess called weakly to her husband from their bed. "John, come hither to me." Startled, John rushed to her side.

"I heard voices."

"Spotted Bird brought us a gift of fresh venison, but it was Henry Beekman whose voice you heard. You do not know him. He stopped on his way to Albany. All is well."

Groggily, Bess asked softly "Have you seen our girl?"

"Yes, and she is as beautiful as her own sweet mother." Tears filled his eyes as he kissed the inside of Bess's palm.

Bess made a feeble attempt to smile. "Do not concern yourself so. I am not desirous of making you a widower again. I will live long and give you as many handsome boys as precious daughters—just as my grandmother prophesized. The women in my family are sometimes troublesome, yet praises to God, we are most fruitful creatures. Did I not tell you as much on the day you proposed marriage to me?"

"Yes, you told me," John whispered. "Now you must sleep and regain your strength. Rest while you can do so. The baby is safe and fast asleep in her cradle."

Kissing her gently upon the forehead, John withdrew as Bess closed her eyes. He walked to the table and picked up the mug of tea that Shasa had poured for him, stepping into the adjacent room where Shasa's eleven-year-old daughter continued to lay asleep undisturbed on the pallet in the corner of the room.

His mind began to whirl with a dozen thoughts. Last week, while at Albany, John had read with great interest a posted notice. A cargo of ninety-four, prime, healthy Negroes consisting of thirty-nine men, fifteen boys, twenty-four women and sixteen girls had arrived and would be sold in Manhattan. It was foolish to think of clearing even the small parcel of white trees that he and his sister spoke of, let alone think of broader plans, until he had purchased the additional field labor; an expensive but necessary proposition if any of this was to go forward. He and David had calculated that they would need no less than five sturdy men if they were going to be able to cut timbers from the forty acre parcel that they had selected for the site of the forge. They required prime workers and only strong male slaves, but if these males had families, John had already decided that he would not separate them. "Only thirty-nine men," John whispered to himself. Surely the best of them were spoken for already. But all things considered, the acquisition of the Negroes was only half of the bitter task that lay ahead. He still had to convince his sister of the worthiness of the forge—and buy out Rachel's interest in the property, provided her husband, Tom Kingman, allowed such negotiations. Mr. Kingman would make a thorny stand for the selected property, part of which he would perceive to be his through right of his wife, or he might demand that he be made a partner; either option left John cold.

For now though, Bess required her rest, and so the intimacy of more tender words he had thought to say must wait. He wasn't sure where his next steps would take him, but at the moment of the child's birth, his fair, delicately featured new daughter had made her position known with an undeniable loud cry. John knew that cry not only heralded little Clare's beginning, but a final ending to his former self-seeking, free-spirited life.

Chapter 16

In the years following Gerritt Vandenberg's death, the long reaching arms of warring European forces relaxed within the American Colonies as the guns of France and England fell silent. As Margaret prepared for marriage, it had been thirty-three years since the heinous 1690 massacre at the outpost of Schenectady where over two hundred French and Indians from Canada had spilled the blood of sixty innocent people. Symon Schermerhoorn's heroic, six hour winter's ride from Schenectady to Albany, warning of possible attack, had become past history.

After the signing of the Treaty of Utrecht in 1713, plans for Peter Schuyler's Colonial invasion of the French enemy to the north had been put aside. Work on his northern forts ceased, and his militia returned to Albany. The natives living within the North River Valley co-existed as peaceable trading partners of the Anglo-Dutch, and rare was the occasion when skirmishes took place between natives and white settlers. It was a time to reinvest in America.

Prior to Gerrit Vandenberg's death, his eldest son, Teunis, had purchased an additional land parcel adjacent to those of his father's from the Mohawk Indians. The deed to approximately forty acres to which his native friends had put their mark and Teunis had signed allowed the Indians to hunt and fish upon those lands for all time. There on the property adjoining his father's, Teunis had, during the last two years of his life, built several barns and a fine stone house for himself and his own growing family. However, despite the contract Teunis had made in good faith with the natives, after he died, and once his widow remarried, all that quickly changed.

London born Tom Kingman had been in the regular British army. Around the turn of the century he had been recruited in England to serve in the colony's frontier garrisons, ultimately being stationed at Albany amid scores of tough English, Irish, and Scots. Although Margaret had never been able to discover how or where the widow Rachel had met her second husband, Margaret suspected it could have been through John Collins, another professional soldier turned attorney who had done very well for himself in Albany. She did know that, during the latter part of his life, Teunis had preferred to use Collins for his legal affairs over Wendell, as had her cousin Peter Waldron. She also knew that Collins and Kingman both had houses on the Southside of Albany. Unlike what most of the English, Irish, and Scots had done when their duty had been concluded, Collins and Kingman, along with a handful of other garrison soldiers, had chosen to remain and continue in their colonial endeavors to better themselves. These were the "facts" from the dribbling of hearsay and rumors that Margaret had pieced together over the years.

The only truth that stood out from all the others was the reality that Rachel had married a stranger within months of her husband's death. Although it was clear to most that Tom Kingman lived in the shadow of his wife's first husband, it was also obvious to all that he did not care to remain there.

Though she was always polite for the sake of the children, Margaret could not embrace Rachel's husband and had as little discourse with him as possible. First, she thought it would be a slur upon Teunis's memory for her to do so. For the most part though, Margaret thought Kingman too full of himself: a man who boasted where he had no quarter to boast and put his nose in where it did not belong.

Her reasons for her summation of the man's character were varied, but primarily Margaret detested Kingman's ill treatment of those he considered beneath himself. Mr. Kingman said that he could not abide the local Indians squatting on his property, frequenting his well, and occasionally borrowing his boat "without so much as a how-do-you-please". It infuriated him that whenever they had a mind to do so, the savages picked apples from the trees in his orchard and even helped themselves to the herbs in his wife's garden.

Rachel's new husband also found fault with Spotted Bird claiming property rights as a tenant farmer upon land that Kingman believed rightfully belonged to his wife. But what really incensed him was that the tenant rents were going to Margaret, not to his wife. Annually on the first of May Spotted Bird delivered his six bushels of wheat, three fat hens, and his promise of the required one day of work to Margaret, all of which Kingman insisted was owed to him. Kingman said that he could accept that Margaret and her brother receive all of this as payment, but only if he too was to receive the same payment. By right of English law he now mastered Rachel and all her properties as her legal husband. Recently he had demanded an explanation as to why this tenant, Spotted Bird, made his annual payments to Margaret and John, and did not share at least a portion of the payments with him who was the owner of the property where the Indian grew his wheat. For that matter, any of the Indian's property claims held no water with him. As far as he understood the law, savages were not allowed to own property. He had threatened to take it all to the courts and let them decide. His threats had come to naught, but had made terrible feelings between the two families; neighbors, and whose children were blood kin.

Margaret thought that none of this was her fault. She had summoned all decorum to explain to Tom Kingman in the most civilized manner that as far as she was concerned the Dutch inheritance laws superseded English law with regard to her rights to Vandenberg land and any other of her properties, including the slaves that had once been owned jointly with her two brothers.

She had pressed upon him that he should indeed be mindful that her family had long ago given these rights to the Indian called Spotted Bird. His marriage to Rachel would not interfere with that which had been written up by Attorney Wendell, witnessed properly, and recorded according to law. Spotted Bird would continue to live at that place in his cabin without dispute as he had done since the early days when John and Teunis had brought the pregnant Shasa and him as slaves from the south lands.

Margaret wanted Mr. Kingman to understand that since the death of Teunis, Spotted Bird had his papers and was free to return to his native Carolinas, or, for that matter, go wherever he should choose. His freedom was granted by full agreement with Rachel and herself prior to Rachel's second marriage. When Teunis succumbed to the pox and then John had not returned for so many years, it was decreed that John be presumed dead. Margaret, knowing John would have lent his blessing to such a gesture, initiated freedom papers, and she and Rachel had signed them.

Indians were not allowed to own property of their own, and so Spotted Bird and his family had entered into the tenant agreement. Margaret had provided him at that time with an ax, a horse, and two hens. He was also told that should he leave he could also take with him his mother and young sister and all the possessions he had acquired. Margaret had prayed that Spotted Bird would not leave for she could not imagine her plantation doing without Shasa. Yet, although she doubted at the time that the Tuscaroran would take up the offer, she would have held to her word and bid him fine farewell. But Spotted Bird had insisted that he would move no more.

As Kingman continued to protest for what he believed to be his rights, in an effort to have him understand the reasoning of her family pertaining to the Indian, she had shared Spotted Bird's tragic history of how he had first come to them. The Tuscaroran could never return to the land of his ancestors. His people had long ago been driven away from their settlements near Charleston. His new friends living along the banks of Munsee Creek told him that many of the Tuscaroran people had fled northward to the security of the Iroquoian long houses at a place called Hoagie. Now the people of the Iroquoian Federation were calling these Tuscaroran Indian refugees, "children of the sixth nation." He could go there and join with them, but he was happy living here at the edge of the mountains, shadowed by the tall hemlocks, where his cabin was cool in the summer.

When Margaret recalled the squabbling that had gone on over these past years between herself and Kingman, she sighed, knowing that their differences were bound to grow if John and David pressed forward with their plans. They had spoken to her of cutting an access road through the woods close to the Tuscaroran's cabin to the site of their proposed forge. Although John had insisted that the enterprise would not disturb the wheat field Spotted Bird sowed and harvested as his own, she had been greatly distressed when she had overheard her brother say that he would use Spotted Bird's cabin to house his new workers. He had suggested to David that he had already picked a site for the relocation of the family, and he was sure that the Tuscaroran would be happy with his offer.

Margaret believed that she knew of the intended spot. It was good land full of rich black soil that the Indian elders said came from the dead lakes of a thousand moons ago. Of course, with no other choice, Spotted Bird and his family would move should he be required to do so, and other wheat fields would be established. Another cabin could be built, but she wondered if John had considered that undoubtedly Kingman would want a portion of any money made from the forge. With a heavy heart she could only speculate on the trouble that could come if this dream of her future husband and her brother was realized.

She closed her eyes, painfully recalling how Shasa and Spotted Bird had first come to them. It was a terrible year for all that had begun with the death of Teunis's eldest son, Samuel. The fury of that winter also took two of Zeb and Eva's little children. As the cold days began to dissipate, but with the ground barely thawed, they saw the departure of fifteen of their workers, a mix of German, Irish, and Scots, who had been hired years before off of the river cliffs where they had camped. The immigrant workers hired to cut timber had all taken their families and walked away to William Penn's "Holy Experiment", a colony where Papists were embraced by Anglicans turned Quaker as vigorously as any other Christian.

Desperate for workers, and unable to find what he needed in New York, Teunis turned to the second largest slave port city in North America. He had learned that Charleston merchants specialized specifically in both Native and African labor, and would be exhibiting excellent plantation workers who had recently been imported from the Caribbean. Having been abandoned by his former workers for what they had called "the grander opportunity", and discouraged by the quality of the Africans the local independent slave traders repeatedly exhibited on the New York block, Teunis had had no choice but to look to other resources. Beside which he made it plain to all that he was tired of dancing with the Scots and the Irish who, although hard working breeds, were obviously not men content in being lorded over. With the Africans, put under Zebulon and his eldest son, Henry, who would train them, Teunis felt his investment would be well seated, and surely he could rest assured that his slaves would not walk away for the grander good.

Once in Charleston, Margaret's brothers had found few Negroes for sale, but they did find Spotted Bird and Shasa amidst seven hundred, wretched Tuscaroran who were being passed among the hands of the slave traders. Both John and Teunis had been appalled at the sad condition of the starving Indians camped within a city that had begun to be referred to as "the city of tears". Teunis had decided that it would probably be best to turn around and leave at once. Home, he could hire the two nephews of his German foreman, Hans Altemouse, who were begging for work, rather than spend good coin on that which could, in all likelihood, bring still more troubles. He had had all that he could stomach. But on the day they were to leave God had intervened as John caught sight of a badly beaten youth of seventeen or eighteen accompanied by an equally fragile woman who was large with child. Later John and Teunis learned that Spotted Bird's father and three brothers had been sold to a Jamaican plantation owner. At first, Teunis was against dragging the haggard Indian family along, but John argued for them, saying that the boy looked strong and the price for two would soon glean three. So four rather than two had returned home, and all on Vandenberg Farm had taken pity upon the two. Eva was soon teaching Shasa how to sew the bags used for shipping their wheat flour. Within weeks Betty was born.

Instead of Henry, Teunis had put Spotted Bird under the charge of Mr. Altemouse, who his father had trusted till the end. Mr. Altemouse, like himself, had no good use for any Scots-Irish, or any Papist, and had been content to spend time with the angry, young Tuscaroran who stood shoulder to shoulder with Altemouse's nephews in training.

Perhaps, Margaret thought, Mr. Altemouse had seen something of himself in the displaced Indian. From the beginning he seemed to understand Spotted Bird's rage and mistrust. Altemouse had claimed that at one time he had the very same fire in his belly. He had left the Rhine Valley to escape the blood-soaked soil of his ancestors. As a young man he saw central Germany devastated by war after the Palatinate district in the western section of the country was invaded by French King Louis XIV, and a short time later by the Spanish Succession. He had been more willing to starve on the high cliffs of the North River than to stay in Europe.

But the history of the Vandenberg family and the acquisition of their slaves seemed to fall upon deaf ears as far as Tom Kingman was concerned. The last time Margaret had seen Rachel and her husband it had been more of the same arguments. In the end, Tom Kingman had sighed loudly, throwing his hands in the air. He and Rachel had turned their backs, climbed into their carriage, and driven away.

Chapter 17

Margaret had not loved David Karski upon first sight, but she had liked him almost immediately. He was never impudent or lording as she knew some men could be, and she liked that from the first day of his arrival he had spoken respectfully to Mr. Altemouse, as well as to each of her servants. He seemed to know how to be appropriately somber, but could also be foolishly frivolous, on occasion playfully throwing one or the other of Henry and Martha's twins over his shoulder or swinging them round, much to the little boys' absolute delight. All loved his deep baritone voice. Sometimes, while lending a hand at the lumber mill, without any encouragement he would break out into song or whistle unfamiliar tunes.

If the man from the west beyond the great waters had no answer to one's query, he admitted such right away, and Margaret was charmed by the way he stumbled over the words in reply after the simplest compliment. Although admittedly not well versed with Holy Scripture, Sally had told her that more than once she had found Master David alone in the barn praying his prayers amongst the animals. David was without a doubt a Christian who loved Christ.

When she had posed any question to him, he had answered her forthwith, looking straight into her eyes. It was brash and unsettling in the beginning, but his honesty had refreshed her soul. Perhaps all of this would have been enough to turn the head of most women, but Margaret had never thought of herself the same as most women, and it was only after she saw how he handled her stallions that her mind unlatched her heart.

As the weeks turned into months, she soon became acquainted with Mr. Karski's steady disposition. She liked most how he told a story as much with his hands as through the spoken word. While acquainting her with his distant family he poked fun at himself. She had laughed uncontrollably as he most soberly tried to explain to her that, according to his grandfather, the Karski name meant a person of stunted growth, or dwarf, but because of his large muscular size, his boyhood friends had called him "Ox". That name had clamped onto him like iron initials against the front of a Dutch house.

When David spoke of his western homeland, his Dutch stepmother, and his expansive family of both married and unmarried brothers and sisters who he had left behind, Margaret saw traces of homesickness in his eyes. For months she tried to ignore her growing feelings, but as September leaves began to fall, and David had not returned west, she took off her armor knowing that she could not deny her heart.

As St. Nicholas Day approached, one late November day David made an awkward confession while they sat alone by the roaring fire in the parlor. He, with the help of another house guest, the Moravian, Phillip Lansing, had composed a ballad in her honor. David had spoken the words of the composition while Mr. Lansing penned them to paper. As he nervously began to sing, Margaret was startled as David's strong baritone voice filled with passion sang out... "*Sweet lips are mine to treasure...*"

She had applauded him enthusiastically intermittently throughout the rendition, and at the end thanked him profusely, saying how he had done her a great honor. After David had finished the sonnet he had knelt before her and professed his love. She had responded that she shared his sentiments, at which time he had taken her hands into his and kissed her fingertips, saying that he was the most fortunate of men.

Margaret could not recall feeling such a sweet tenderness ever before in her life. Of course, there had never been a serious suitor such as David Karski. There was Harry Stoddard, who after a stolen kiss had filled her dreams on many occasions, yet what she felt for David was far different. She had tried to imagine Harry's face, his smile, and the warmth of his lips upon her own that evening long ago. She had written every detail of their brief encounter into her journal and reread it frequently. But, alas, when nothing had come of Harry Stoddard, she had suffered dreadfully. She should have been able to vividly recall every detail about the young man who had caused her so many sleepless nights, but without the journal, all about Mr. Stoddard was no more than a distant blur.

As spring blossomed into the summer of 1723, tiny yellow birds and red-throated humming birds returned, as did long leisurely garden strolls in the evenings. Along with all else the new season had brought, it had also ushered in a more intimate period of courtship between Margaret and David, each of them yearning to know the other better.

In the past John Vandenberg had shared pieces of his and his sister's childhood with David, often speaking about his father and elder brother, but rarely did he mention his Indian mother. He had left the telling of this narrative to his sister.

As David and Margaret's courtship progressed, little by little Margaret had shared her own childhood remembrances, but only when specifically asked about one thing or another. However, after professions of love, and possibilities of marriage, she felt compelled to open her heart completely.

She introduced David to Gentle Heart and her family, at a place that she knew her mother would have considered an appropriate beginning, and that was with Kishelemukong, the god believed by her Indian ancestors to be the Lenape creator god. As a Christian woman, Margaret had hesitated after mentioning the pagan god's name, but David had dispelled any fears, and so she had continued pouring out her heart. She told him of how the night her mother died she held her Ohitas, a little cornhusk doll, and shed tears until there were none left. She told him of how deeply she had loved her dear mother, and the great loss they had all suffered, she being only twelve when her mother had gone to be with Almighty God. She quickly added that her grandmother, mother, and she had all been baptized, and from then forward had always practiced the true faith along with the Indian customs of her ancestors. After all, being a Christian paved the way to heaven but to forget Kishelemukong would have dishonored the memory of her ancestors.

Her Lenape grandmother had taught her daughter that her ancestors believed that all that is seen: the water, the rocks in the stream, the trees, all of this and more, are alive and speak with one another throughout the seasons as if family. The creator, Kishelemukong, built the world on the back of a giant turtle that he found in the deepest part of the great waters. Kishelemukong created men and women from the trees that grew upon the turtles back, and made the sun, the moon, and the animals to live together with men.

In sharing her story Margaret told her prospective husband of the ways of the Indian marriage. When she was young, her Indian grandmother had married, and as was the custom, her new husband came to live in the lodge that was owned by her mother. The women owned all the land in trust for Kishelemukong. In the old times, Margaret had explained, a bride and groom would live in the longhouse with the bride's mother. It was that way for her grandmother when she wed her grandfather. Unlike the Europeans, the bloodline was traced through the women and not the men.

Margaret said that she could not recall arguments among the tribal women. She imagined that there must have been disputes, but she had left the longhouse with her mother and brother as a small child, and according to her mother, her grandmother and her sisters all loved one another, as sisters should.

When speaking of their cultural differences, David mentioned that he had heard of the tradition among the native peoples that the brave lived with his wife's family, and he had heard also that a man would sometimes marry two sisters, but had smiled shyly as he assured Margaret that as for he, one wife was more than enough.

David did not mention that he knew of white traders in the wilds who had multiple Indian wives. Personally, he could not consider the prospect of his own household with many women all serving him as wife. It was true that the Old Testament was full of such marriages, but he was convinced that such men, although righteous, must have walked a fiery path.

On another day, Margaret told of Buka, her grandfather, and his two younger brothers who had been unjustly accused of murdering a white man. Buka, because of smallpox and other European diseases, had witnessed the annihilation of more than half of his people in his lifetime. Through terrible hurt Buka had learned many things. He understood that Indian land was the natives' most valuable asset and also the one most coveted by the whites. Her grandfather had tried to use his knowledge of those early Europeans, who lived by greed and not by kindness, to protect the remainder of his kinsman. When his two brothers were unjustly accused of murdering a white man, he negotiated with the officials for their freedom. His brothers were released once he had signed the land deed handing over a large section of his land to one of the local court officials. It was not an uncommon arrangement, Margaret explained. Eventually this same land would be owned by her father. Many old Colonials founded their estates in such a fashion.

It was around this time that her grandfather had delivered to Gerrit Vandenberg his beautiful young daughter, Gentle Heart, who would become a wife to the near forty year old Dutch widower, and who would take over the care of his young son, Teunis.

For many years thereafter, as he struggled to survive hard times, Margaret's Indian grandfather made similar contracts, until one day, drunk on the white man's rum and disheartened over a bad land transaction, he killed a land speculator. A few days later he surrendered himself to the English officials, who, after a brief trial, hung him. Margaret told David that thereafter, most of her grandfather's relatives were forced off their lands, and that these lands ultimately mainly became Anglo-Dutch estates. Most of the Lenape then migrated to the west lands, others to the southlands to sympathetic and peaceful Moravian Protestants where, it is said, they were baptized.

On another separate occasion while they picnicked by the stream, Margaret had broached what was for her a most delicate, as well as painful topic. She started by first recalling what she believed to be the greatest of her native mother's teachings: Gentle Heart's interpretation of God's gifts. Her mother had believed that all gifts are provided by God to all peoples, and the responsibility inherited from The Almighty at birth was to share the gift given to each human being. Her mother had said that powerful humans who refused to share their blessings of wealth would soon lose everything.

On this occasion she began to tell the story of her Negro family. Commencing with her father's acquisition of Zeb from Waldron farm, and Eva's first owners, the Royal African Company, Margaret traced their journey to Vandenberg manor, punctuating her recollection of the elderly couple with that which her father had told to her. She recounted how Zeb had built up their herd of cows and helped to build the gristmill. She told how Eva had been personal maid to her father's first wife and a mother to her in the years following her own mother's death.

She spoke of her deep affection for them, as well as their family, but especially for two of their children, Marie and Lizbeth, each of whom, as a small girl, Margaret had held in her arms. She also told him of her father's promise to Zeb and Eva to never sell away any of his servants, and how after her father's death, for reasons that only she could justify, she had given freedom to her two favorites. Tearfully she had poured out her heart of how her gold had bought freedom for Marie as well as for her younger sister Lizbeth, and of how she had sent young Lizbeth to New York City for what she had believed would be a wondrous opportunity, yet her well-meaning endeavor had ended with Lizbeth's tragic, untimely death. She could never forgive herself for sending Lizbeth off—she should have known that a freed Negro country girl would be prey to others wanting to make no good use of her. Marie, on the other hand, had accepted her freedom papers with but a grain of salt it appeared, and when Margaret had suggested that she could arrange a good position as a maid for her on Manhattan Island or one of the finer houses in Albany, Marie had begged Margaret not to send her away. Margaret confessed that she was relieved when Marie had said as much for she would be lost without her.

Lizbeth had responded to her proposal far more enthusiastically.

From the time they were small girls, Margaret said she had enjoyed tutoring her favorites. She taught the girls how to sign their names, how to recite their daily devotionals, how to decorate their moccasins with glass beads, and how to do needlework. Marie did well, but her younger sister did better. By the time Lizbeth was fourteen she had become an expert dressmaker, and Margaret often loaned her to friends, allowing Lizbeth to keep half of whatever she earned. Several of the women gave her remnants of the expensive cloth that had been used in their dressmaking, and from these pieces of fabric she had adeptly constructed many fine quilts. Some of these she had also sold and was allowed to keep every coin.

Stroking her hair tenderly that afternoon, David had observed Margaret's tears as she spoke of the young woman and had suggested that she not go further, but Margaret had insisted that she be allowed to continue, saying that she wished for him to know everything there was to know of these things before a marriage contract was signed.

As David had pulled her close, wrapping his strong, muscular arms around her, Margaret felt loved and protected. Thoughts of the five hundred Lenape or so who remained scattered throughout the Colonies; a society of natives who once numbered many thousand, were not as painful.

For her, where Lizbeth was concerned there was no absolution from guilt. She would always carry the hurt within her soul. She knew that had she not sent Lizbeth to the city, she would not have died in the fires of the rebellion.

Margaret told of how as a young woman she had met and befriended Mary VanWie of New York City, a friend of a prominent Dutch ship captain's wife, and how she had made arrangements for Lizbeth to be employed by Mary. Mrs. VanWie had written a letter of gratitude, expressing her delight not only with Lizbeth's needlework, but her appealing countenance as well. She was never sullen and was always helpful with the younger children. Mary reported that Lizbeth was a most gifted seamstress, that she had already made a new friend of a neighboring servant girl, and that she was keeping company with a freed African man who worked at the livery stable four streets away. Mary tried to put to rest any anxieties that she suspected Margaret had, saying that, should the friendship progress any further, she would speak with Nathan Seamon at the Trinity Church so that a marriage could be arranged. That is, provided that Margaret would agree that this would be best for Lizbeth. After the tragic events that followed, looking back, neither Margaret nor Mary had any idea how, or when, Lizbeth had become acquainted with the Negro called Silas Bowman.

A few weeks after Mary's glowing report the slave insurrection had erupted. At midnight one April eve, twenty-three Africans armed with guns, hatchets and swords set fire to several buildings within the city. Nine whites and four Negroes were killed. Some were shot and others had been brutally stabbed to death.

It had been Captain Waldron who gave Margaret the devastating news. Her beloved Lizbeth was one of three young women who were caught between the crossfire. Margaret had been told that her sweet Lizbeth was found dead just outside one of the burned houses. It would be a kindness to think that she had been killed instantly.

No one, of course, could have imagined that the Negro liveryman was one of the core members of that terrible uprising. After the killings, the New York militia, who caught the Negroes involved within a few days, quickly subdued the revolt, but a time of frenzied hysteria had commenced in the entire colony. Six of the Negroes committed suicide rather than face the punishment they knew would come. The rest were executed, several publicly; burned alive at the stake.

John was not at home at the time, and so Captain Waldron and Benjamin Lapett collected Lizbeth's body. She was brought home and her mortal remains buried on the hillside behind the mill alongside of two of Zeb and Eva's other children who had died when only babies.

Knowing something of the circumstances of the death of the Vandenberg servant woman who had been freed, and tragically died, as Margaret composed herself, David had gently suggested that ten years was a long time to mourn, and that no one, save Almighty God, could know all that was to come. Surely, had Margaret known of the slave rebellion that would erupt that year, she would have undoubtedly kept the young woman to home.

Margaret had agreed that there was no going back, but she was not sorry for providing Marie or Lizbeth their freedom, but only for sending Lizbeth away. She had long wished to see these two, who were as sisters to her, freed. Years before she had heard it preached that bondage of the Negro and the enslavement of the Indians were not sinful, but she could never accept those words. She prayed for guidance and was answered when her mother's words came back to her. "Generosity is expected from those who have more, and those who do not share blessings will lose all."

She could not deny that she felt that the trouble they had all most recently suffered was rooted in some way back to Lizbeth and that terrible night all those years ago. It was no secret that there were those who did not trust her because Lizbeth was known to have kept company with Silas Bowman. Some were so cruel as to say that she deserved her death.

Prior to the shocking revolt in Manhattan, slaves and freed Negroes alike had little restriction placed upon them as they completed their errands within the city. With consent they were even able to carry arms, and in general come and go as they pleased. In those times slaves in New York City as well as those living in the North River Valley had little trouble as they went about the duties of their masters.

But now all was different. Fearful Colonists everywhere vowed never again to see such a bloody night as had occurred in New York that spring of 1713. New restrictions were imposed throughout the colony.

From Anna Stoudt's recent letters Margaret heard of the confiscating of Negroes' guns. She had been even more dismayed to learn that catechist instruction was once again forbidden to the Negro slaves. The hate crimes of those twenty-three had spoiled the peace for thousands. Most believed that the trust extended to the slaves of New York would never come again.

Chapter 18

Margaret watched Eva's fattest goose give vigorous chase to two of Henry and Martha's small, squealing children playing outside the window near her desk, at the same time wondering if any of their lives on the plantation could ever be peaceable again.

The unthinkable had happened. Her countryside cocoon had been penetrated, her slaves violated, yet despite all vulnerability, she would do her best as Mistress to regain harmony and continue to conduct the business of her estate. Not knowing who these men were who had come upon her land with swords and guns, she was finding it impossible to concentrate on her accounts, let along conduct formal business meetings for the sale of her crops. Would she be doing business with those responsible for the treachery without knowing it? She had done nothing but think of this and had come to no resolve. She must do what she must do. She must put on the contented face of the bride-to-be, despite knowing that suspicion, mistrust, and even hatred awaited her from these men who must be captained by the devil himself.

Most importantly though, she wondered if David regretted that he had returned with John last summer, and now privately admonished himself for asking for the hand of a half-breed who could not, it seemed, efficiently manage her own properties. Though she had kept Marie's secret, she was sure that David comprehended something seriously amiss had prompted the savage attack at the mill. But, as quickly as the thought crossed her mind, she heard the whisperings of her dead Indian grandmother: *Pray. Remember your gifts. Be strong.*

Beyond the squawk and flutter of geese, and the children at play, lay neat rows of late summer's faded gardens. Further still, the soaked, tasseled cornfields awaited harvest, and beyond all that, the hollowed out forest of hickory bordered the horizon. It was in their depths that Margaret assumed the native peoples had most likely already begun to celebrate the harvesting. How she would like to turn back time and find the girl she had once been when under a warm sun she took pleasure participating in the *Green Corn Ceremony*. The ancient Indian tradition was being celebrated this week. She began humming the old Lenape harvest songs. The joy of the music recalled memories. The tune swirled and leapt throughout her entire being, guiding her to another season in a happier time. It was then, only a year ago, when she had met David Karski during the Pinkster celebrations. Through David's strong baritone voice she had discovered his wondrously amusing spirit. Although it was unseemly to consider, she was strongly attracted to him in both body and soul. He had captivated her long before she knew that she loved him. David had arrived exactly fifty days after the glorious holy day of Easter, a time which marked the first day of the weeklong festival celebration of the Colonial New York holiday of Pinkster, a week of frivolity where neither free, freed, nor slave men worked. She had thought their meeting must have been arranged in the heavens.

She recalled their introduction amidst the raucous celebration of wild beating drums, melodious flute, and jumping dark fiddlers. Margaret recalled how David, full of rum, had danced at the tail end of the line of the Africans, yet how enchanting it had been that the newly arrived outsider was immediately absorbed into this African and Anglo-Dutch carnival. She and David had a rambunctious start in a season which could have brought none other than the stirring of the blood.

That first night as they walked together, with John and his new bride strolling an appropriate distance behind them, the whole of the countryside glowed with hundreds of blazing bonfires up and down the river way, all lighted by folk jubilantly praising the Lord for the return of life after the lift of the heavy footprint of the long, northern winter.

Whatever had gone wrong with the rest of her world? It seemed to her that, save her romance and the birth of sweet Clare, nothing at all had been right with anything since the census taker arrived. Of course, there had been those troubles in New York City, yet before Anna's letter a fortnight or so ago, she would have said that this was the best of all the years of her life.

All that she knew now was that if her reputation as a reputable slave owner had been compromised, a marriage might also be in jeopardy. Peaceful negotiations with merchants ensured everything for her. She was not comely or young, and if not for her wealth she would not make a desirable wifely prospect. Although she believed that David loved her truly, she had always understood that she would not be on the cusp of taking vows had it not been for her wealth and position. She had to keep the peace at all costs. Exasperated, she put down her quill and closed the gristmill's leather-bound ledger, pushing herself away from her writing desk.

Deciding to check on Moses, she left the house and walked along the pebbled pathway through lame gardens planted alongside rows of young tulip poplar trees, continuing on past the cornfields and several slave cabins that lined the path to the Vandenberg wharf where her sloop was moored.

As she approached the river's edge, she caught sight of Henry's twin boys, Sam and Joshua, who made a comical sight curling their small dark bodies into balls rolling down the gentle grassy knoll of the embankment toward the edge of the North River. At the bottom of the hill, the twosome began to meander further along the rocky shoreline, soon picking up handfuls of small pebbles. Their heads together, Margaret surmised that they were challenging one another to a game of pitch, just as she and John used to do. Before long the water was filled with giant rippling rings. As boys do, they soon tired of this sport and proceeded down the beach in search of other amusement.

They were not lacking diversion for long. They came upon an unsuspecting target, their Uncle Moses, sitting by the wayside, intent upon cleaning his catch of fish. Margaret watched as the pair quickly ran to the nearby rushes and stayed poised perhaps fifty feet away, whispering what no doubt was an earnest and, most certainly, ominous plot.

As Margaret turned her attention back to Moses, she was pleased to see that, although it had been only a few weeks since the attack, he was moving about well with the aide of a crutch, and the bandages had been removed from his head. In fact, this morning his mannerisms seemed almost lively. But then, it was already three hours past dawn on a Wednesday, and the allowed mid-week free time for his fishing or tending to his assigned personal garden would soon come to an end. *He's working against the hourglass,* Margaret mused, *and he's in a great rush to get those fish he's caught into his sister-in-law's cooking pot.*

As Moses pulled himself up with his crutch and prepared to leave the beach, the mischievous boys inched their way closer to him. Margaret merrily slapped her side as she noted that the slave never saw them following him as he headed back toward Martha's cook's pot.

Unable to hold herself silent any longer, she laughed out loud at the sight of the trio: the barefoot young man who hobbled along the shoreline as proud as one of her peacocks, the leather strap of his full calabash pail firm within his grip, followed by the rambunctious boys who sallied a safe distance behind, every so often slinging fistfuls of mud at one another. None of them, though, seemed to hear her outburst, and they continued along their way.

Wait until their mother has a look at those two, she thought, knowing they would receive her harsh tongue at the very least. Furrows began to appear on Margaret's brow. *Oh, Martha, be not too harsh with them.* She stood transfixed, watching them, the one legged man and trailing boys as they disappeared around the river's bend under a thick umbrella of green tinged with gold.

Though Moses' actions regarding the runaway slaves had undoubtedly brought down the wrath of God upon them all, Margaret's heart broke as she thought of the suffering he had done these past weeks. It did no good for any of them to stay angry. He had suffered much loss himself.

* * * *

When she returned to the house, Marie had just finished working her way around the parlor room with her feather duster.

"You missed seeing our comical two young jesters down by the river," Margaret chirped, coming through the door.

"Sam and Joshua, I presume?"

"Do we have others who would qualify for the English court?"

"I pray not, as two be enough," Marie replied.

"Oh, come, my spirit rejoices as I watch them frolic."

Marie replied sternly, "They ought to be dancin' out yonder in the laundress' tub. Martha told me that is where she would have 'em at first light, but you tell me they be runnin' wild."

"They are children, Marie," Margaret sighed.

"My nephews are in want of good keepin' and I will say so to Henry when he comes up to the house kitchen for today's three o'clock meal. I will say that you saw those two by the river."

"You will do no such thing."

"I will," Marie muttered.

"You will be silent about the boys and say nothing."

"Peg, you may be amused today, but will not find the boys so funny when tomorrow you discover that the table linens remain soiled—not having had a proper good stompin' in the tub."

Obviously choosing to ignore Marie's prophecy, Margaret's eyes twinkled. "I think they had a mind to be bothersome to Moses, but he did not see them."

"Moses? Where was Moses?" Marie asked.

"Do not fluff your feathers. There was no trouble. He was fishing; that is all."

"It is past fishin' time."

"Yes, but we will not chastise him for fishing a little longer than allowed after all the hurt that has come upon him."

Marie sighed. "I am not hard-hearted. His wounds heal and I praise God for his mercy, but I fear for my brother. I am at my wits end about him. As for the boys, I think the two need discipline and I will speak to Martha."

Margaret stepped toward Marie. She put her lips close to Marie's pristine white cap. "Do not be mean, my dear, and take out your frustration upon the boys. A harsh face does not become you, and you will do as bid and say nothing to Henry or his wife. Do we not have enough disruption in this house?"

Marie was startled and stepped back. When she spoke her voice trembled as she replied stiffly, "I am no shrew, Peg, and you know that I am a truthful woman. By God Almighty you know that much! My mother coddled Moses from the first time he was put to her breast, and now we see what has become of him! I know it is a terrible thing to say, but I would not see the boys go down the same path."

"Marie!!"

"Beggin' the Lord's forgiveness and yours, but none of the other children are allowed to romp as they please and where they please."

Apparently tired of the confrontation, Margaret replied, "I imagine Martha has them well in hand by now, but I think that the laundress coming from Van Horn's must have been delayed. Otherwise, they would be in the washhouse tub. Those two little frogs would never jump away from that which is more of a frolic than a duty."

Marie sighed. "As you wish. I have said my peace."

"Come now," Margaret soothed, "no harm was done this morning. And I have given up the care of Moses to the Almighty and would suggest that you do the same."

"Of course, you are right. I will pray that he be preserved, for I have do doubt that my words of rebuke are meaningless to my brother."

"I had forgotten that the laundress was to come today. How the months do fly by. It seems only yesterday that it was June and wash week."

"You had instructed that she be employed sooner so that all your people can look their best for your wedding."

"Ah, yes, I remember now."

Marie proceeded to outline the planned agenda, "The women are to gather on the morrow and the men later today...."

Margaret heard not a word. Babies and children had consumed her thoughts these last months as much as the begetting of them. She thought of Martha who was once again pregnant though she thought the slave was nearly as old as herself.

Sheepishly, Margaret whispered, "If it be God's will, I would be glad of heart should a child or two fill my womb, and I would be most happy to see them grow into playful frogs."

Marie raised an eyebrow replying, "You might complain if they came from your body made like either of those two."

"Marie, I should take a reed to you!" Margaret flushed. "You mistake my meaning."

"Pardon, me Mistress," Marie apologized, trying to keep a sober face.

"I give you my pardon. Marie, I would ask you a question that has been put upon my heart."

"Yes, Mistress. You may ask me anything that you wish."

"Did you give thought to childbearing when you were to be wedded to John Stoddard's Matthew?"

Marie straightened. "I did not dwell upon such thoughts, Peg. Of course, then I was not freed and it was your father's will that I should marry. I met the man intended but once. And now it has been all these years. I do not recall thinkin' of children. I think upon it now though, and...."

Suddenly Betty appeared at the door, beads of sweat rolling down her forehead.

"Mamma Eva sent me from the kitchen. She boiled clean the table linens herself and has hung them on the racks. They be good and damp now. Soon I put them on the linen press. Do you have more for the washin', Mistress Marie?"

"Oh," Margaret interjected, anxiously glancing at Betty then back to Marie. "We shall require plenty of cloths. There are several dinner parties planned for the next three weeks, with the first, of course, on next Monday with Mayor Schuyler. All must be in good order, and we must have a clean cloth on the table after every meal."

"Go down and say that I will come shortly," Marie replied to Betty.

"Yes Mistress."

After she had gone, Margaret asked eagerly, "Now that that is under control—you were going to tell me something before Betty came in. What was it?"

"I can not think of it now. I am sorry, but my thought flew away."

"It was something about the marriage that was arranged. I do not know if I ever told you of my letter to John Stoddard.

I wrote to him of my disappointment as soon as I had knowledge of his abrupt decision to place his man elsewhere, I would have you know! I conveyed to him that he was no man of honor, being that he would switch oars in midstream that way, and we did not take his slight kindly."

"You did say as much to me, Peg."

"I would want you to know that I have never been against a proper marriage for you, Marie. If you were so inclined I would look for someone suitable and believe me he would be a far better match than the zealous carpenter I have watched you with over the summer. Now that your circumstances have changed, you are in a better position as a freed woman. Why, not long ago, Mary Beekman mentioned to me her driver, Charles."

Marie winced. "You know I have never asked for a husband, Peg."

Margaret added defensively, "What I meant to say is that the marriage would not have been a favorable one for you, and we should thank God for guiding Mr. Stoddard's prospect away from this household to Mr. Livingston's seamstress, Fanny. As things turned out, Mr. Stoddard's offer of a marriage was far below your station, Marie. Besides, I have been told that the man—I believe he is called Harmon; yes that is his name—has become fat and slothful, and he has sired but three babes who all died as infants. Poor Fanny."

Marie paused; staring at the last of what had been a beautiful garden's bloom that she had arranged in the vase a few days before. "To all eyes, even to the slaves hereabouts, my position is seen as changed, yet, in truth, Peg I am no different. I am the same since the day I was baptized. I have always been free within my heart."

Margaret flushed. "Yes, of course," Margaret replied, tenderly fearing that she had frightened poor Marie with her outspoken thoughts on matchmaking, but in the end Marie would see what is best.

"I should go to my mother and see what must be done. Might I take my leave?"

"Yes, surely, go to her and say that I will come down myself to see what is what after I have finished with my correspondence."

As Marie turned away, Margaret added, "And Marie..."

Marie stopped and turned toward her mistress. "Yes?"

"Fret no more over Moses. With God's help, all will be well."

Marie nodded. "I pray it be so," she replied hastily, obviously glad to escape to wherever the disturbing notions of her Mistress could no longer be heard.

Margaret shuffled through her letters. She began reading a quite unexpected, and somewhat stiffly written, piece of correspondence penned by Mary Beekman. *Unfortunately,* Mary wrote, *the Beekman's will be unable to accept your kind invitation to witness the celebration of yours and Mr. Karski's exchange of the marriage vows.* This was all Mary wrote.

The brevity of Mary's letter shocked her. In all the years that she had known Mary Beekman she had never received a letter from her that consisted of less than a page.

When last they had spoken, Mary had said that she and Henry were delighted by her invitation and looking forward to the wedding with great anticipation. In fact, she recalled thinking how amusing Mary, the buxom, violet-blue eyed mother of five, was as she struggled through her terrible quandary over which color dress she would wear...the red or the indigo blue. Always the social center at parties held in all the grand homes of the more prestigious Anglo-Dutch families in and about the North River Valley, Mary Beekman would be missed terribly.

Mary had obviously been completely captivated by David when she had been introduced to him; Mary having commented upon, "....Mr. Karski's most invigorating and brash rugged manners."

There was just no sense to be made out of her sudden change of heart, although Margaret did begin to think something else very odd. When Mary had stopped by last week while enroute to her sister's, she had never said a word about the rather unusual impromptu visit her husband had made to John's house the morning after Clare's birth. Margaret had expected a good prodding, but other than her normal excited chatter about the proper attire that should be worn at a fine wedding, now that she thought more about the visit, Mary had seemed rather distant and had few questions about the wedding plans or guest list or anything else, for that matter. She had never mentioned sending Henry along or anything about any foreboding, gossiping rumors. In retrospect, Margaret did think Mary's closed mouth demeanor strange because she knew how Mary could prattle on and on, making conversation out of nonsense.

Working toward sorting it all out, something John had mentioned suddenly came to her like a star falling out of the sky. According to her brother, Mary had specifically sent her husband with a precise warning...she was concerned for her safety.

I ought to stop reading something sinister into a simple refusal of an invitation, she thought, but try as she would, she could not put her thoughts to rest. The last she saw of Mary she was waving her fancy embroidered, white linen handkerchief from her carriage window, promising to bring along her widowed mother for the festivities. Of course, now, Mary's sister, Susanna, would not be present either. Margaret tucked Mrs. Beekman's letter of regret into the mantle letterbox.

Returning to her accounts at her desk, she glanced out the window, noticing Zeb bracing himself against a tree, the twins beside their grandfather, all eyes of the threesome lifted toward a nearby tree branch. Margaret craned her neck in the direction of Zeb's pointed finger to see what it was that had caught their attention. There, on a branch of the old oak tree, sat a magnificent large hawk peering back. Margaret wondered how long he had been so stoically perched, realizing now that the old slave was sharing the significance of the hawk's visit. When the giant bird spread his wings the children whooped and hollered enthusiastically. As the bird soared away, a calm that had not been present within her soul for weeks came upon her being as she recalled God's promise to his faithful: peace comes to all peoples on the earth on the wings of the hawk messenger.

Chapter 19

Placing a pile of folded linens onto the kas shelf, Marie wondered what her station would be after Peg's marriage took place. Undoubtedly it would not be the same as it had been all these years between the two of them. There would be little time for strolling through the gardens whilst Peg read to her from her books of poetry, or lying across the Mistress's bed sharing gossip. She supposed that she would continue to travel with Peg as she had always done in the capacity of her personal maid, but she would no longer also be her sole companion. Already she could sense the change that had come between them. It seemed to her that Peg had become higher-minded during these last months, and, since the attack, Marie felt hurt that she looked at her through eyes of suspicion. Marie sighed. She had naught to blame but herself for Peg's feelings of mistrust; she should have gone to her right away when she saw Moses in his mischief that day. Perhaps, had she done so, her brother and the others would have been spared injury and young Peter would still be among them.

Reflecting upon the past, it had always been Marie's assumption that Peg preferred her to remain a single woman. The old Master's plans for her to marry had never come to be, and she always assumed that Peg had something to do with her father's decision. Plainly, an unmarried woman, freed or not, could devote herself to a Master (or a Mistress) without the many distractions of a married woman. The married woman's heart's first concern was most always the care of her dependent children. Although in many instances slave husbands were often separated from enslaved wives, from what Marie had observed, a servant woman wrought with anguish over her children made for a distracted worker.

Her Mistress' recent questions and her suggesting that she would encourage a marriage for her had come as a surprise and left her nervous as to what future Peg was contemplating. It was becoming more apparent that great changes were coming upon them all with this marriage. She could see that every time Margaret held tiny Clare in her arms. Peg said little of the possibilities of motherhood for herself, but every inch of her joyful demeanor gave away her innermost desire for such a possibility to all in her presence. The Mistress had warmed to every aspect of marriage. Marie sensed that many of the slaves thought their aging Mistress hilarious with the infant, but she did not laugh with them. She knew differently. Peg was a strong woman who might well bear several children for Mr. Karski.

While visiting with her sister-in-law Martha at her cabin one Sunday afternoon, Marie had sat through the arguing going on between her four brothers on how the Master wanted them to dig the pits out in the west field for his mine after the hickory trees were cut down. James suspected that, "….there be hundred or more of those hickory that have t' fall before next spring's plantin' 'cause I hear tell one hundred trees need be to make a furnace run for a year. The new Master he be wantin' his furnace be ready to be runnin' all day, all night, everyday in summer season. They be no time for fishin'. Master John expects that they be beginin' to cut the trees down right when the marriage bed be warm and the harvest time done. All us be cuttin' till our fingers be froze to the ax. If new slaves be found, you Henry, you be over those newcomer African boys good so the trees fall right." But James had added with much exasperation, " Which one of them was gonna' be workin' the mill and keepin' the mill stone picked sharp while all this other work be done?"

Henry had tried to calm his younger brothers by saying that Old Master Vandenberg, rest his soul, had always been a fair Master, and their Mistress was a good woman. Their sister's killing in the slave riots could not be put upon her, anymore than the wickedness of the white men who attacked them. It was only right that she would want a husband and one had come.

Marie sighed as her thoughts returned to the present. Hard changes were just over the rise for Vandenberg Farm, and they still had no word on young Peter who had disappeared the night of the attack on his way back from the Kingman place.

Her freedom had never meant anything to her one way or another. She wasn't like young Lizbeth had been, all silly and eager to get away and to live in a stranger's fine house in the big city. No, she had never felt that way at all. Freedom to her only meant being content with the path that God had provided: to accept the freedom papers that her Mistress insisted she have, and be grateful for the good status within a house where she was treated kindly.

She began to wonder if, now that Peg would herself be married to Mr. Karski, the Mistress had not put thought into finding her a husband as well. Undoubtedly if a match were to be arranged, the intended would surely be expected to live upon Vandenberg lands. Her freedom to stay gave her great comfort.

Perhaps keeping her silence about poor Moses had thrown mud in the butter as it was being churned. It was true that a proper suitor was not to be discovered upon every stoop, yet something more might be in the brewer's pot. Perhaps this was what Peg had meant in saying, "...it is wrong to 'wish backwards,' as my good father would have said."

Ah, well, at this point in her life, unlike her Mistress, she had no wish at all to spend what was left of her remaining years catering to the domestic needs of any man, whatever his fine position. This included the Beekman driver. Her mother had laughed when she heard of the suggestion, saying she knew the old widower to be sixty if he be a day. Of course, there was the Van Rensselaer carpenter...

Stepping back from the massive oak kas, Marie surveyed the filled shelves. Margaret would be pleased. The linens were splendid.

Chapter 20

David easily lifted Margaret from her horse, pulling her close to himself as her feet touched the ground. "You said not a word to me on the ride all the way out here. I am not a man good with words where women are concerned, but I know well enough when I have displeased a lady. It is clear to me that I have brought your wrath down upon me, and all the worse if I have I lost your heart. Have I lost your heart, Peg?"

Margaret gently nudged him away, "My heart is still here," she said pointing at her breast, "and you have not lost it. But so is my mind up here," again pointing, this time to her right temple. "My heart and my mind speak to one another. My brother has every right to do as he would do with his inheritance and to build a forge, David, but he goes at it all too fast, and with little care for the work that he puts upon the backs of our slaves."

Letting her go, David's retort was fringed with indignation. "What do you keep your slaves for if not that they should provide the necessary labor to sustain your enterprises?"

Margaret's voice rose. "My people perform their duties well, and you have no right, Sir, to speak thus. You shock me, as I have not before seen this side of your disposition!"

David stared despairingly down at his boots. "I meant no disrespect to you or to your people. I believe that you will agree that after this time spent on the manor I know their duties." He replied in a voice that was barely audible.

Margaret tried to compose herself, but a furious fire had built itself within her being. She knew that this was an argument that had been brewing for days, as she listened, and had said nothing while David and her brother had made their arrangements for a trip to the New York slave block. "I have no stomach for the acquisition of additional slaves, and yet I see no choice but to open the gates of hell! I loath to be backed into such a miserable corner!"

Gripping her shoulders, David forced her around to face him. "I would not have this come between us, Peg. I will tell John that I am out of it, and will no longer partner with him. If you say this is your desire; it shall be so."

"Oh, God save me, but I do not know what it is that I want if it is not to be at peace once again. I can not tell you to abandon my brother. John has come home, and I have vowed to help him, and I know that you are not a man to discard a pledge."

Holding her close, David whispered, "Then we must help one another. I must help you to keep your vow and you do the same that I should keep mine."

"I suspect from discourse that we have shared that you would prefer to seek another path, yet I also know that John has given you reason to believe that the Africans are our only choice."

"Make no mistake, my love, I agree with your brother. We both prefer the African labor to the flood of mother England's convicts who are being imposed upon us. There are plenty of those who we could take on, and as you have heard, they are eager to serve as a slave to any man who will have them. We all know that hard-hearted British murderers serve Masters in these colonies and that after only fourteen years the crown forgives a death sentence. I have come across their sort in the wilds of my western country. After the completion of their servitude they often become merchants; some have established farms, themselves owning slaves. Once convicts destined for the gallows, many of these murderers have become wealthy men."

"The Almighty preserve us all. What terrible fate awaits little Clare? Rest assured, Vandenberg's will have no convicts," Margaret snapped.

"I would have none myself, but we are in sore want of men to cut the trees, and we do not have the labor to continue."

Exasperated, Margaret leaned her head on David's chest. "I wish we had more time to give all of this proper thought."

David stroked her long, black hair that hung loosely to her waist. "My family having lived among the French Jesuits, I have no grudge against the Papists, and I have naught against the Irish, or the Scots, yet John's heart is set against them all."

"I know his heart," Margaret responded softly.

"I am an experienced woodsman, Peg. I will be in the forest with John and the men to guide them rightly. I give you my solemn promise that we will treat all justly."

Margaret looked into David's eyes seeking his heart. She wanted to believe that her newly found happiness was unshakeable, but events of late had dictated otherwise. Men often too drunk to ride their horses roamed the hills, creating a lawless clamor that had swept away all innocence. She could not imagine a worse time to engage in a new enterprise. On the threshold of marriage, how good it would be to have no other thoughts but those of a joyful bride's expectations of passion to be released.

"We are soon to be wed, David, and I have made promises of my own. I have promised the Almighty that I would be with you as one within our marriage. I am a woman to keep my vows."

"I have known this, Peg, since we first walked in your garden." David smiled, "I believe that John knew us to be a match when he persuaded me to come along with him to his homeland."

"I would think that he would not have done so well in his matchmaking, as I fear my brother no longer knows my heart as I have come to know his."

"Nay, John has the greatest affection for you, Peg."

"Perhaps, but affection is not always partnered with respect."

"It hurts me to hear you say as much."

Margaret patted her black stallion, reaching for a bottle of spiced wine and some cheese stored in the leather bag across the horse's back. "The sun soon will sleep. We must return to home, though I wanted to bring you to this place of the old hickory where we could talk alone."

Seating himself against a tree trunk, David said, "I am happy that we came; it was important that we talk, but it is not so late that we must rush to home. Should we delay a short while, we will still be back to the house before dark. Come sit by me that we might take the time to enjoy that which you have brought along."

Joining David, she said, "See how tall this one grows up into the sky."

"Yes, they are grand to gaze upon."

"I will soon return to this grove one early morn with Shasa to gather the sweet, brown, hickory nuts before the squirrels, deer, and the fox have their way with them. We will make the nut and venison stew that you loved so well last autumn." Glancing at David sheepishly, she added, "I would hope to keep this patch of my woods away from the ax."

"I give you my word, Peg: these woods will never see the ax."

"Let us seal the contract then," Margaret said, breaking the cheese with her fingers. The two took turns sipping the wine from the jug.

Having finished the cheese, Margaret licked her fingers. She began to understand that serenity amidst a world filled with greed was not easily attained, and a marriage with David would not always be a soft bed. She thought it might be wise to consider the recommendation of the well-known Jonathan Swift who had advised that the road to a happy marriage was not in the net, but in the making of a proper cage. Her wealth made her an attractive prospect for a spouse, but the deed to her property would not become a part of her dowry. Though her passion for David burned hotter than coals, she would speak with Attorney Wendell on a marriage contract, and if he could not accommodate her, surely the English lawyer, John Collins, could.

"Then we have made resolution?" David asked, finishing the last of the wine.

"Yes." Margaret answered. "I am feeling far better on the matter."

David smiled contentedly. Reaching for the reins of the stallion, he threw the blanket back onto the animal. Cupping his hands together, he boosted Margaret onto her mount.

Margaret smiled too, thinking of words of wisdom the recently married Albany socialite Ariaantje Coeymans had often shared. She had quoted Joseph Addison who once wrote: *Admiration is a very short-lived passion that immediately decays upon growing familiar with it's subject, unless it be still fed with fresh discoveries and kept alive by a new perpetual succession of miracles rising up to its view.*

Chapter 21

Lapett believed that he had never admired Margaret's staunch tenacity so much as during the days leading up to her October marriage to David Karski.

He, along with many others, he suspected, had questioned whether or not she would go through with the marriage. As for himself, he had always had a difficult time envisioning Margaret Vandenberg bowing to a husband's rule, and, of course, the late summer attack had been without a doubt a jolt to her very core. After weeks of searching to find her young slave had failed, she had locked herself away for days of fasting and prayer before finally emerging to announce that she would accept God's will in all matters.

Weeks later, the impressive ceremony took place within the strong walls of Vandenberg Castle, as the manor house had come to be known, and was guarded by several Albany militia men assigned to the duty by Colonel Peter Schuyler to ensure there would be no disturbance.

Wearing a traditional tiara-like, Indian felt head band decorated with hundreds of small, white beads with one upright turkey feather in the center, Margaret spoke her vows. Afterwards, she moved the feather to the back of the headband, openly signifying her new status as a married woman.

Sipping sweet wine, the newlyweds toasted each other and their guests from Peter and Catharina Waldron's wedding gift: a double handled, silver cup engraved: *"When this you see, remember me"*. It had been crafted in a similar manner to the one her father had given as a gift to Peter and Catharina many years before when they had wed in New York City.

If any of the guests found Margaret's headdress or adherence to other Indian customs in any way heathenish, or so disturbing to their senses as to be shocked, there were no whispers to be heard.

It appeared to Lapett that there were several prominent names absent from the ceremony, having turned down their invitation, he assumed, for various reasons known only to them. Fear of another attack might be one. As for himself, he would not forget that it was Margaret who opened many prestigious doors for him during recent years, allowing him to compete with the most highly regarded local portrait painters, such as Nehemiah Partridge and Peter Vanderlyn, both favorites of the affluent New York Dutch. Margaret had also recommended his wife, Helen, as a skilled hat maker to Mary Beekman, who had in turn recommended her to several ladies of fine standing. She had all she could do to keep up with the orders. He had, for many years, called the Vandenberg's friends. Then again, all things considered, it may have been too late for those who had received notice that the wedding date had been postponed (because of the attack and it's aftermath) to adjust their schedules, for it was his understanding that some who had been invited, and who did not attend, came from as far away as the Forks in Jersey,

Philadelphia, and Boston. And he could understand how some might have fears arising from the recent Negro insurrections in the city compounded by the attack upon Margaret's own slaves.

Among the extensive gathering of well-wishers were neighboring farmers Nicholas Bonastale and his wife Anna, and Simon Yates, the robust, sharp-tempered minister from the Kinderhook Dutch Reform Church, who had officiated the ceremony, while his unmarried daughter Deborah acted as witness. It had always amused Lapett that, while in the city, Margaret presented herself quite Anglican, speaking nothing but English and often worshiping at Trinity Church, while at home to all eyes she was anything but Anglican. Although the official language of the colony for many years had been English, the ceremony and two hours of Dominie Yates' preaching thereafter was done entirely in the Dutch language.

Lapett recalled the ceremony with a mixture of amusement and chagrin, as his distressed daughters sat politely, but snobbishly still, his eldest rolling her eyes at Anna Stoudt's shedding of unprompted tears at the most inappropriate moments. Later his wife recalled overhearing Anna complain to her companion that she had always thought it would be she who would be Margaret's choice of witness to her marriage.

There were several interesting events that day. Every jaw fell open at the sight of Widow Bender, who near eighty years of age and dressed in her finest purple velvet gown, arrived holding the reigns of her own buggy. The widow, who first came to the colonies as an indentured girl on the ship the *Princess,* had traveled by herself many miles along the dusty old road leading from Connecticut between her plantation and Margaret's. As she slowly and most gingerly climbed down from her rig an aghast Margaret frantically beckoned to her Negroes to come to her aid. The widow reported that her driver was down with the fever and she had not another driver for her horse. After barking orders to the servants to bring her trunk inside, she insisted upon going directly to the stable with the Negro to be sure that her mare was properly secured.

Elizabeth Kidd, daughter of Captain Kidd, arrived unescorted two days before the ceremony, openly defying the gossips who spoke ill of her friendship with Margaret. Just prior to the ceremony Lapett and his wife had seen tears in Margaret's eyes as Marie ushered Elizabeth in. These tears could also have been brought on by sorrow as well, as her eldest niece, Teunis's daughter, Christina, was also ushered into the parlor about the same time.

He was surprised to see Captain Waldron's father, the elder Will, at the wedding, recalling that it was he who was the first to captain the *Rebecca*. He and Margaret's father were acquainted since the days of the Dutch West India Company. Seeing old Will Waldron brought back a flood of memories. His grandfather, along with a man by the name of LaCroix, and Captain Will's grandfather, Resolved Waldron, had long ago been partners in the fur trade business. Lapett marveled at how ageless the Captain's father appeared. The man seemed as upright and vigorous as he remembered him from the Old Dutch festival days in Harlem. Both Captain Will and his father, Lapett thought, had the staunch ways of their forbearer, Resolved. He was also delighted to once again see Peter Waldron, Captain Waldron's brother, a bricklayer and Albany chimney inspector.

As Margaret had promised, the soft-spoken, very talented Phillip Lansing had come to entertain all. A Pennsylvanian

Moravian missionary and flutist, Phillip had apparently become acquainted with David Karski while ministering to the Shawnee Indians in the lands of western New York. In time, Lansing would become acquainted with John through David, and it was John who had invited Lansing back east for a visit the summer he had returned to Vandenberg manor with David. The missionary, having been away from his homeland for many years, had long wished to revisit his father's farm in the east near Philadelphia. Somehow John had persuaded Lansing to stop at Vandenberg Manor before heading southward. However, once back east, Phillip had taken a chill along the road and was forced to remain at Vandenberg Estate for nearly a month before continuing on the second leg of his journey to Pennsylvania. So, while Phillip recuperated, Margaret and her servant women tended him, she often reading to him. Certainly it was not odd to imagine that the unique brilliance of Margaret's well-trained mind had quite captivated the deeply sensitive Phillip. Perhaps it was precisely the kind of reception John had hoped that his friend Phillip would receive from his sister. Who would have thought that, although Margaret liked the sensitive, well read Phillip Lansing very much, he did not turn her head in the same manner as did the robust David Karski who could barely read. That summer, Lapett had the opportunity of becoming acquainted with the Moravian and found him to be most agreeable. After meeting him he believed that it was Phillip Lansing who John had intended as a prospective husband for his sister, and not David Karski. Apparently, the Almighty had already decided who would make the better partner for Margaret.

As Margaret had also promised, the ceremony was attended by many of her Lenape cousins, Schoharie Indians, and Mohawk from the distant village of Kahnawake, all of whom had been packed into the grand manor house entrance hall. Surrounding the front stoop and spilling out onto the front lawn leading to the river were the Tuscaroran, Spotted Bird, and his family, as well as every one of Margaret's estate Negroes, and many of her tenants who later celebrated the occasion with a magnificent feast, set out for them under the shade of the great red oaks. Lapett's eldest daughter had had to be discreetly nudged into a thank you by her mother as she stood agape when one of the Indian women had offered her an apple.

Lapett thought of his mother, now long departed, who had claimed that her own grandmother was part Indian, and she, in her later years, would often proudly proclaim that she was a distant cousin to the famed Iroquois Indian chief, Tee Yee Neen HoGa Row or Thoyanoguen (his Christian name being King Hendrick). After returning from his visit to London with Peter Schuyler, King Hendrick and the other three chiefs who accompanied them had became renowned all over the lands. However, all those who openly bore witness to the secret of their family lore had gone to their reward in heaven. Here, this day, his four, well-dressed, English speaking daughters would rather forget the possibility that one drop of Indian blood could be flowing within their veins or for that matter that the Iroquois even existed.

Lapett had the opportunity to talk with his old friend Elias Neau. Life was indeed an abstract drawing. Had he not married and joined the Anglican Church, he might never have had the opportunity to work beside Elias. It was this devout catechist who, through his appeal for the salvation of the soul of the poor Negro slaves, had drawn his, Margaret's, and Anna Stoudt's families together. And of course, he would have also missed one of the most magnificent weddings he had ever attended!

The newlyweds presided over a scrumptious feast. Their lace covered bridal table was laden with seemingly countless silver platters and delft bowls, each overflowing with wondrous bounty: roasted pigeon and squirrel, quail pie, pheasants in cream with apples, smoked ham with peas, sage flavored parsnips, and innumerable other fine and delicious delicacies. The finale of the supper included two of Margaret's favorites: Baked molasses Indian pudding and, though she would never admit as much amid so many of her Dutch friends, an old English favorite, Maids of Honor: irresistible cake and apple jelly tarts just like the ones that had been sold on London Bridge since the days of Queen Elizabeth. All of this was washed down with several barrels of beer: the dark Dutch kind as well as a pale English Ale. There was also much Madeira to accompany the deserts.

Lapett found himself charmed by the glowing locked gaze of the newlyweds as they toasted one another. The scene brought to mind the story of ex-Governor Lord Cornbury, cousin to the late Queen Anne, who insisted that he had fallen in love with his wife because of her beautiful earlobes! As Lapett sat at the table thinking of the lady's earlobes he had lapsed into an unseemly fit of uncontrollable laughter that must have been quite loud considering the glances of reproach he had received from his wife and others.

He hoped that the newly wed Karskis' love would endure. The attraction between man and woman, this overwhelming desire for the sole company of another, was certainly a blessing from the Almighty to be protected and cherished. *Love*, Lapett reflected, *was a natural tonic for the worst that life sometimes had to offer.*

After the feasting someone suggested it was time to form teams for a good game of lacrosse. The clamor of approval that arose could have been heard all the way to Albany as one of the Indians fetched his fur-stuffed deerskin ball. Several others had brought along their netted sticks, as did Peter Waldron who pompously declared, "My cousin is a Captain of the river, but I am your Captain for this game."

John Vandenberg was selected as the other team captain and came running out of the house with a three foot stick that had belonged to his father. Loudly he boasted that even though Peter was once faster than the bobcats, Waldron had slowed considerably in "old age". Everyone knew that speed was the champion of this sport. He declared that those who ran on the Vandenberg team would beat the breaches off Peter and his team.

Each captain quickly picked players who he surmised would be the best for his side. John immediately grabbed two of his tribal cousins, suspecting that they might be good selections. He exhorted his players, causing many of them to begin hooting and hollering, and provokingly exclaimed that Peter Waldron was far too old a cat to master a good game any longer.

As Peter gathered his men around himself, John disappeared into the woods behind the house to search for more good size sticks, and reappeared, tossing the best of those he found to Simon Yates and his cousin, Cornelius, while the others still argued over team positions. Peter Waldron's young son-in-law, Derick Bratt, had also brought along his stick and went to Peter's side. Waldron's robust daughter, Cornelia, stepped forward, but was soon booed away by the men, including her husband, Derick. Makeshift nets were strung between trees at either end of the large, flat field.

By late afternoon the ferocious clash of wood sticks propelled by Indians and white men half stripped of their grand wedding attire was only to be outdone by the excited, hearty cheers of their women and the wild, rhythmic beat of Indian drums. Hours went by as the latest chapter of the old game devised by the northern Indians and the French hundreds of years prior (somewhat reinvented by the Anglo-Dutch) played to its ultimate conclusion. Clearly, the gentlemen, as well as their ladies, were in desperate want of a bit of wild abandon, tempered, of course, by good sportsmanship partnered with Christian fairness.

It was a wonderful scene. The splendor of the birches, elms, and maples that surrounded the playing area, dappled by the angled sun, provided a perfect backdrop for the activities. It was as if the participants and nature were combining for one last glorious outburst before the long days of winter were to set in. The scene, coupled with the unexpected warmth of the October day and the crisp, clean air, made for an invigorating afternoon that bled into the evening. All troubles were forgotten, and everyone, participants and spectators alike, basked in the pure joy of the day and the occasion.

As the sun set, amid the clamor, the bride and groom bid farewell shortly after the fruit and best cheeses were served to their guests. Then, as was customary, they slipped away unnoticed to the intimacy of a first night's bed. With the exception of the servants and Widow Bender, who had begrudgingly accepted Marie's bed shortly after the ceremony, everyone else remained to watch the game wind down in the fading light and approaching cold of the evening. Without question, the wedding had proceeded surprisingly well.

Two days following the nuptials, several families' returned home to Manhattan on the sloop with Captain Waldron, whilst others set out by foot back to Albany with an escort of militia men sent by Schuyler. As David and Margaret made ready for a short wedding trip to Witwyck, Margaret readily agreed that it was better that many of the women, unaccustomed to the roughness of frontier life, not be exposed to any further possible threats from nature or from man. Still blind to the men who had perpetrated the hostilities, the possibility of another raid still existed, although there had been no further threats. All the same, John had insisted on riding along with his sister and her new husband halfway to their destination.

Lapett now understood, for the first time, how deeply Margaret was resented by many of her neighbors, as well as by a few who call her friend. They saw only an Indian woman of great wealth who lived in a 'castle'. Though many had personally experienced her generosity, they disliked her for her position. In addition, her past works of charity with the Negroes in New York City with Elias Neau just prior to the slave riots, and then Lizbeth's untimely death, had made her resented by both Dutch and English, who opposed teaching the slaves at all, let alone teaching them to read the Scriptures. The fear brought on by the volatile mixture of envy, unwanted interference, and perceived arrogance had continued to allow her enemies' emotions to smolder.

Chapter 22

"You have a sweet on John Waldron," ten-year-old Hannah Lapett, puckering impishly, warbled to her eldest sister.

"Good gracious, be quiet will you!" Yvonne admonished nervously. "Papa will hear you, and he will forbid John from ever calling on me again, and then I shall be confined inside this house for the rest of my life!"

"A sweet, a sweet, and you would like it beyond anything else if he would kiss your lips," Hannah said dancing around the room. "That is what you replied to him when he said he would like to kiss your 'beautiful lips'. I heard you say so."

Fourteen year old Yvonne reddened. "Oh, you are the most brazen child I have ever known!" she whispered sharply yet quickly composed herself as her father entered the parlor.

Benjamin Lapett crossed the room toward the window's ledge where he opened an ornately painted, wooden box resting on the sill, gently replacing the family bible. He stood pensively looking out into the street as a cold relentless rain pounded against the glass panes.

Only moments earlier, the customary Sunday afternoon Scripture reading following the meal had been abruptly interrupted when his wife's cousin, Phillip, had appeared at their front door, his face wrought with tension. Although soaked through to the skin, and despite Mrs. Lapett's urging, the young man had declined to step inside. His Mary was about to be delivered of their first child, and his mother-in-law had sent him to fetch Helen along with other neighboring women that they might pray beside her through the birth. Time was of a critical nature. Phillip had to make two more stops at houses along the street before returning home. After apologies for interrupting, thanks, pleas—all in one breathless sentence—Cousin Phillip had pushed off down the block like a powder shot.

Lapett could hardly make out the image of his wife, or their servant woman, as the two dashed away from their front stoop in the direction of Pearl Street. *Nary a soul but thee would insist upon walking those wet bricks this afternoon,* he thought, but his heart warmed all the same. Another cousin awaited God's command to take his or her place within his wife's large and extended family. His precious spouse would ignore the pain of her stiff joints, joyously eager to be part of the favored summoned group.

As daughters Alice and Martine bounced into the room, Benjamin seated himself comfortably next to Yvonne who lifted her sewing basket into her lap. It wasn't long before Hannah came up behind his chair, putting her small, delicate arms around his neck. She leaned forward, her cheek next to his, and he could not but grin, suspecting what was coming next. His little butterfly was bored, and would momentarily charm, and then undoubtedly prod him for a story.

He patted her arm. "Yes, Hannah?"

"Papa…"

Alice giggled, anticipating the familiar scene between her father and her sister, who was younger than she by two years. She knew that Papa could never say "no" to Hannah who without further invitation plunked herself down on the floor by her father's knees. "Yes, Papa…. would you tell us a story about the old times, when Great-grandpapa Jacques lived with the wild savages in the northern woods above Albany?"

"Wild savages you shall have, Hannah. But on the Sabbath?" Benjamin tugged at Hannah's long, copper braid that her mother had lavishly tied at the end with light blue, silk ribbon from the remnants in her hat box.

Alice giggled again, knowing well the game.

"I would have it so, Papa."

Yvonne put down her sewing. "Yes, Papa, it is such a dreadful day, and Mama is sure to be gone for hours. Tell us about how Great-Grandmother and Great-Grandpapa LaCroix married, even though he was a professing Papist and her family were Huguenot's. Is it true that Great-Grandmother's brother tried to slay Great-Grandpapa Jacques because of his bold attentions to his sister, but the couple's strong love saved them?"

Hannah, with eyes closed, faced her eldest sister, smacking her lips in a mock kiss.

Ignoring her sister's taunt, after a moment of silence, Yvonne added, "For the life of me, Papa, I cannot understand how they managed to wed."

Hannah whined, "I want to hear about the Indians."

Martine sighed. "Yes, I agree with Hannah. I would rather hear the tale of how young Great-Grandpapa survived the Indian's gauntlet, and because he was brave and withstood the ordeal he became half-brother to the Indians. I would be most happy to hear about our ancestor's adventures as he roamed the wilderness among the savages and the wild mountain men, and became known as the 'Great Voyager'."

Lapett observed his two eldest daughters. "You, Martine, would have us all see Grandfather Jacques as a man akin to Daniel, who fearlessly made the lions lay down before him." Lapett chuckled, yet paused to contemplate his own words more seriously.

"I confess that there may be some similarities between Jacques and Daniel. Back then, in those times when our great city was known as New Amsterdam, Great-Grandmother Marie's family was indeed a lion's den for Jacques, but with the help of God he did eventually win their friendship."

"Love conquers every obstacle," Yvonne breathed.

"Yes, my dear, love is the desire of all men and women of every faith. Of course, you must remember that it was the Lord's will that my Grandfather would become a Protestant."

"Mama says that there are good and bad Protestants. Was he a good Protestant?"

"Of course, he was, Yvonne."

"Martine, I can see that you are more interested in hearing about Jacques the Papist warrior, who spoke words of love, than the converted Protestant. Alice and Hannah, would you both agree?"

Hannah and Alice nodded.

"But you, Yvonne, I suspect, carry the blood of Marie's obstinate brothers and would smother the forbidden love with a thick, hot sauce of rebuke, most likely chasing away poor Jacques as he pursued the beautiful young widow, Marie."

Hannah quickly interjected, "Oh, she would, Papa!"

Yvonne shot Hannah an unpleasant glance.

Lapett smiled. "Do not interrupt your Papa, Hannah," he admonished gently. "Think, daughters, none of you would be here today with your Papa if hard hearts remained closed."

"Oh, I should not have wanted that at all, Papa," Yvonne whispered.

"Perhaps now, whilst I have you all together around me, I would say a few words regarding your conduct at the wedding we all most recently attended. Martine, think not that your Papa or your Mama have deaf ears attached to both sides of their heads. I will say no more on this, but know that we were not pleased. I listen to everything and I see all.

"While the bride and groom feasted, I too, listened with great enjoyment to all of Captain Waldron's amusing discourse. I suspect that his aunt, the Widow Vermilye, found her nephew equally interesting that day. Yes, yes, your Papa knows from whence these notions about the old times and our family have come into your pretty heads. Your mother and I have agreed that Captain Waldron is an interesting man to have at one's table, but at times we find it difficult to see where the truth lies in his tales and where the Captain's gift of imagination fills in.

"But, I do not wish to imply that Captain Waldron tells only fables. I am sure that as a boy he heard many tales from his aged Grandfather, Resolved Waldron, whilst visiting the old Waldron farm at Harlem. I believe that he relates what he recalls. Captain Waldron it appears has inherited his Grandfather's talent for storytelling, and old Baron Waldron, Great-Grandpapa, and Mrs. Karski's father, Garret Vandenberg, are adventurers who were a part of the early days of our colony."

Flushed, Yvonne lifted her eyes. "I must admit that the Captain's version of our Great-Grandfather's partnership with

Baron Resolved Waldron and his tale of prior Dutch time in our colony were fascinating. I had never heard as much of the olden times as what he told us that day over cookies at the wedding, and I found myself wishing that he had more to tell. I will be sorely disappointed if the Captain has charmed us all with nothing but a sweet fable."

"Nay, daughter, do not mistake me," Benjamin exclaimed. "'Tis true there were no braver men alive than those who first came across the sea to settle our sweet land, and for we today to sing fondly glorious ballads in praise of their heroic deeds brings joy with the remembrance. Men such as Jacques LaCroix and Resolved Waldron are to be held in high regard in the memories of those who knew them in those hard times when the houses here in our city had thatched roofs and the animals roamed freely about our streets unrestrained by any fence.

"Yet, after so many years that have parted us from those early settlers of New York, I suspect that some of the lyrics have gone aground, so to speak. I have no doubt that Marie's brother Roland did look unfavorably upon Jacques LaCroix as a suitor for his sister, but I assure you that no murder was ever attempted."

"Then, amid the Captain's narrative where do we find the fact, and where the fiction?" Yvonne asked.

"Yvonne, consider that old Captain Waldron is a grand champion of tales, even better than your Papa, or his Papa, I believe," Lapett replied winking.

Yvonne wrinkled her brow. "But, what then is truth, Papa?"

"This is what I would have you think. Sometimes, dear children, we are better off not to take the remnants of every tale that we hear about our ancestors to be the complete truth, yet we can appreciate the wonder of the story told.

"I am certain that your mama would approve if I told you a little of what has been passed down to me of the love of Jacques and Marie. And I assure you, Yvonne, I speak no fable, but the truth of a love that was as great as that sung about in the most romantic of sonnets."

Hannah giggled. "Yvonne likes to hear of love."

"Daughter, be silent. I think that having so recently attended a wedding of two who overcame great obstacles to become as one, the story of Marie and Jacques will lend some understanding to those who must endure much to be together."

"Please, Papa, go on," Yvonne replied sheepishly, now eager to hear the rest of the story.

Benjamin cautioned, "I will speak little of Great-Grandfather's early years spent as a Papist. Your mother has told you that he was baptized by the Jesuits. I would ask each of you to recall that Great-Grandfather Jacques found peace with Christ at the end of his life, and believe your Papa, it is best to leave all talk of Papists in Rome."

"But... may we at least hear of the Indians and how he lived with them and fought beside them against opposing tribes?" Martine whined.

"Gracious," Yvonne mumbled in a perplexed tone.

"Yvonne," Martine snapped snidely, "we are each of us akin to the natives of this land. Don't forget, before Great-Grandfather Jacques married Great-Grandmother Marie, Mama said that he was married to an Indian girl, and before she died she bore him two sons."

Yvonne mumbled, "We are no blood kin to any of the first wife's children, but I must say, Martine, based on your love for feather and beads you will make a fine partner someday for the pipe maker's son who caught your eye at the wedding. I hear his grandmother is Iroquois."

Martine stuck out her tongue.

Benjamin reproved the two girls. "Let us remember that kindness to others, whomever they may be, is what our Savior taught. And..." he added slowly, "a prudent young lady is silent as she listens considerately to the words of her Papa." Yvonne's deep blue eyes registered her embarrassment while Alice leaned close and whispered, "You had better keep your lips closed."

Martine interjected eagerly. "Mr. Yates' pipe shop is the grandest in all of Manhattan. John Waldron says so and told us that they sell hundreds of tobacco pipes every year."

Continuing, Lapett said, "Thank you, Martine. It is good to know Mr. Yates prospers. Now, I would like to get back to the story at hand. We know that Jacques and Marie came to the colony during the time of Dutch rule, but they married in 1666, which was nearly two years after the Dutch were replaced and the English King became our Sovereign Majesty. Marie had been married before, but there was no issue from her first marriage."

Martine could not contain her question: "Why did Great-Grandmama's brother hate Jacques so? Not all Papists are hated by everyone. Celine Dumont's Grandmother was a poor servant girl raised in the Protestant faith before she ran away to Maryland, a Catholic colony, to marry a Catholic nobleman."

Lapett smiled. "As I recall, the lady returned to New York after the death of her husband and married a magistrate by the name of Taine. Ever since then, the family has been pew holders at Trinity Church.

"Your mother and I choose to believe that Roland never hated his brother-in-law. From all family accounts, Roland was a kindly, jovial man, and it is difficult to imagine a man with such an inviting disposition harboring a murderous heart. But, it is understandable that he was cautious about such a man as Jacques who was reared by the Indians since a boy of twelve or fourteen and had become a kinsman to them. I think that this is what Martine means when she speaks of her native kin."

"We are not blood kin," Yvonne repeated flatly.

Ignoring his eldest, Lapett continued dramatically. "I am sure that when Roland saw Jacques, Roland saw not a lovesick suitor, but a bloody sword at his sister's throat. Had Jacques remained a Papist in word and deed, of course, the marriage would have been impossible. French Protestants suffered in France and had come to America to escape persecution.

"Colonial Jesuits professed it was their love of God that brought them here, but it has been said by more than one that many French Papists went along with their Jesuit priests living among the Mohawk more out of love of the beaver pelt."

"If that be true, Papa, they would have committed a terrible sin,"

"If that be true, Yvonne, you would be right in thinking so. I make no judgment upon the Jesuits or any other ambassador for Christ. You have heard before that many missionaries were martyred while leading the Indians to knowledge of Christ's Gospel."

Alice grew somber. "You mean they were killed, Papa?"

"Yes, dear one, Papists and Protestants alike were murdered while attempting to bring the true faith to the native people."

Alice winced.

"Yes, terrible deaths came to many who thought only to bring the Christian faith to the heathen. There are few colonists who are old enough to recall the days of Dutch rule in the colonies, but many remain whose families have lived here on Manhattan Island since before the time of William and Mary's rule. Papists, both in England and in New York, lamented James's loss of the English crown when he was thrown out of power by his daughter, Mary, and her husband, William. Yet Protestants recall with disgust the three years of chaos under the reign of the Papist, King James. Those colonists still harbor old wounds of their ancestors. There is a lesson to be learned today, my girls. Society will smile as they face you, but should you mention a Papist or Indian in the bloodline, beware... for their warmth will soon fade."

"I think we understand," Yvonne said, glancing at Martine.

Lapett's voice rose emotionally. "Some Priests held their crucifix high and bid the Indians follow them to Kahrawake near Montreal where the Indians took up the European French Catholic's grievance against the British people. Because of this, many, many good colonials have died."

"But, Papa," Alice interrupted, "Did you not say to us that the 'Great Voyager' once saved a Jesuit priest from the savages?"

"He did indeed," Benjamin answered, softening. "LaCroix, according to family tradition, was blessed to be of service to Colonel Nichols, who was the first English governor of this colony. He took part in the ransom negotiations for several settlers who were captured near the northern village of Scaticoke, which is not too far from Albany. The Jesuit was among the poor souls. Twice before the Jesuit had been captured by the savages, and both times tortured to the extent that two of his fingers had been cut off. But still, as it is told, the Jesuit returned to the same tribe and persisted in bringing faith to the unbelievers."

Hannah, who had nestled herself into her father's lap, wrinkled her forehead thoughtfully. "Great-Grandpapa was brave. Jesus teaches us to love everyone. Do you think we should even love a Papist?"

Startled, Lapett hesitated only a moment before answering, "I do, my darling girl."

Yvonne added. "I think that the Jesuit was also brave, and he must have truly loved God. Mama says we must pray for the immortal souls of all those who know not the true message of Christ."

"Your mama is the wisest of all women. But come now. As I have said before, it is best to leave all talk of popery in Rome, or perhaps within the confines of the private chambers of King George and his councilmen."

"But what of Great-Granduncle Roland?" Alice asked.

"I am of a mind that it is also better to allow Roland to rest in peace," Benjamin answered quickly. "I will tell you though that Roland made his peace with Jacques long before the two saw the face of God."

Alice's eyes widened. "You mean they became friends?"

"I believe they did."

"I'm glad."

"As for the savages, Yvonne," Benjamin turned toward his eldest, "do well to remember what I have said about the words you form in your mouth. And have a care about what you say to your sisters who love you."

Yvonne's eyes misted over. "Forgive me. I will try to be more sensible before I speak."

"I am pleased to hear so. But, come now, I will not have tears."

Martine twisted a piece of her hair uncomfortably. Rising from her chair she declared, "I will set the kettle to the flame for tea. Mama left us fresh bread to sprinkle with sugar. I don't know about any of you, but I crave a slice."

Hannah jumped up. "Papa may I be excused? I would like to be in charge of the sugar."

"Yes, of course. Go with your sister that you might be of help to her."

"I do not need help, Papa," Martine said as Yvonne put away her sewing.

"Come along, Hannah," Alice ordered, dragging her sister from the room.

Yvonne bent over her father and kissed him on the forehead. "It will be dark soon; I will light the candles."

"Yes," Lapett agreed, turning toward the window where he watched the rain drops sliding down the glass panes.

"Shall you join us, or should I bring you a cup of tea, Papa?"

Lapett looked up into the loving eyes of his first born daughter wondering where all the time had gone.

"I think your Papa will sit here awhile, but a cup would be welcome, thank you."

"I will bring one in to you as soon as the pot is brewed," Yvonne whispered, adding, "Do not worry about Mama: several of the women will be there, and she has promised to return home before we girls retire."

"Yes, of course," Lapett replied softly.

As Yvonne swished away, Lapett sat pensively thinking of his own boyhood days in New York, and the stories that were told to him upon days such as these, and how his father throughout his life had kept alive the history of his family and the colony he had so dearly loved.

With Margaret's wedding still fresh in mind, and having just finished relating tales of old regarding his Grandpapa and Resolved Waldron, Lapett found himself thinking of Jacob Leisler who had been connected to the Waldron family through Resolved Waldron's daughter Aeltje's marriage to Johannes Vermilye.

Captain Vermilye had been one of those appointed to the province's "Committee of Safety", a watch group formed in 1689 meant to keep order during the perilous transition while awaiting the coronation of William and Mary after King James vacated the English throne. During those times Vermilye had a seat in Jacob Leisler's council. Leisler had appointed himself Lieutenant Governor of the province without authority from the British crown. Shortly thereafter, Vermilye began signing as 'Commander in Chief' of the Province. Through a series of political misunderstandings, Captain Vermilye was one of the unfortunates arrested along with Jacob Leisler and his son-in-law, Milborne, for High Treason. Vermilye and several other committee members languished eighteen months in prison following the hanging of Leisler and his son-in-law before Governor Fletcher liberated Vermilye along with the others. How unfortunate that Resolved Waldron died in 1690 with his son-in-law still incarcerated. Lapett could only imagine his sadness, having given half of his life to his adopted homeland. After the death of her father, and a few years later her husband, Aeltie Waldron Vermilye sold all her Harlem properties to a nephew and moved northward to Yonkers.

Perhaps though, Leisler came to mind now, because as a young boy, Lapett and his father had witnessed Leisler and Milborne's sad execution on a dismal day such as this one.

A decent, yet overly ambitious man, Leisler had been caught up in the confusing political circumstances of the transition of power between England's monarchs. Lapett recalled how his father often said that had Leisler been patient, and waited upon King William for his appointments, he might well have been properly empowered and both he and his son-in-law Milborne spared the rope. His father knew well the story of Leisler, having been one of the soldiers with Milborne who had been sent to Albany in 1690 to defend the northern city against a possible attack from the French from Canada. In a twist of fate, the attack had been upon the outpost at Schenectady, a village seventeen miles from Albany: a brutal massacre that took the lives of sixty men, women and children. Had the French attacked Albany, there would have been another story to share, or not, had Milborne and the others not survived.

Leisler, a Huguenot, was, after all, a Godly man, born of a prominent Calvinist family, who, prior to his rise to power and the terrible misunderstanding, had spent many years establishing himself as a respected merchant in New York, often socializing with the soldiers at the old Dutch fort. Lapett remembered his father's account of how LaCroix, Sheriff Waldron, and Leisler had on more than one occasion played at bowls on the Common. Leisler was much in favor of a government headed by William and Mary, having sworn his oath against all popery, and to defend the majesties of King William and Queen Mary. Although history would write him differently, Lapett came to agree with his father that Leisler and Milborne had meant well enough, and the men hung in New York that May of 1691 had been many things, but never traitors.

In time he would tell his girls about the staunch Dutch inhabitants of the village of Schenectady, who for the most part favored standing with Leisler, and who had misjudged the danger that was at hand; a terrible costly mistake for many poor souls.

Whilst Milborne was at Albany with his soldiers, the fort of Schenectady was surrounded by a palisade guarded by only ten or twelve Connecticut militia men. Instead of securing themselves inside, and locking the gates, the villagers had scoffed at the notion of an enemy attack in the frigid, mid-winter of northern New York.

The night of the assault, many of the Schenectady men had drunk too much rum, and lacking sobriety they laughed and left their gates open. They were so belligerent that they made a public mockery by forming a snowman and dressing the cold sculpture as a sentinel. Apparently, neither the commander, Lieutenant Talmadge, nor any of the guards had any indication of the approach of two hundred men, half of them French and the other half Indians converted to Christianity. All had, amazingly enough, traveled with muskets and ammunition on snowshoes for weeks from areas near Montreal.

Some distance outside of Schenectady, the French and their Indians found an Indian hut with four Iroquois squaws inside, who they promptly captured. After warming themselves by the squaw's fireside, they tied the women's wrists and forced them to lead them to Schenectady. In the darkest part of the night the assailants surrounded the village while the inhabitants slept.

A war-whoop sliced through the silence of the night. Doors were broken down with hatchets, and the terrified villagers were torn from their beds. Many were hacked to pieces within minutes.

Lapett would tell them of brave Adam Vrooman who saw his wife and two-year-old child's heads smashed against the doorposts of his house. A survivor testified that Vrooman battled the enemy like a wildcat to save his family. After the attack, a Mohawk brave who had been camped with friendly Indians at Schenectady and witnessed his valor, stepped forward for the bereaved man, begging the French soldiers to save the desperate fellow's life. The Indians, even those with the enemy, respected Vrooman for his courage in fighting fearlessly for his loved ones. Adam Vrooman was spared by the French who did not wish to insult the Mohawk's or antagonize the local Indians.

The minister, Peter Tassemaker, was mutilated with a hatchet, and his body was left in his house which was burned to the ground along with all of his papers. In later years, it was said that the French had meant to save the minister for questioning, but so wicked was the attack that even God's appointed representative was not spared.

A few had survived. A village official, Captain Sander Glen, was spared. The French had their orders not to hurt Captain Glen or any of his family. The reason for this generosity was that he had on many occasions saved the lives of French colonists living thereabouts.

None of the Mohawk Indians who were in the blockhouse were harmed. Their attackers insisted they had no quarrel with them, only the English. Eighty were taken prisoner. A few old men, women, and children, not fit for work, which would be demanded by their captors, were left behind at the smoldering village. Months later, Glen helped to secure the release of several captives, but some were not recovered for years, while others were never seen again.

Lapett sighed, remembering that his father had told him that some of the captured women married the heathen by whom they had been captured, and later would not leave the tribe, although a rescue had come, because they had born babes fathered by their captors. The Jesuit Priests, he understood, had performed the marriage ceremonies.

The scourge of Schenectady was rarely spoken of any more as it was a cruel part of history that those fair complexioned and faint of heart would have difficulty in listening to. Yet, Lapett believed that the brave acts of those who had long ago passed into the hands of the Almighty should be recounted so that not only might a prayer be whispered in their memory, but also that vigilance would never again be discarded.

Suddenly Helen's footsteps could be heard ascending the front stoop. Lapett rose to greet her at the door just as Yvonne entered the room with a cup of tea.

"You are home!" Yvonne exclaimed.

Helen smiled wearily. "Yes, dear, and we have a new citizen; a boy, John Paul."

Chapter 23

In silent peace Margaret followed her husband along the winding pathway toward the river's edge, glad to have given in to David's plea that they leave behind the harvesting of trees and late crops for a few hours of picnicking. Discourse was unnecessary. She was perfectly content just to be in his company while enjoying the splendor of the burnished fall colors along the trail, smiling as David pointed toward a small brown-speckled hawk hovering high over an open clearing ahead. Obviously, he felt the same as she.

They had been married for over a fortnight, and, other than a brief wedding trip south to the farm of friends along the Wallkill, had had little time together alone on the estate. She had promised to show David more of the secret places that had so stirred her senses since childhood. The bright sun and clarity of the air lent warmth to the day, encouraging appreciation of every morsel of nature in sight. *If there was any tangible and consistent comfort within this wearisome life,* Margaret thought, *it had to be the land upon which she and David stood.*

Further into the woodlands she took the lead, and they had walked a short distance before they came into a small clearing where a narrow walking bridge had been built over the stream. Margaret commented softly, "The Walkill River is not as wide or as deep as is our mighty North River, which travels, I have been told, over three hundred miles of New York ground. Some consider the Walkill no river at all, but more of a generously filled creek, but that does not disappoint me. I do so love the creeks."

"What is it that endears you so?"

Thoughtfully Margaret answered, "I suppose it is the unusual life that can be found within the water that passes through many wayward chutes of wood and then over fallen logs and moss-covered boulders. I have long found a fascination with Munsie Creek's rippling water journey into shallow, spring-fed pools. I do not know how such things be in your home country, but here in proper season the little polliwogs leisurely swim together beside schools of small fish. Next summer we will come here again, and you shall see that during the evenings their familiar song gives definition to the word 'home'." Margaret paused at the center of the bridge, adding demurely, "This is how I have come to know the place, and I hope that you will too."

David waited for his wife to enjoy her quiet moment before he answered. "I am most certain that I will find every part of our adventure today as delightful as do you. Remember that I spent many years in a wilderness similar to your country, yet truly, here, with you, there is no place in any country that could be more beautiful."

Margaret looked at her husband and smiled appreciatively, "Sometimes when I have been here I think that the water speaks as it feeds the roots of the pink and white wild azaleas that come into flower here in the summer. Their sweetly fragrant blooms cast a delicious spell over me. For me this precious early summer scene encourages me to remember Psalm 150:6 'Let everything alive give praises to the Lord!'."

Margaret continued across the bridge. David followed, noticing that her long black hair hung far below her buttocks. It seemed that every day he saw something new that he had not noticed before about his Peggy and all that surrounded her.

"Your sentiment is most tender," David responded. "Have a care here," he added while Margaret reached to grasp his outstretched hand, thus navigating a tree limb that had probably fallen across the well defined path the stormy night that Clare was born. After crossing this obstacle, Margaret began to ponder out loud the cycle of life.

"My native ancestors knew this patch of the world to be a precious gift of the Great Creator. In those old times my mother's people said that human beings could own no part of the earth. The earth, like the air, was not something that could be selfishly captured for one's own personal profit. The land was to be appreciated and cared for by all people, and not to be considered as an acquired possession such as an ax, a good blanket, or an iron pot."

"Ah, Peggy, my love, you speak of times a hundred years gone."

Margaret nodded. The path had widened and she continued to hold David's hand as they walked side by side. "It is true that our country is changing, yet I think that the more things change, the more we should recall the wisdom of our ancestors."

"The country is bound to grow, Peggy. Life will continue in ways different from those of our grandfathers."

"Yes, life will go on, Almighty God willing."

As they continued on in silence, Margaret believed that as a child, with a heart open to God, what she had learned at the knee of the wise Lenape was a sacred truth. As her Indian mother's daughter, she understood the legacy of her responsibilities toward the land: that it should be held close and cherished. These were lessons of blood that the white settlers who had come over on ships could never understand; lessons that even those born here, such as her David, would have trouble comprehending. Yet reality was that the Indian way had all but disappeared. The teachings of her Lenape ancestors must live only within her heart.

As a woman she had become very much a daughter of the Dutch. Still, after her Bible, it was the land that was her staff of life, lifting up her damaged soul. Her mother had never put any stock in her dwelling place. As long as the house was warm and protected from the harsh rains and snows she was content.

In contrast, her father had imported from Europe the finest furnishings and strove to the end to constantly improve upon their house and holdings. When Margaret walked the plantation grounds, and looked upon her house and barns, she knew that it must be his blood that stirred within her body, as she took great pleasure in her house, as well as all that had been built up around it. Sitting grandiose upon a well-groomed hillside slope dotted with excellent hardwoods (elm, oak, hickory and chestnut), her castle-like, brick and fieldstone manor house, with its multiple, finely set, deep casement windows gave her a sense of pride. She knew that the estate made quite an impression on anyone who saw it. It was well known that city folk often drove their carriages all the way from Wiltwyck and Albany just to see the 'Castle'.

Though such pride might be considered sinful, she never stopped enjoying the view.

Indeed, her father's dream for a mighty plantation had become a glorious reality. Yet she wondered if one day, hundreds of years hence, all of their structured endeavors would fall to dust just as easily as had the simple structures of the original people of the land whose civilizations had endured a thousand or more years before the appearance of the white man. She supposed that, if the past did cut a path to the future, then Mother Earth, like her faith in Christ, would remain a faithful companion. Everything else was fragile. Everything else could be gone forever within the blink of an eye. Margaret shook herself; she hated to be gripped by such perplexing thoughts on a day the Lord must have meant to soothe the soul.

David spoke first, "I wonder if Dan Bloodgood has come by the mill this afternoon as he had arranged last week?"

"How I enjoy Dan's lively discourse every time he comes to grind his wheat," Margaret replied.

David nodded. "'Tis true, Dan gives flavor to the day."

They walked along in silence for a few minutes before David said, "How far are we, Peggy, from the spot you wished me to see?"

"Not too far; let me go in front of you again, and lead the way. The path narrows again up yonder."

Margaret went ahead of David, her thoughts turning toward the operation of both her mills. When she and David were visiting the Clarks near Wiltwyck, during their absence (much to her annoyance) John had left Mr. Altemouse in charge and taken the opportunity to make a business trip to New York where he had purchased what he called "three of the most handsome Negroes he had ever seen". One, a man of perhaps thirty years of age, spoke excellent English, the other two spoke only the old talk of their country. Upon return, John had put the English speaking slave under Henry, who spoke Dutch, and no English. John wanted desperately to make a mill hand out of his new English speaking charge. He felt that putting an English speaking Negro into the mill would make future business transactions with English customers much easier. James took charge of the younger men, working them in the field.

Margaret wondered how the new slave, who John had decided to call George, in honor of England's King, was doing. It was no easy task to train a man to work within the thick stone walls of her mill. This was a work place where prosperity became reality six days a week, from before sunup till after sundown, as corn was made into meal and grain into flour. Only on Sunday did the mill grow silent. Henry certainly had his hands full.

Her grist mill was a bustling hub of social activity, with neighbors often linking the news of other neighbors as well as the gossip concerning England's monarch while bringing in bushels of their own harvests to be ground. Margaret felt pangs of guilt knowing that it should be she who should be back there taking care of business. Before she was married she enjoyed taking over for Mr. Altemouse and clerking in the mill office just to have the opportunity of conversing with neighboring customers. Of course, after being wed, David had raised an eyebrow over his wife standing behind a public desk and had quietly suggested to her that Mr. Altemouse should handle all the clerking henceforth. Thus, Mr. Altemouse had been given the title: "Overseer General of the Vandenberg Estate". He took his lead from John in all matters with regard to the mills.

Until recently, Mr. Altemouse had handled the desk at the lumber mill as well, but with all the trees being felled, the lumber mill's production had increased greatly, and John had been forced to leave David and his crew camped out in the woods while he tended the mill. Thank goodness David had made no protest over her going down to the sawmill to see her brother at work, as she liked watching trees made into planks, and there was something absolutely irresistible about the aroma of fresh cut lumber.

Stopping to pull a few deep purple berries from an elderberry bush, she offered the fruit to David.

After popping the berries into his mouth, he puckered his lips. "Tart, bitter," he mumbled puckering.

"Nay, they are good to eat," she said, surprised by his reaction. Trying one herself she grimaced, "I usually find them sweet and most pleasing. I have collected among these thickets since I was no higher than Sam and Joshua. I do not understand the taste; the crimson and red is the same as always."

As David put another handful of berries into his mouth, he shrugged his shoulders while puckering once again.

She resumed her lead with David trailing behind. Thoughts of the twins brought her to Peter, recalling how, after Peter had disappeared, John had gone to Albany to report the attack and the missing slave to the appropriate officials, and while there had stumbled upon Seth Thomas. Matty's eldest son said he had overheard a conversation at Green Brier Inn where a trapper claimed that he had seen a young Negro boy in black woolen breeches in the harsh hands of two sailors. The young slave might have been about the age of Peter. After John had heard this he had gone to the printer who made notices concerning a Runaway Negro, with a description and promise of a reward for the boy's return. John had then spent the better part of three days posting the notice in a dozen or more of the taverns between Albany and Wiltwyck. Margaret had also sent a courier carrying the printed notices to several ship merchants along the wharf in New York. Despite all these efforts, there had never been any response. Hope for Peter's return diminished with each passing day, and now she was almost afraid to think of the terror her slave may have faced. She would rather that Peter be dead than in the grip of some torturous barbarian who had him stowed away upon a slave ship bound for a foreign plantation where he would be absorbed into the darkness.

Since her marriage though, there had been little time for further investigations. Everyone in the valley now spent every hour of precious daylight gleaning the last fragments of food that had been grown; drying and hanging beans and squash, salting fish and meats, and storing all for the long, bitter winter months ahead. To this end, she had driven herself and all those working with her to the brink of exhaustion. She could not save Moses from the mutilation he had suffered, nor Peter from the hands of peril, but she would not fail to keep her people from starvation and cold before the dandelions were ready to be picked early next April.

Today's Sunday afternoon dalliance bordered upon sinful, but when she wed, did she not promise herself that she would put her husband first? With Marie in charge of the house servants and Mr. Altemouse and John at home, all was in good hands. A few stolen hours of happiness could be forgiven. The harvest work was almost done... the house account books and the world at large could wait... or so her husband adamantly stated while he had been nuzzling her neck this morning as she was about to sip her chocolate.

"We are here!" Margaret proclaimed as they neared the edge of the narrowest part of the stream.

"Thankfully!" David called jovially from the rear.

Settling on a clearing of tall grasses, Margaret threw open the multi-colored, indigo blue and red blanket she carried. Glancing at the water, the day being unseasonably warm, she suggested they remove their silk stockings as well as their matching bead-decorated deerskin moccasins, a wedding gift from Mamma Shasa. Without waiting for his reply she hiked her yellow dyed linen skirt and her chemise undergarment exposing her bare legs to her knees. David put down the filled rush basket he had been carrying on his shoulder. He stood over her, his hands on his hips. "Your will be done, my lady. I will say you are a most talented wench when it comes to persuading your husband."

Soon the two traversed hand-in-hand through the inlet's brisk waters, careful to avoid the creek bed's sharp bottom stones buried halfway into the silt, the cold mud squeezing up between their toes. From afar they could hear the dull sound of the rotation of the Vandenberg's waterwheels.

After a short time they had tired of the cold waters and sat down on the blanket. Harmony filled Margaret's soul while they languished stretched out beside one another, picking at small squares of chestnut bread, strong cheese, and cold mint-spiced tea she had packed for their picnic. Here, for the moment, all burdensome responsibilities and hopeless thoughts were banished. Here, for the moment, all that existed was the serene ecstasy that comes to a human being who is loved and allowed to love in return.

Propping herself up on one elbow, Margaret studied her husband's firm jaw line and his face, centered by a rather crooked, broad nose that he had explained was so shaped because his brother had broken it during a fight when he was fifteen. She had no notion what brought about the skirmish, but David had said that after that dispute they had never fought again. The man she loved was not handsome, yet unmistakable; there was something in his face that she had fancied from the beginning of their acquaintance: a quiet reassuring assertiveness that encouraged her to believe that anything was possible.

"Your eyes could bore a hole into my head, woman. What think you?"

"I pray that you have no misgivings, having married a woman so lacking in joy these past days," she whispered.

David wrinkled his brow. "You are not a silly girl, Peggy, and that you are a woman of tender thought does hold my heart."

"As do you hold mine," she said rubbing one bare toe against his naked foot. To her great surprise, though the air was pleasant, a shiver ran down her spine.

"Dear Peggy, the time is long past for second thoughts, but rest in knowing that I have no regrets over our marriage. Try to enjoy the beauty of this day, dearest." Reaching for her hand, he kissed her fingers lightly.

Margaret said, "I hear that there is constant chatter in Manhattan with regard to our King and England's investment system which from all accounts is falling apart. Perhaps it is God's wrath."

David groaned, "You never rest. God's wrath? What are you talking about?"

"I have heard that King George is a disgrace, not fit to rule beggars at the backdoor of the local tavern. Many speak ill of the German raised King, saying he is a brute."

"Where did you hear this?"

"Here, yesterday at our mill from that Mr. Clark who is visiting Groesbeck. Yes, yes, do not look so skeptical. I know what I heard. I was aghast when I overheard the men jesting, just as fine as you please, about the King, saying he arrived in England in 1720 with two Negroes, and two mistresses, all four of whom he claimed to be just 'good friends'. His Majesty, it is said, looks to them for advice. You can imagine if he looks to such persons for advice why the financial system is in ruin."

David, though somewhat surprised that his bride would speak so openly about such things, could not suppress a chuckle, but quickly sobered under his wife's raised eyebrow.

Margaret continued, "The Negroes had been captured in the Turkish campaign, and since the King had imprisoned his wife, Sophia, for adultery, the two consorts kept him occupied in the bedchamber. I fear our King must be mad. Praises to heaven, King George spends most of his time in Germany, and leaves the government to the new and worthy Prime Minister, Mr. Walpole."

"Dear Peggy, I have far too much on my plate to worry over the sins of England's German King, and I suspect Mr. Walpole, being new to the position, has his own troubles."

Margaret quickly added. "It was obvious that the English Parliament was forced to make a painful decision when it took George as King, for the alternative would have been The Pretender, James's son, and none of them could stomach another Catholic on the throne of England. Of course, English law forbids it and the law would be upheld. Well, in the end God took good care of England's politics and sent along Mr. Walpole."

David laughed. "I would hope that Mr. Walpole has no regrets for his calling."

This time it was Margaret who became serious. "There are some who may indeed think you have cause for a great many regrets," she persisted.

David responded, "Why would I care what others apart from us think, my love? I care not what Kings or beggars would have to say. And who are they who would utter a foul word in our direction? I should think that anyone who would speak bitter words against us would be better to have a care in keeping their tongues silent, for we might think them a part of a conspiracy to bring us harm."

"We would report them."

"Serious talk, even of the smallest measure, against any one of us would be foolish while the officials are combing through the countryside looking for those who have committed such crimes as stealing our slaves and destroying our properties. Gossips will be gossips, but who would dare be so impudent?"

Margaret shrugged. "The gossiping woman, I fear, does not think beyond the length of her nose."

"The chatter of women folk, under normal times, flows into my one ear and quickly leaves through the other, but truths can sometimes be found when a treachery is followed by gossip."

Margaret nodded. "Of course, you are right."

"Still, Peggy, I would ask you a question?"

"And I will answer if I can."

"I do understand your lack of joy because of the missing boy. Who has such a hard heart as they would not think of him? But I think something else worries you. Perhaps something that has to do with the round woman who came to the mill yesterday afternoon? She was present whilst I talked with Henry about the new man."

"What makes you ask such a question?"

"I saw the look of worry that crossed your face when you were leaving. You and the round one had some discourse."

Margaret smiled. "Ah, you speak of Mary Moak, the cheese maker. You are most observant, husband. Mrs. Moak is a woman who does try my patience yet I suffer through it, for I and others—even Colonel Schuyler—crave her cheeses for our tables. But, no, she had nothing amiss to say to me."

David reflected further. "Then perhaps you have heard something more from the spoiled tongue that belongs to Abigail Rye. I recall how salty she spoke to you on our wedding day. She be the sour mouthed one. We should have thrown her out!"

"She drank too much strong beer. That was all."

"You are forgiving, sweet. She is to my mind a jealous woman; that is what she is, be she drunk or sober. John tells me that she prays daily that she be blessed with a suitable prospect for the sacrament of matrimony."

"You surprise me that you listened to such foolishness," Margaret said tensely, withdrawing her hand.

David lay back, cupping his hands behind his head. "You are right, Peggy, I should not make light of any good woman, and I am far too new to the role of tolerable husband to understand a woman's way; yet I sometimes think that every wife must think her husband deaf and blind to all that fills the day."

Margaret reached for the wine. "I do not think you either deaf, dumb, or blind."

"Ah, some good news."

"Would you have some more to drink?"

"Nay, I have had my fill. Peggy, I hear the talk about us as much as you do, and I am angered by such talk. I know that many think me a man who married you for gold."

Margaret laughed. "Gold! What gold have I?"

David sobered. "I do not know and do not care. You might have ten thousand pounds and a ship full of gold or not a skuiver to your name. It would make no difference to me as I have told you many times. I have pledged my love to a woman, and that is all."

"And I to you, husband," Margaret whispered, laying her head against David's chest.

"Be comforted, Peggy. Had I not the desire to wed, I would not have done so. I have no need of your money nor your lands, and as well you should now know, I care not as much as a rat's hair for the opinions of the unhappy unmarried maids hereabouts, or of anyone else for that matter."

"Abigail Rye," Margaret whispered quietly, "is an unhappy woman and she truly must be pitied. I will say no more of Abigail."

"You need not say a word. I know all about Mistress Rye and the doctor for whom she has set her cap."

"You do?"

"Recall you, I am not deaf and blind."

Margaret laughed. "Indeed. Oh, David, I must say that you do astonish me in how you see all. You are a shrewd man." There was a humorous ring to her voice.

"Shrewd?"

"I mean to say that, being so quiet, most would not know you to be so smart of things that happen around you."

"Thank you. I see your meaning now."

Margaret lifted her head indignantly, "If I were to speak unkindly of a woman's actions, or to mock her over her desperate yearning for a gentleman, and perhaps drinking more than was wise at a celebration, would my mouth not hold the same sharp tongue as Abigail's? I am as curious as any other woman, but I should hope that I am no clucking hen."

David laughed, "Clucking hen does not suit you at all, my love."

With her face to the purplish blue of the fall sky, Margaret said, "I wish that Abigail becomes as happy as I am now, and of course I would wish that the good doctor be inclined to feel the same about Abigail."

"I have wed the most generous of all women."

Pulling herself closer, she whispering into David's ear. "You are much mistaken if you believe that I heed what our neighbors say. I care not what the whole of the colonies say or think about our marriage. So we are of one mind."

"This is very good to hear as well," David replied, closing his eyes.

Margaret took her husband's lead and closed her eyes. She wasn't completely honest when she said she didn't care what anyone thought, and she was angry with herself for having given in to foolish feelings over Abigail Rye's prattling. She doubted that David knew, but Mistress Rye was only one among many who had pitched their hurts from the side of the mouth. But, it did no good to share the pain of such bits of unpleasantness with her husband or anyone else.

Leaning toward her, David said, "I have wanted to tell you something for a long time, and..." David was about to say more when Margaret interrupted.

"Do you hear?" Margaret whispered, drawing close.

"I hear," David whispered back.

Margaret jumped nervously, "What is that cracking sound?"

"Be at peace. It is no woodsman come hither, I assure you. Look over there. See the tiny wood thrush nestling himself into the bush?"

As the two settled back the noise returned, growing louder.

Margaret jumped to her feet. "That is no bird. Something is over there in the bushes!"

David cried out, "Who goes there?" No answer came to them, yet it looked as if two wolves darted from the thicket.

Margaret and David were astonished. Margaret said, "Did you see what that was?"

"Wolves perhaps, you stay here and I will go to investigate."

As David reached for his musket, Margaret grabbed for his shirtsleeve, "Oh no, husband, you will not leave me. I will come with you."

"Come if you will," David sighed. The two of them followed the creek's edge. Suddenly Margaret gasped, "Look, over there near the tall grasses. I see something!"

"Where?"

"There, yonder where I am pointing to, near the clump of fallen trees. Dear God in heaven, David, I think there is a body in the brush!"

"I see it. Now stay behind me," David ordered. He made his way through the low brush to the cluster of fallen trees near the edge of the creek, discovering the corpse of a black male face down in the water. Margaret, ignoring his command, followed him halfway but stopped, while David waded into the knee deep water and pulled out the body, legs first, from under the clump of old tree trunks and brush. He flipped the corpse over. Immediately Margaret let out a scream, "Oh no—this can not be. Oh Lord, no, it be Peter!"

Standing over the young boy's body, David's mind whirled. Without thinking, he muttered, "Young Peter was brutishly killed. See how the side of his skull has been crushed."

Her head spinning, Margaret had begun to pray, but soon her voice trailed away as her heart filled with bitterness. "A murderer lives among us, husband."

David lifted his eyes from the partially decomposed body. "The lad has been dead for many weeks I would say, and hidden thus, his body not seen when we searched."

"I can not understand why we were not able to find him here. I am certain that all parts of our property were covered during our many searches."

David sighed. "Perhaps the heavy rains pushed him forth or perhaps the boy was put here after we searched no longer. It is of no consequence. His immortal soul is now in Our Savior's care."

Chapter 24

Pulling back hard on the reins, John Vandenberg, red-eyed and coughing, brought his chestnut-colored mare, Molly, to an abrupt stop amid a choking swell of clay colored dust that had all but blinded him. He cursed under his breath. The seizures were more violent, and the spasms came more frequently as well.

A man in his prime should not allow a bout or two of the shudders to hold him down, he reasoned. All the same, he had been thinking of making the trip up to Albany to call upon the Physick, Jacob Staats, who had been so highly recommended by the Dominie. The minister had said that with the help of the Almighty the Physician had concocted a remedy that had cured his mother, who all had thought to be near death, herself having suffered what sounded to John as much the same sickness. Mama Shasa had prepared him her strongest herbal bag and despite sleeping with it on his chest each night, it had done him no good. Struggling to clear his throat, he leaned over and spit out another thick wad of brownish phlegm.

"Hold up, John, will you?" David shouted. Trying to keep his brother-in-law's pace along the narrow, tree-lined road that connected Vandenberg and Kingman land, David feared his horse would drop out from under him. He had ridden to Kingman's place before, and he found the route a rigorous one, but today was all the more difficult because he dreaded what was to come. But he had felt obligated, and he knew John didn't want him along. "Hold, hold!" he yelled again.

Over his shoulder John shouted, "You should have stayed home!"

David had grown accustomed to the notion that John was not a man given to idle discourse; usually though, he could coax something from him, yet they had barely said a word for the last two miles. Spurring his horse so that the two of them rode abreast, it was obvious from John's sullen face that Clare's sweet smile played no part in his thoughts. "So you mean to confront him?"

John's eyes remained fixed on the road ahead. His answer came out hard. "I do."

"I would ask you again then that we turn around and return home," David said. "I ask, knowing you to be a Godly man who does not give over to the vile work of the devil."

John shook his head. "You do as you will please, but I will not be turning back. I have bitterness in my belly that will not be soothed, David. My wife, herself a loving, patient woman, cannot tolerate me these days. I cannot tolerate myself, but I know what needs doing. I am resolved to get answers from Kingman today."

David felt his insides turn over. "So you said when we started from your place; all the same, I feel compelled to dissuade you."

Nodding his understanding, John leaned over the side of his horse and spit again. "I hear you, friend. I know your sentiments. You are a man to be concerned, and were I in your stead, I would be at you the same."

"There is no evidence, John. You can not go at a man without evidence!"

"I feel that there is, but, as I have said, I will not grow angry with you, or frown upon you for your prodding. My grievances against Kingman began long before you and Peg found poor Peter."

"Yes, I understand, John."

"You do not understand. I tire of my sister's complaints over the man's demands, I tell you! I am done with being treated the half-breed neighbor instead of rightful owner every time I approach Rachel's property! Ah, yes, I must remember it is Kingman property now...!" John growled through clenched teeth.

Unaccustomed to such a blow of words, David hurled back, "Do not think me insensitive to my wife's needs or hurts, John. I see your meaning, although I would have you see mine. It does not make any sense to continue the battle until we know our enemy."

"There are some things that cannot be left to burn in the bottom of the kettle," John grumbled.

"Yes, yes, I know we have spoken on numerous occasions of this rift you and my wife have had with Tom Kingman. It is true that Kingman as well as his wife strike me the same as you. They do act the part of insulted majesties, but that and shallow suspicions are not enough to ride up onto their property throwing insults at them like they were common folk."

"Aye," John replied flatly, kicking his horse.

David called after him, "Loathing this man provides all of us nothing but hurt. What will he say to you today that he has not already said?" John made no response as they advanced toward the Kingman house.

For the next half mile David kept silent, thinking that, as for himself, what he needed least of all in the world today was a confrontation with Tom Kingman, or for that matter, anything more of family animosities. John and he had trouble enough with trying to partner up their new Negroes with the old. The English speaking Negro had taken to looking down at Henry, which had provoked Henry. The next problem to solve would be Henry's rebuke of the stubborn new slave.

Although the new field hands were peaceable enough, they could not speak Dutch. James, though he tried, could not communicate work instructions beyond a basic command. David felt that their new Negroes understood James well enough, but the new slaves, having discovered that they were safe from the lash, were of a mind to have James endure their pigheadedness.

Even the slaves who had long been a part of the Vandenberg family were giving them trouble. Moses, complaining of pain, had been allowed more molasses rum and was often drunk on spirits and forgetting the simple chores that had been assigned to him. Martha, David felt, was not the same, pleasant woman whom he had first met, and this distressed him greatly as he struggled to find the reason for her change of disposition toward him. How had he insulted her?

All these domestic problems could probably be remedied, yet the rift between the Vandenberg's and the Kingman's was not so easy a problem to resolve. David knew that somehow he had to find a way to get at the truth of what was behind the attack on their properties that had led to the young slave boy's death. Had the boy seen and recognized the culprits that day following the violence, thereupon being murdered by them to keep his silence? David and John both thought this the most plausible notion, and David suspected that this was the root of what drove John onward, but there was something more to all of this hatred between John Vandenberg and Tom Kingman. What was the core of all of it? The situation between two families that aught be agreeable to one another had confused him since he first arrived.

Perhaps, David thought, if the door could be cracked open between his wife and her former sister-in-law, Rachel, some progress could be made. It was his understanding that at one time the two women had been close, and he could see that Rachel's slights dearly hurt Margaret.

After Peter's body had been found David had suggested that Margaret write a note to Rachel, and she had done so, requesting that they meet. But Mr. Kingman, obviously a man characterized by a blatant lack of sociability, must have intercepted her correspondence since there had been no reply. Clearly, Peggy insisted, it was Rachel's husband who saw fit to promote rather than heal the estrangement. It had to be he who had forbidden his wife to accept any of her invitations. This morning the sands of time had run through the glass. The worst was that if his heart be known, David had begun to think of Kingman much in the same way as his wife and her brother. What did this man have to hide? All the same, approaching a man in anger would not answer any questions.

David speculated that the problem might simply be that Kingman, a born Londoner, saw all of life through English eyes, and Margaret and John through the eyes of Dutch colonials. When Kingman made reference to them of his country, he meant mother England, but, of course, country to the Karski's and Vandenberg's was not, nor would ever be, England. Without a doubt Kingman viewed what was his by way of the King's version, which was that a born Englishman's rights were never to be questioned by a colonial. The problem of rights apparently had become more complicated over the last four years when Rachel gave birth to three boys. From what David heard from Margaret, he was convinced that Kingman's small sons by Rachel only added salt to the wounds as he proclaimed himself English lord with dominion over Teunis' lands.

Slowing Molly's pace, a more composed John turned toward him. "I am sorry that I spoke so sharp to you, David."

"You should not have to walk softly for anyone," David commented, feeling more sympathetic.

"Amen to that, but the worst of all these troubles has been the changes in Rachel's ways. Years ago, when she married Teunis, I welcomed a kind-hearted, bright-eyed girl by the name of Rachel Koch as a sister-in-law. When I returned, I found a distant woman who has become a stranger."

"Difficult times make changes in people. Have you not said to me that you are not the man who left your father's house?"

"Yes, this is true," John reflected.

"We have all changed; I too. I fear I would endure much jesting should my boyhood companions discover that I have spoken marital vows. It is unnatural that all things remain the same."

"Still, this Mrs. Kingman is not the beloved Rachel of yesteryear who graced my father's parlor."

A smile crept over David's lips. "Had your brother not died, most likely you still would not have recognized her after a separation of many years. None of us are the person of our youth, John."

"'Tis true, 'tis true, and I cannot fault Rachel's harsh treatment of me since those hard times when she lost her husband. I thought only of my own pleasures. Had I been at home when I should have, perhaps today I would not be wondering how to extract a truth from her repulsive husband."

"And what truth do you have in mind to extract? Do you believe that Tom Kingman is behind all and would be so cruel a man as to brutally murder the boy? Do you believe that your sister-in-law could marry such a man?"

John struggled for a reply. "I was not here when I should have been, David, and now I feel I have a debt that is owed to Teunis. Though Rachael might hate me for doing so, I must protect my brother's rights for the sake of his children."

"Perhaps you should not think so much about all of this. We have much put upon our own table."

"I would leave it if I could, David. I would wish unhappy times and sore duties away, but God has made plain to me that I must stand for what is right. He has blessed me with a good wife and precious daughter. For the sake of Teunis I can not remain silent."

"I pray that we both be wrong about this man in our suspicions," David replied.

John's voice softened. "Often when holding Clare I caution myself of being too hard-hearted. I would have my daughter grow to maidenhood knowing her father as a righteous man and not one who is anxious to condemn any man. Understand, I do not want her to see her father as a sorrowful man, as was my own, one whose heart is heavily weighted by bitterness. Nay, I would much rather my child knows me as a joyful, patient, true human being, yet as I kiss her soft cheek, a voice inside fights my good intentions. I can not help myself."

David remained thoughtful. What could he say? Contrary to John's conciliatory sentiments where Rachel was concerned, David felt John sought every excuse to damn her husband. At length he turned to John, who seemed barely able to remain on his horse. "I understand your feelings toward a brother. I would feel that same for one of my own: I would want to protect his widow and children, yet, John, no man, brother or not, has the right to step between a man and his wife. You know that it was Rachel's right to remarry, a sacred duty to her children. You know that this is a truth," he said forcefully.

John reddened and then glanced away while nudging Molly into a slow trot, "I know more about this man than you think."

David proceeded, hardly recognizing the tortured soul riding ahead of him. His heart ached for John. The fair-haired young man he had met back home at Peek Bend's springtime horse race had never been sullen. The John whom he had followed east was a quiet, amicable fellow who was ready for every challenge life offered. He appreciated the clear blue of the sky, as well as the blessing of a soaking rain. He had found love back in the west, and David knew him to love his Bess to near distraction. It frightened him to think that John's zealous, vengeful desires might rob him of all his blessings.

"What is it that you know? Tell me, I beg of you," David asked, pulling up beside John again.

John shrugged. "I watch what I say when I am in the taverns, but it is important you know that my suspicions are not completely unfounded with regard to Tom Kingman. What I speak about now could be considered evidence, and the evidence is the ear that was sliced from Moses' head."

"What of the ear?"

"I will explain. Tom Kingman is a London born Englishman who came to New York Colony by way of the Virginias, where I have learned that he was reputedly an owner of a small plantation a number of years ago. In Virginia, according to Mr. Randolph, who once lived in the Virginias, if an owner suspects his Negro has been involved in a conspiracy, he will cut off his ear. It is a common practice there to do so, but we Dutch along the North River do not treat our Negroes so coarsely.

"Now, think of Moses who will pass the rest of his life with only one ear, and who cannot work because of his lost limb. And then think of Mr. Kingman who is thoroughly English and who spent his time in Virginia before coming to Vandenberg land. I am not a fool who makes idle complaints. I watch. I listen."

As they approached the ridgeline, once again John stopped along the roadside. He was breathing heavily and spat again. He made no attempt to dismount, but sat upright on his horse, thoughtfully gazing over the river valley and the winding waterway below that stretched toward opposite steep cliffs. "I never tire of this view. It nourishes my soul. I have always found strength in the waters of our great river."

David said nothing of John's suspicions but joined him in surveying the impressive cliffs that were a part of the section of the mountains that settling Europeans had long ago referred to as the Blue Mountains. His eyes scaled the jagged rocks from top to bottom and then followed the shoreline two hundred feet or more down to the river's rough, racing waters. From when he had first come to this part of the country and looked upon the northern water highway, he had thought the North River grand.

Visualizing John as he must once have been, an eager woodland adventurer, it was easy to see him a part of the river below as a young man navigating his canoe alongside his stalwart father as the two maneuvered their way over the perilous lower end rapids. He could almost hear the elder man whooping and roaring like the maddened lion John had often described. Indeed, so often had John spoken of his and his brother and father's exploits that he felt as if he knew the geography of the place long before he arrived.

John remarked pensively, "The cliffs put me to thinking of Mr. Altemouse. How often my elder brother must have been knee bent, head bowed in prayer, asking for patience when I first sent him Altemouse. 'Twas a terrible game that I played with he and Peg."

Happy to see some interest other than Kingman return to their conversation, David asked, "I would hear of the sport."

"I took great pleasure in taunting Teunis."

"Your sister tells me that you often enjoyed taunting her as well?"

David was astonished as John smiled wanly, "I was a placid lamb when it came to what I put upon my sister compared to the jesting of my brother. Since a boy I was a terrible trickster to my brother; the worst of all the tricks played upon him, he would say, was when I sent him Altemouse."

"I can hardly imagine the solemn Altemouse, our bear, a party to jest."

"In those times he was a shadow of the man you see today, I can imagine my brother's expression when he awoke one morning and was faced by a thin, desperate man who would become his overseer in my stead."

"Altemouse... thin?"

"Like a stick insect. Teunis would not accept him in the beginning. It was the same, though, with Spotted Bird, but the Tuscaroran and Mr. Altemouse proved to be two of my better decisions."

"A blessing for you," David replied.

"I found Altemouse close to here."

"Here?"

"Yes, not far, he was camped with his family by those yonder cliffs; ragged and starving they all were in those times. It was not long after my father's death. The English navy had brought shiploads of German Palatines: men, women and children; Rhine men they were, over to cut down a forest of pines in the big woods beyond the cliffs of our North River."

"I have heard that he was one of them."

"Yes, Altemouse and his family were first in Holland, and then to London where he and hundreds of refugees lived in huts they had constructed along the Thames before they came over. They were first put ashore to live on an island just off the coast line of New York City before finally arriving here to the cliffs. They were promised bread and beer for sustenance. But the English reconsidered and decided they had no use for lumbermen when they discovered that most of the pines in these parts were unsuitable for making tar."

"What foolish person captained that venture?"

"One would be Livingston, who had sold thousands of acres of his manor to the navy for the purpose, but you will not hear your wife say as much."

David said. "Mr. Altemouse was a fortunate find."

"My brother did not think so at first."

"But your sister told me that Altemouse was hired by Teunis. Is this not so?" David asked curiously.

Seeming not to have heard David's question, John gazed toward the large boulders of rock that jutted forty feet over the river. "There were hundreds like Altemouse and his family living over there in those ancient Indian caves," he recalled. "I went to them to see why they were there, and they received me cordially, telling me their story of hope that was drowned in a sea of English incompetence. The immigrant Germans were to cut down the pine trees, but the English mistook a northern Colonial tree for an English tree, and the sap was not suitable for making tar. Truly, I pitied them all, knowing myself how it felt to be the likeness of a drowned man: one who breathes, yet is dead.

"A few days later, I put a few bits of my clothing into a sack and returned to the cliffs. I told Altemouse to wash and to put on the clothes I had in my sack and in the morning to go to Teunis. I promised him that he would have a position if he could convince my brother to keep him. I remember that he thanked me many times, saying I would never regret my kindness to him and his starving family."

Observing David for a moment, John said, "I can see from the expression on your face that you wonder where in my tale is the jest? I shall tell you. After I left the Rhine man at the cliffs, I went away on the journey that would last many years. How could this poor Rhine man know that I chose him to walk in my shoes? My brother was sharp witted, and I knew that he would see the same as I had seen in the eyes of Altemouse. God knew Mr. Altemouse was a better man than I in those days.

"Peg has told me that the German came knocking when the rooster crowed, and after my brother discovered that I had abandoned him he cursed me many times over."

David sighed, "I would have done the same."

John nodded knowingly and reached for his leather pouch, drinking down several swigs of rum. Wiping his mouth on his shirtsleeve he said, "If Teunis expected a soothing hand from our sister, and that she would go against me, he was sorely remiss. I am ashamed to say that I have often outfoxed my sister. I knew I would have her silent approval. Although I loved her, I could not stay.

"The night prior to leaving, I went to Peg's bedchamber and woke her. I sang her a song of my great need to be parted from the farm. It was a ballad that I had sung before, and at first she waved me away, but I pushed further and made justification for the course I wished to pursue. If you do not know it already, brother, your wife is a tireless champion for those oppressed, and my desperate cry touched her heart. She understood the yoke our father had laid upon our shoulders, and I believe she saw that Teunis meant to enforce the same restrictions upon us. I told her about the Palatine and his gaunt-eyed babes. She urged that I walk with Christ while I climbed the back of the turtle."

David nodded. He understood, although John continued explaining. "It is an Indian expression. The meaning is to see all the earth."

"No one can deny that my wife is a woman generous in thought and deed."

John said, "When Teunis cursed me, and cursed Altemouse, Peg told me that she replied to him that she would not be the one to withhold the ladle of sustenance!"

"Yes, I can hear her say as much," David chuckled.

"Teunis was not heartless and sorely needed the help. He soon found little fault with Altemouse," John said. "He was even happier with him after my sister taught him to cipher."

"I can see no obstacle that good men cannot overcome together."

"Good," John replied.

"I should hope that my own father and brothers do not hold it against me that I have left them. If I could write and they be able to read my words, I would like to send them news of me, but alas the best to hope for is that the French trapper, Lapett's cousin, will come upon them this year and give them all the news of my marriage. As you know, it is hard to leave obligations behind."

"It is harder still to return to obligations," John replied. "My regrets aside, you have many brothers back at your homeland that would take up the slack caused by your absence. I had left but one good man behind to bear the burden of the whole of my father's legacy, who was, of course, Altemouse."

"You have returned, and out of love, your sister has pardoned you. Now you must forgive yourself."

"If only I could."

David gently ventured, "I can see that your belly is full of remorseful hard thoughts, John. I think that you believe that had you been here when your brother died that your sister-in-law would not have remarried. But, as I have said before, it is only sensible that a woman in her position would marry as soon as possible after her husband's death. After all, Rachel is comely, and was left with dependent children. What would you expect?"

"From what I have heard tell of Rachel, the woman is a meek soul who cannot function without the direction of a Master in her house. I mean no slander toward Rachel, or insult toward you, but it does seem to me that you take much upon your shoulders in consideration of Rachel. You say you wish not to be judgmental, that it is your desire that your own child does not think you a brutish man, yet your own words give me cause to wonder if you believe yourself."

John heeled Molly into a trot, "It is impossible for you to understand," he called over his shoulder. "I am sure that you think me too suspicious, but I am not alone with my misgivings. There is something else of which you have no knowledge. Peg was the first acquainted with Tom Kingman."

Confusion registered across David's face. "I do not understand."

"Kingman pursued your wife before he reached for Rachel, but his interest faded when he received no encouragement. Peg never trusted Kingman's intentions, but I will speak of this by and by. Yet, it is true as you say that Rachel was lost after Teunis died.

"Rachel's kinfolk live to this day near Schenectady, which is where Teunis met her while traveling with our father. She was eighteen when Teunis wed her. Her father and mother had been killed during the massacre upon the village and Rachel and her infant sister left behind. An uncle raised Rachel and her younger sister with exceedingly protective hands. I suppose a tender manner should be expected from a man lamenting the violent loss of his kin.

"The uncle was not happy to let his eldest marry so young and then to have her husband take her to live at such a distance. I was told that Rachel would beg Teunis not to leave her alone in the house with her babes even though her servant, Dago, kept watch all the night through for her sake. She was much afraid of the dark. You are right about a widow's needs, and had Kingman been a different man I would have embraced him. But he is who he seems, and, Rachael being one who requires protection, she would accept the first proposal offered. Tom Kingman went to Teunis's widow when she was most vulnerable."

David stiffened. "Considering all of this, I know the aggravation Tom Kingman offers, but I just cannot understand how you came to such a severe opinion of this man. I suspect I know your suspicions, but John, you have no proof that Tom Kingman had a hand in the treachery last August. Yet you talk as if you would put a rope around his neck. It is not like you to judge a man without good evidence."

The rigid lines around John's mouth softened. "You are an honorable man, David, and I am glad of heart to call you friend as well as kin, but this with Kingman is my business."

"I see turmoil that need not be, that is all," David replied, heaving a heavy sigh.

John coughed hard, this time spitting up a little bit of blood along with the phlegm.

"Friend, perhaps we should turn back. You are not well."

"Nay, I am well enough—and I find talking with you a comfort. Do not be so concerned, David; I will survive this. I will go to see Jacob Staats in Albany on the morrow or the next after, though I hate to go."

"You will please me to do so."

John looked over his shoulder at his brother-in-law. "I have kept much of my feelings apart, but it is good now to speak. While I lay a drunken youth, Teunis sowed the fields. Teunis was the man that I had never been. I have a great sorrow for these fences built by Tom Kingman, which not only severed Vandenberg land, but hearts."

The two continued on, and as they rode by Spotted Bird's cabin, David waved a greeting to Shasa and Betty who sat weaving baskets beside their home. John's arm, too, rose in greeting. "Greetings, Nentpikes," John called over. "Greetings to you also girl."

Shasa is usually a better Nentpikes than Staat's is a physician, but this time her cure has been of no avail. "

"Nentpikes?"

"Ah, yes, I forget sometimes that you have only been here a short time. Shasa is an honored herbalist."

"I agree she is a valuable servant. Look how she has healed Moses. If it were not for her good remedies the man would have perished. If only she could do the same for you, but I agree—you should go to Albany," David stated bluntly.

"Remember someday that I have said this to you, David: when the times are hard—and believe me, more troubles will come to us—recall that I said that the heart and not the eyes are the better tool for considering a man's actions."

David frowned. "That is why I worry. You go to this man's house today to make strong accusations because of what you feel and not what you know to be true. You have malice in your heart for Kingman because you say he lived in the Virginias and learned the wicked ways of those English men."

John responded indignantly. "I harbor no such grievances against a man solely because he be of English blood. I call many English 'friend' and they call me 'brother'!"

Frustrated, David argued, "You say naught against the Palatines. You knew nothing of Altemouse, yet you trusted him. Yet the Englishman is judged before he is tried. Why can you not endeavor to calm yourself and attempt a peaceful questioning?"

John jerked his horse to the side of the path for a second time. "Except with respect to one, there is no man I do not tolerate. From our discourse I take it you think me hard and partial to kicking a man who by birth is English, but 'tis not so. The Englishman with whom I take issue is the one who sails over only to prey upon the frailty of a woman who is suffering within her darkest hours."

David considered thoughtfully before he spoke. It had come to him earlier that although his Peggy, her brother, and Kingman all spoke the Dutch language, John thought only in the Dutch, whilst Kingman could understand but the English way, and Peggy's thoughts, David surmised, blossomed first in Lenape. "You must take care, John. All that you have said might be evidence, or all could be only coincidence that would harm not only Mr. Kingman but Rachel and her children."

John pulled his horse beside David's. "Before you speak so defensively for Tom Kingman let me tell you something that may change your course. I have heard that long ago, Kingman passed much of his time at Fox Hill Tavern, where he once wagered that he would have Margaret married and to bed. You know Bob Perry, who operates the ferry down yonder?"

"Yes, we are acquainted," David answered curiously.

"The ferryman heard this vulgar wager made by Kingman with his own ears, but I need not have taken only Bob's word of what was said. Seth Thomas, who I have called friend as well as neighbor ever since I was a child, was also present to hear the boast. None of Kingman's brag came to pass because when he presented himself to my sister, she rebuffed him. Kingman did not take well to my sister's refusal. Bob said he was back in the tavern two weeks later cursing her for her high and mighty ways. After failing to attract my sister, he obviously set his sights upon a less agile prey."

David smiled. He could not imagine his Peggy the prey of any man. "If the story you heard be true, I should then compliment my wife's prudence and praise God for Tom Kingman's vulgarity."

John sighed. "I see that you do not take me seriously."

"Nay, but I do," David insisted, thinking to himself that John was right about a few things. He did have much to learn. He knew little of the life demanded of one who would be master to such an estate as was Vandenberg manor. He had come from the western part of the country where few, if any, Negroes trespassed, and those that did were rarely held in bondage. He knew little of the English language let alone Anglo lords or fancy Virginia men, but he would learn. David was certain of one thing if nothing else and that was that he would learn.

Chapter 25

As John and David passed Kingman's barn, several of the slave children played happily in the dirt by the side of a corral containing eight milk cows. David recalled how on the day of his departure Lapett had insisted that sad circumstances would dim in the by and by, but as Kingman's large brick house came into view, it seemed to David that there would be no end to painful confrontations in the near future.

Passing the hay barrack, they tied their horses to the post near the well. Immediately Tom Kingman came out the front door, rushing down the steps of the porch stoop. Stepping toward them, after a few feet, Kingman stopped. He dispensed with any form of polite greeting. "You come here uninvited, John Vandenberg, and you as well, Mr. Karski!" He bellowed. "Why do you persecute me this way? I have told you that I am not responsible for the unfortunate death of your Negro, nor do I know who is responsible for the boy's death. I do not know who inflicted injuries to your man servant. If I knew, I swear by the Almighty God that I would bring the criminal to you myself!"

Approaching Kingman with his hands outstretched, well away from his saber, John declared, "We come peaceable. A good talk is all I ask of you."

"Peaceable? I see you come armed with saber and musket."

"We mean you no harm," David said.

Tom Kingman threw his arms into the air in frustration. "We have talked before! You know that I was at Margaret's side as soon as I saw the smoke that terrible day, yet you still come at me this way! And do not say that you come here peaceable for you have made it known to everyone around that you think me a murderer!"

David watched Nettie, Kingman's Negro cook, run from the house toward her small children. Most likely she had seen them ride in and must have known that the serenity of her afternoon was about to be broken. But the cook might not have seen a thing, David suddenly decided, for the ruckus that Kingman had made, first inside the house and now outside, would have awoken the sleeping devil himself. For that matter, it could raise the dead buried in Trinity Church yard in lower Manhattan. The cook made quick, beckoning motions to the little girls huddled in fear against the side of the barn. Soon the terrified mother had secured her children safely in the house, away from the volcanic commotion outside.

John glared at the handsomely featured, dark-haired man. Tom Kingman, at over six feet in height, was an exceptionally big Englishman who towered over many of his neighbors. "You may not have been the one who wielded the sword, but I know that it was you, Kingman, who had some part in the wrongdoing that day."

David quickly forced himself between the angry men. This was a fight that he had tried to defuse for as long as he could, but he doubted that simmering embers would be extinguished today. "Come now; hold your tongues, both of you!"

"You have no right to interfere, Ox," John protested.

"You told the man we come peaceable. Now keep your word."

John stepped back and David turned to Tom Kingman. "We came today that we might civilly question you, Sir. We did not come to join in accusations or to be a witness to bloodshed."

John called out, "I ask you, Tom, will you speak the truth? Will you give your oath and make your mark before the Sheriff that you had nothing to do with the troubles that were thrust upon us?"

Tom Kingman glared. "John Vandenberg, you speak of truth, but as anyone can see, you know not the meaning of the word. You do not see me, Vandenberg. You only see a man who lives in your brother's stead. How can a man blinded by hatred see anything of the truth? You refuse to acknowledge me to be the respected, honest man who I am, despite that I came to you with my wife, sons, and slaves in your time of trouble. I risked my life and the lives of many of my own people to save Margaret from harm's way."

John snickered, "David, why not ask him to say how he really feels about your wife?"

Kingman turned toward David. "Ah, I see now the road my accuser would travel. I am not afraid to say the truth. When your good wife was still unmarried, I came to this place myself, a gentleman in good standing who was without a wife, and I did call upon Mistress Margaret at Vandenberg manor. She received me kindly, but that was the whole of it. There was no further discourse between us. Soon after, Margaret made it understood that she, in those times, had no interest in a husband, so I made Rachel's acquaintance, herself a widow of nearly two years. Widow Vandenberg found me pleasing, and was kind enough to become my wife."

John began laughing sarcastically, but soon his laughter gave way to a fit of coughing which required a good half minute to calm. "Did you not once refer to my sister as the vine that withered?"

"John Vandenberg," Kingman said disgustedly, "Surely you have lost all sense of propriety."

"You were heard to have used those words in reference to my sister one night after many tankards of ale. Many recalled your vicious slanders, but perhaps you were too drunk to remember."

The Englishman was quick to retort. "Back in those times you were not about, and I would say it was you who was senseless. Do not play the high and mighty kinsman who would avenge his wronged sister, for everyone in this land knows the careless man you have been."

John fell back as if he had been struck.

"Hold, both of you!" David shouted.

"This Englishman," John replied, cocking his head, "played his games with a fair lady in the Carolinas before he came to New York. I have heard such. That widow's brother soon showed him the door, and he then found another in Virginia, which yielded him a small farm when the woman he had taken to wife and her boy were found dead in the woods—by the hand of the savages he told the authorities. Soon after, we find Mr. Kingman in our country. We all know a hound comes to scent, and he…" John pointed to Kingman, "sniffed at the hem of my sister's frock, but she would not have him, and so he found Rachel."

Kingman faced David squarely. "My intentions were never dishonorable, and I will not explain my personal tragedy or my business before I came here, or my business now, to any man. I assure you that I never held any disrespect toward your wife, or any other lady, Mr. Karski."

John plodded on, "My sister may have received you kindly when you came to her door a first and second time, but she was swift in her judgment knowing a fox when it is in the coop; despite your testimony to the contrary, Margaret did rebuke you."

Tom Kingman's face went scarlet red. "Have care in the vile words you say to me, John!" he shouted furiously. "I have answered your damn questions! Now, leave my land or force me to commit a crime for which I have not the heart!"

Once again David stepped between them, but in the middle of the conflict he caught a glimpse of a tearful, much distressed Rachel, who was encircled on the top of the porch by her servant women and several children.

Kingman followed David's stare and turned, readily observing his wife's anguish. Her eyes pleaded with her husband for tolerance. He turned back toward the men. "Go home," he said to John, his voice breaking as he desperately tried to control his anger. Finally he half whispered, "I beg of you both, go home before we say more." Kingman then turned his back and walked toward his family.

Taking hold of John's arm, David pleaded "Come, it is best to leave and resolve all of this at a later time. Have respect for your dead brother and his distraught family. Look at them. Would you have them all hate you? It is plain that they suffer greatly from the hard feelings you carry in your heart. Consider how your angry words are affecting not only them, but your sister at home who almost nightly cries herself to sleep in my arms these last weeks."

John stared up at Rachel. The encounter had exhausted him. He no longer felt so righteous. "I did not wish for my words to come forth ugly; I wish only to find the truth. I do not wish to hurt Rachel or her children."

"Then for the sake of honor, come away," David urged as he turned and then untied and mounted his horse. When he glanced back toward the Kingman house all had disappeared behind the closed door.

John followed suit, and the two of them headed back home. During the first few miles of the ride David kept to himself, not wanting to be swallowed up by the desperation of the moment. He knew he must find a way of helping John excuse his grievances. He needed to find a way that they could get back to the business of building the forge.

Suddenly David remembered that Phillip Lansing had promised to return to Vandenberg manor before returning westward to his mission among the Susquehanna and Shawnee Indians. If anyone could bring joy to a household it was the multi-talented Moravian musician. Both he and John had been glad of his company along the trails in the past, and had it not been for Phillip, he might not have been persuaded to come east in the first place. Perhaps he and Peggy would be able to persuade him to stay a few weeks before the cold weather set in.

"John," David said at length. "Margaret tells me that Phillip will be arriving within a fortnight."

"In a fortnight?"

"Yes, and I will be most happy to see him."

"I pray God I am well when he arrives."

"The Physician will have a cure, but you are in grave need of rest, my friend."

"How can I rest, David?"

"You must. You are no good a dead man."

They rode on a little awhile, and then David said, "John, you will not like me saying so, but I do not believe that Kingman had any part in any of that which has befallen us."

John shrugged.

"What is important is that you be well, John. You must take care of yourself for the sake of your wife and child."

John was deep in thought. He tried to contain himself, knowing any further argument would be useless with David, but it was apparent to him that his brother-in-law would never understand anything until he could prove without a doubt that Tom Kingman was a murderer and should be forced from Vandenberg land by the authorities. He was convinced that it would be better for all if justice was served.

"I will make no further arguments. Although we will disagree on Kingman, you speak true of Bess and the babe. I will keep myself from harm's way for their sake."

"Then we will leave it for now," David replied.

John didn't answer. He needed his partner's expertise if the foundry was ever to become productive and not remain merely a distant vision. David, although young, had more than ten years of experience as Iron-Master with the forge that he had begun with his grandfather. His knowledge of charring would be invaluable, and business aside, he was fond of him.

All the same, John wondered if David would ever make a proper fit. An honest man who obviously believed that any man's sins should not only be forgiven, but forgotten, John could see how little Ox knew of the world beyond the boundaries of his father's house at Rupert's Landing. David knew well the Susquehanna Indians, but had little knowledge of ambitious men. Why, until little more than a year ago, his brother-in-law had never seen a settlement populated by more than fifty. David, his father, uncles, nine brothers, as well as numerous cousins, worked their farms and hunted in the thick woods. They bred horses, mules, and sheep. They lucratively traded beaver pelts, but a good part of the acquired Karski wealth came from their successful ironworks. From the start, John could work and jest beside him, but he wondered could such a simple man from the rugged wilderness, who was unaccustomed to eastern civilization, ever be the Master of Vandenberg Manor?

Chapter 26

For the annual November plantation owners' race, Margaret had dressed herself and her four-year-old Friesian, *Sassy Sam*, more opulently than any lofty Provincial, or for that matter, she believed, any of Europe's most high and mighty royalty. Exhilarated by thoughts of introducing one of Holland's favorite breeds to the New York North River Valley region, she proudly led her beautiful best trotter down River Road and through the anxious crowd that had begun to gather at sunup from as far away as Maryland and the Jerseys. Anticipation for today's race had been building all week, and this morning the butterflies that had been flying around in her stomach had begun to feel more like bats. Every nerve in her body tingled as she admired the black horse at her side, and Margaret had no doubt that *Sassy Sam* would bring home the Vandenberg team, producing the grandest triumph ever seen in the New York colony. Soon her *Sassy* would be considered the finest horse in all the colonies.

Only sixteen hands high and not as large as other horses of the breed, *Sassy* might not pose much of a threat to the competition at first glance, but Margaret knew better very early on. When he was just a wobbling spring colt, *Sassy Sam* began to shine in that special way horse breeders dream of, and she was moved to place him into the trusted expert hands of her Negro stable overseer, Titus. She had always been sure that *Sassy* would come to greatness under Titus's care, who years before had trained her father's magnificent *Swift Powder*, who had brought in numerous victories before the Livingston's horse bested him.

Anyone who had ever watched Titus guide *Sassy Sam* around the Vandenberg fields could see that he paced far more naturally than any Livingston horse, and Margaret took old Titus' words straight to heart when her servant had assured her that *Sassy* was far more powerful than any horse he had ever worked with...including *Swift Powder*. How glad she was, she had confessed to David, that she had stayed the course by navigating with her instincts, explaining how months earlier, in anticipation of racing season, she had decided that nuptials or no, her horse would race this season. But then the unthinkable had come, and she had not had the heart for the September or the October challenges. Still, those that *Sassy* had run, he had won, validating Titus' praises. He was the long awaited champion.

Nodding politely to Ann Rye and her daughter, Ava, as she paused with *Sassy* in the parade lineup, a smile crept onto Margaret's lips when she overheard her neighbor's escort remark, "That horse is superlative and the one to watch."

Quelling the urge, Margaret thought better of turning to the man in response, but how she wanted to shout over her shoulder like a bawdy tart, "Aye, he is the best!"

Sassy had been meticulously garnished with an impressive string of wampum generously entwined with eagle feathers as well as gray and white ostrich plumes plucked by Martha that very morning. The ornateness of *Sassy's* adornments had heads craning. Margaret took her turn parading her newcomer horse twice around the field before guiding him toward a chariot-like cart. There, the stable boy, Ishmael, hired specially this past springtime from the Schermerhoorn's at Kinderhook, awaited the command to *"hitch 'em up"*.

The river road had taken on the usual, noisy, pre-race carnival atmosphere. Already the Albany brew master and his sons were hastening to set up his barrels under a colorful red and blue tent across from the baker. As the aroma of roasting foul, ham, pea soup, and freshly baked seed cakes filled her nostrils, Margaret searched eagerly past jugglers and fiddlers for David who had promised to join her as quickly as possible after stopping off at the mill.

Wondering if he had encountered a problem, Margaret tugged at *Sassy's* rope and had almost arrived where Titus and the boy stood waiting when Tom Kingman's dark stableman appeared. Hatter—named for the belief that he owned more hats than any man in the Colony, black or white—ran ahead of her bowing low, making a grandiose gesture of sweeping the dirt in front of her footsteps with his fur cap's red foxtail.

Sassy Sam was unaffected by the commotion Hatter caused and kept perfect stride which caused Margaret to beam with pride. She made a feeble attempt to wave Hatter away, wondering if from some obscure place his master was watching his slave make his flagrant and very audacious display, which was recognized along the flat track as one of respect reserved only for the owner of exceptionally fine horseflesh. "I thank you most kindly for the compliment," Margaret said, and she curtsied deeply before the Negro danced away. Rising, Margaret felt the stares of two finely dressed young women whom she did not recognize who were standing a short distance away. Apparently the two had watched the amusing scene and had remained transfixed observing her colorful attire. The expression of envy displayed across their young faces made Margaret feel quite proud of both she and her horse despite the chastising glances of the Dominie standing within their circle. Margaret thought, what did it matter what the crusty Dominie, or for that matter, anyone else, thought of her attire? Buckskin boots, trousers, linsey-woolsey shirt, gold threaded stomacher, green velvet waistcoat, and her grand hat—she fancied she was dressed as colorfully as one of her peacocks. Like her wedding day, it was a happy occasion that she had accented by smothering her neck and arms with rose water that morning while dressing. Her husband had approved.

Undoubtedly her trousers had raised an eyebrow or two, but what she suspected most drew the coveted glances of the young ladies was the brazen, wide-brimmed, marigold dyed bonnet that Marie had sewn for this special day; a hat every bit as flamboyant as any that Mrs. Lapett could have designed from the finest fabrics, and a hat that surely had prompted the attention of Kingman's man.

Marie had insisted upon a wide pink ribbon to be tied under the chin, and both she and Bess had assured her that neither the ribbon nor the feathers bound by a large, gold buckle were overdone and were quite appropriate for this special anniversary of this race. Margaret promised herself that tonight she would reward Marie with a bottle of rose water.

She smiled at the Livingston girls as she passed their party. The older girl was breathtakingly beautiful in an indigo blue brocaded dress, the cuffs of her sleeves obviously the finest of Holland's lace. The fair-haired, stalwart English Redcoat whose arm she clung to returned pleasantries. She thought his striking presence equal to the young woman's. In the same instant Margaret wondered if any owner of any substance was left at home. The well-publicized race had, it seemed, brought out everyone in the late autumn sun.

Patroon Livingston claimed on his race notices posted in every tavern within a fifty-mile radius that this year would be the twenty-fifth year the horses had run the flat track at River Road. Almost immediately a flurry of debates had erupted. The designated number, twenty-five, had given cause for brisk discussion among many locals up and down the North River, and Margaret's family was no exception.

* * * *

Waving to Bess who she spotted making her way through the crowd, Margaret recalled the table conversation of the previous evening. Horse flesh and the breeding thereof was once again on everyone's lips. John had suggested quite openly that, had it not been for a horse, Margaret would have remained unmarried. The first time he saw his would be brother-in-law, he said, was mounted upon the back of a grand black beast. He had been so drawn to the magnificence of the horse, who John extolled brought to mind William Penn's beloved *Tamerlane*, that he was induced to strike up a conversation with David.

As John was telling the story the previous night of his and David's first encounter, the mention of *Tamerlane* had prompted a half an hour of reminiscing over youthful days spent at the manor in the land of Penn's Holy Experiment riding some of the finest animals stabled within any of the colonies.

Eventually the conversation that evening had returned to New York, the race, and the days of old in the North Valley when their father had so loved to see his horses compete against neighbors' horses. Margaret thought it only natural that the impending race would bring back old times. How could they speak of this race and not recall so many others? In the course of this discussion she disputed Mr. Livingston's calculations because she clearly remembered far more than twenty-five annual races. John suggested that the first horse race was run during the old Dutch administration of "Peg Leg Pete" Stuyvesant.

Their father had told the story of a windy October day long, long ago when hundreds of festival-minded Dutch settlers mixed with equally enthusiastic local natives to watch and cheer two Spanish-bred horses gallop a fast quarter of an English mile. The horses ran along the rutted, newly widened dirt path, a road that accommodated six horses across, the same road that connected New Amsterdam to the outpost village of New Haarlem. Their father was then a young soldier employed by the Dutch West India Company, and he, like many other soldiers, had witnessed the race. He told them of a terrible dispute that had erupted following the race between two soldiers who had wagered heavily, and of how Sheriff Resolved Waldron, then a strong arm to Peter Stuyvesant, had been summoned to suppress violent tempers. Both wagerers had lost more than just their horse money that day as the two men were bound and carried off to a New Amsterdam jail by Resolved and thereafter fined stiffly for benefit of the poor before their release three days later. Remembering such a time, the talk had expanded to other members of Resolved Waldron's family: his grandson, Captain William Waldron; his cousin, Peter; and Widow Vermilye, the former Aeltje Waldron.

All grew somber when John spoke of the heavy heart that old Resolved must have taken to his grave; he dying whilst his son-in-law, Vermilye, was still imprisoned on false charges of high treason. Unfortunately, Waldron had not lived to see Vermilye's good name cleared, or his son-in-law's confiscated properties restored to his daughter, Vermilye's widow, Aeltje. Vermilye's tragedy, John observed, had made a sorrowful end for the old constable. It was a shame, especially so because Resolved Waldron had sorrowed many times over during his years in America because of his ill-fated family.

He had lost his first wife, Rebecca, before coming over. Years later Waldron had lived to suffer the loss of his brothers living in Holland and the new world.

Whilst the English ships lay in the harbor, poised to take over New Amsterdam in 1664, the sheriff's younger brother, Joseph, had run away with Resolved's Negro slave woman. As Captain Will had told it, his grandfather never saw his younger brother or his slave again.

Years before, another elder brother, also called Joseph, had been captured along with his family by Indians. For years the family thought them all dead at Kent Island. Eventually though, Resolved's elder brother and family did return. He ultimately died in a powder blast at the old fort.

At that point Margaret and John's conversation had turned to their cousin, Catharina Waldron, and her husband, Peter. John related the lore surrounding Waldron's elderly slave woman called Sarah. Resolved's wife Tennake, being very attached to her Negro woman, Sarah, the one who had gone away with her brother-in-law, Joseph, found herself another young girl who she called Sarah in remembrance of the first. When Resolved Waldron's widow, Tennake, died at Harlem, she left her beloved Sarah to Peter Waldron and his wife, Catharina.

During the relating of this part of the Waldron family saga both David and Bess, newcomers to the old family stories, had sat silent, seemingly spellbound by the tale.

Later, as the discourse had returned to the glory of the old Dutch days and the New Amsterdam race, John had remarked that he often wondered if their father's zest for breeding the best of stallions was birthed that long ago October day.

As they sat around the table, Bess rocking Clare to sleep in her arms and John remembering fondly days of old, Margaret thought how good it was to see her brother, for the moment, at peace. Prayers had been answered: Physician Staats' remedy had seemingly produced a cure for her brother.

Continuing their remembrance of the old New York families who had embarked upon colonial journeys more than a half century before, ultimately each story joined the current excitement at hand: the annual race. After placing the sleeping Clare into her cradle Bess suggested that the number of the year attached to this should not hold such importance. God forbid they be the census takers of the races. It was only a number and what difference did it make what was the tally? Her husband had laughed and patted her shoulder.

Margaret had recalled the first race she had attended with her father, mother, and brothers at the place called Brier Lane, a long level road that connects Kinderhook village with Moose Lake. She was not yet eight years old. The crowd was not nearly so large as those who would be gathered for this one, but numbers of spectators were all that was lacking. Certainly there was no lack of enthusiasm for the sport, and the beasts that took part in that battle for the prize of two beaver-skinned hats were magnificent.

Stubborn Pete, a long legged stallion that was named honorably for old Peg Leg himself, had been raised by her father with tender care. As it turned out, he had torn up the dirt track in record time. Margaret and her mother wore wreaths of dried wild flowers in their hair, and she remembered how her laughing father had exuberantly lifted her tiny mother into the air, twirling her around and around so that when he finally put her down she nearly lost her balance. She could still see barrel-bellied Hans Miller, the appointed race official, offering congratulations. He slapped her father on the back good-naturedly and handed him the two fine fur hats which were, many years later, presented to Teunis's boys.

But it was the finale to that long ago day that made the greatest impression upon Margaret's memory. Her father had done something very unusual that day. Garret had never been prone to outbursts of emotion, but with tears in his eyes, he had placed one of the fur hats on her head, adjusted it properly, and swung her up onto the champion's back. She felt like a princess, she would often say, as they paraded their victorious *Stubborn Pete.* It was a happy time that she cherished.

It was that same girlish pride that she felt now as her horse *Sassy Sam* awaited his own glory.

Chapter 27

Making her way through the thickening crowd, Margaret's eyes once again found the impish Hatter before he disappeared behind the elaborately decorated horse carts lining up along the far side of the dusty road. Though she had heard that Tom Kingman's horse would be a contender, surprisingly, there had been no sign of him or Rachel.

Across the field she was relieved to finally see John by the baker's tent. They did not agree on all things, and he could provoke her to complete distraction, yet she loved him, and again thanked God for returning him home.

It had, however, become apparent that although many things had changed since their youth, many had not. She was not going to win every debate with John, despite the logical presentation she felt that she made to him on many occasions. She had come to realize that she would not bring him around to her point of view on slavery, the need to reach a truce with Tom Kingman, or even such trivial matters as the anniversary number of this race. On this latter matter her young sister-in-law was right: dates were unimportant. Festivals, after all, were to be celebrated, not argued, and as Bess had suggested, numbers were best left within the confines of the ledger book. Arguing was a sin, while a woman's silence surely put her in the company of angels.

Margaret doubted her worthiness to be embraced by God' angels, but had been able to let go of the argument on the dating of the race only because she was confident of the answer. She knew that the number of the anniversary could only be considered official if this race was calculated from the ruling of the English Queen who had become much obsessed with the sport. In 1702, England's Queen Anne gave her Royal Blessing to horseracing along these flatlands of New York. From that time, summer and autumn races had become a high point of entertainment not only on Manhattan Island, but also in a dozen small towns dotting the North River all the way to Albany. By this accounting, the number was twenty-five. However, if one counted the number of races from Dutch times the number would be much higher.

Hearing an unabashed swell of cheers, Margaret turned to see Patroon Livingston, his lavishly powdered wig topped by a broad brimmed, plumed, scarlet velvet hat. The enthusiastic Livingston was being carried onto the track in a painted blue chariot pulled by four, very large, fawn-colored, Flemish horses that she had never seen before. With his Negro driver standing beside him maneuvering the fragile, but superbly painted coach past dozens of excited bystanders, Patroon Livingston gallantly waved his white silk handkerchief. Margaret had to admit that the Livingston horses were majestic animals. As the Livingston cart passed, she bowed to one of the Colony's wealthiest landowners and most powerful men, once again awkwardly attempting the best curtsy that she could manage in her buckskin trousers

Finally having arrived with *Sassy Sam* at the designated area, Titus and Ishmael began to hitch up the horse to the vibrant red rig upon which was painted in gold a remarkably detailed "V". Horses together with their drivers, coaches and accompanying owners began moving from the lineup area along the road to assemble in the race positions that had been determined that morning by drawing of lots. It would be less than a half hour until the starting time.

Returning to her servants and horses near the assembly point, Margaret patted *Sassy*, whispering words of loving encouragement.

"Fear not, he is destined for victory," David said, coming up behind her. He slipped his arms around her waist. "You feel good to me, woman," he whispered huskily. Margaret reddened. Glancing in the direction of her servants, she turned and whispered back, "Watch your company, husband." David laughed, releasing her.

"I will tell you what I feel," Margaret said playfully.

"I await your reply, Lady."

"Ah, my reply is that I feel silversmith TenEyck's magnificent, silver, brandy-wine bowl in my hands."

"Look there," David announced, pointing to a group of giggling young girls.

Margaret's heart skipped a beat as she saw her niece, Alice, Rachel and Teunis' youngest daughter, centering the cluster.

"You should go to her," David encouraged.

"Yes, I would like it much if I could, but when I sought her audience at the Schuyler festival last summer, she avoided me. I have not recovered from my hurt, and we have not exchanged the simplest discourse for more than two years. She must be..." her voice trailed off as if taken captive by her thoughts.

"What are you trying to say?" David queried gently.

Distractedly, Margaret answered, "How I miss Alice. She was always my favorite of their children. My deceased brother would say that her smile lit the darkest room, and so it did, from the first time I cradled her in my arms."

"You have told me as much, Peggy. Why do you not go to her? She is only a child. Perhaps she waits for your approach."

"Nay, not today, but it does warm my heart to see her merry, as radiant as a summer's sun in her yellow dress. I would imagine suitors upon the Kingman steps."

David again moved close. "Do not worry over Alice," he consoled sympathetically. "She will come around, as has her elder sister, Christina, but today, why cry over amends not made, my love? It serves no purpose."

Margaret forced herself to smile. "And the day is too grand to spoil with laments."

"Here, I will have the brush," David called to Titus. "I will have a hand at some of this myself." Titus handed the brush over, bowing.

While brushing *Sam*, David looked over his shoulder, "By the by, though you should not covet, my compliments to you, Peggy, for pulling the grand prize from the Albany silversmith."

Margaret smiled. "When I asked him to consider a small donation of his craft, he told me that he would be proud to do so, but, of course, I was astonished to see the splendid bowl he brought forth. Everyone is talking of it."

"It is the finest prize I have ever seen for any contest. On the frontier, even a barrel of beer is a grand prize that is rarely seen. I only wish that my brothers could be here to enjoy this festival and to see such an outstanding offering."

"A barrel of beer is a fine enough prize in any part of the country."

"A truth, a truth, well said, wife. But a silver bowl is even finer! And much more likely to set a fire underneath every driver!"

"I believe there may be a reason for the tradesman's generosity," Margaret suggested pensively. "Years ago my father financed a small shop for the man. The arrangement was that the debt be paid over the course of three years. Two years later my father passed into the hands of the Almighty, and I was moved to forgive the remainder of the debt."

"You laid aside his debt?"

"Yes, but I felt none other than obliged. On the document that I penned for TenEyck as legal satisfaction, I wrote a few words of my gratitude, for when my father was grievously ill, many times his wife came to comfort me. The last year was dreadful for me. I was quite alone as few came to call. Mrs. TenEyck was a compassionate friend who gave me respite when I was so tired I could barely stand. I shall never forget her kindness to me. Forgiving her husband of his debt was of small consequence."

"And it pleases you to believe that an honorable man repays his debt in one way or another."

"It does."

"Of course, it is possible, Peggy, that the silversmith also sees the wisdom of such a momentous gesture. All will see his outstanding work and will be encouraged to trade with the generous benefactor."

Margaret laughed. "I can do none other than agree with your sentiments there, though I would prefer to think that the friend to all is not so devious."

David surveyed the grounds. "Have you seen Tom Kingman?"

Following her husband's lead, Margaret scanned the area. "No, I have not, but Alice is there, and his man, Hatter, is yonder. Tom Kingman must be close."

"I have seen John and Bess. We spoke but briefly earlier as he was in discourse with Henry Beekman," David said. "Bess told me that the infant is home in the care of Sally."

"Wrapped tenderly within Sally's arms to be sure, and Bess need not fret over the babe as Eva will be close at hand with her." Stepping in front of David, Margaret eyed him levelly. Abruptly she blurted out, "Now is as good a time as any that I would speak with you on another matter. I can speak my heart none other than bluntly. I have a mind to drive today."

David stiffened and handed the brush back to Titus. Putting his hands on his wife's shoulders, his return was stern. "Not you. I put my foot down on this, Peggy. We agreed that you would have John take the reins. You are accustomed to do as you please, and most often I say nothing, but I am unyielding today."

Margaret's dark eyes flashed. "I did not agree, husband. John said that he would ride and you agreed. I recall no such conversation between us. I do not believe that it is good that John drive since he is still recovering from his illness and even now gets the tremors upon occasion!"

"I took your silence to mean that you did agree, and it is just as well. I have seen you this past week looking poorly, and I will not have you sick to bed suffering though the sickness as John has done. Besides which, you know, Peggy, it is not right for any owner to drive, and a married woman driving her own cart is just not proper."

Agitated, Margaret snapped, "I feel well enough today; married or nay, I am ready. See—I wear the proper breeches. You worry needlessly, David. I have ridden my horses in races before I knew you, and I am well accustomed to riding *Sassy*; far more so than John. I can handle the cart too, as well you know. "

David folded his arms. "Yes, you ride as well as any man, and I see the buckskins, woman, but I had it in my head that your costume was but a fancy."

"I am going to drive the Vandenberg rig." Margaret insisted stubbornly.

Lowering his voice, David whispered, "Wife, you have the mouth of a salty wench today. Surely it is not the same that spoke loving endearments whilst the moon rose high last night. What was accepted a year ago will not be tolerated today. Will you remember that you are a married woman?"

Margaret grabbed the brush from Titus and laid it hard against *Sam*'s back. "You knew me to be a woman who speaks plainly from the first. Well you know that I am *not* salty." Pausing as *Sam* neighed, Margaret tried to control her emotions as her eyes filled with tears. She returned to stroking the horse's mane. After a minute she stopped, and turning toward David, said resignedly, "But if you be resolute, I will bow to your wishes, husband. I will not have bad temper between us. John will take the reins."

David sighed. "Ah, well...'tis good. You know I only think of you. That is all."

"I understand, husband. As I say, John will take the reins."

"Indeed, he expects to do so."

"You spoke with him again?"

"Yes. Now come, love, please do not be surly with me over this. John is happy to oblige."

Margaret turned looking into the face of her husband. Though it was true that she held great reservations over John being *Sam's* driver, had she not sworn to God that she would be a loving wife, and that she and her husband would be together in all things? A test had come. Reluctantly she relinquished the last of her resolve. "It is a sin to argue."

In a gesture that expressed understanding, David raised her gloved hand, holding it endearingly against his cheek for a moment. "Knowing my friend, John, he will have no interest in TenEyck's grand gesture, but Bess would be well pleased; we would all be glad of the three barrels of Hendrickson's beer that I heard this morning the brew master has added to the prize pot. I recalled John telling me that he considers Hendrickson's far better than ours, Ryckman's, or even the English Burton brews that he once shared with your father at Grays Inn in London. Of course, if we were to win, the barrels would be divided between us."

"It appears that it is God's will that he should drive."

"Without a heavy heart, you will relinquish the reins?"

Margaret sighed. "Yes. You are right. It would not be proper, and I would not invite more scandal or bad blood. I have had my fill of all of that."

"Good, then I shall go to find John, and convey in all haste that he should fear no unpleasant words from his sister who wishes him only Godspeed."

Margaret nodded absently, forcing back her disappointment, her thoughts drifting back to her girlhood. She saw herself and her Indian cousin, Flower, two happy ten-year-old girls, bareback riding her pinto, *Sugar*. Her long black hair flew behind her, tickling Flower's face as she drove her *Sugar* madly through the fields, over and beyond every knoll. Flower laughed infectiously as she tried to keep her cousin's hair away from her face with her one free arm while the other was wrapped tightly around Margaret's waist. In her daydream, Margaret could hear her frantic mother calling, "Come back, come back..."

Catching up to David as he walked away, Margaret put a hand on David's arm. "Before you go to John, I would have you know my true concerns. I am not so much interested in a silver bowl or beer that will gratify the winner of this contest. What summons my attention is that I, too, have heard things this morning, principally that Tom Kingman will drive his trotter himself today. I know that John is well enough in body to drive our *Sam* to victory, but after the visit to Kingman's farm, I fear that his spirit is not in such good form. He can not control his anger toward Kingman, and this could be disastrous if he allows his hate to overcome him whilst he holds the reins."

David stood quietly observing his wife, but the hair on the back of his neck began to rise. He had never considered the possibility that John's confessed mortal enemy would be holding the opposition's reins. Until now he had thought Hatter would drive the Kingman rig. Now he came to understand that he had mistaken much of what had stared him in the eye these last weeks. Nothing would give John more pleasure than to pull to the knees the man who he suspected was behind the murder and brutalization of their Negroes, and he would do so at any cost.

Margaret's voice was tight. "Look yonder."

From far across the field Tom Kingman, with his two small sons in the cart on either side of him, rounded the corner driving a stunning, rare, chestnut brown Friesian. As he approached, the crowd applauded raucously.

David looked at Margaret. His voice was filled with worry. "I am off to find John."

Chapter 28

As David disappeared into the crowd, a gruff voice called to Margaret from behind. As she turned, a short, rugged looking man in his forties approached, arms outstretched.

"Seth Thomas! Good gracious, the sight of you is a blessing this morn!"

"And you, Peggy," Seth replied merrily. Without hesitation the two embraced. "How good to see the grand mistress looking so fit and ready to ride."

Sheepishly Margaret replied, "Ah, well, I will not be riding today. John will be the one to ride. You recall I am a married woman?"

Seth laughed heartily. "A married woman, indeed you are. I would have much liked to be to the wedding but was away."

"Yes, I know. When did you return, Seth?"

"I've been back quite some time from London town, but went up north to the farm at the Half Moon village. I had a mind to see how my youngest was doing with our trading post up there, but came back to my own farm here a week ago. I could not miss this race."

"And your youngest—that would be little Tom?" Margaret interjected.

"Little Tom, say you? Tom is taller than I. He is seventeen; a grown man. As I say, I wanted to know how he fared with the trading post whilst I was away to England, but I need not have lost my sleep. He has one of my best Negroes with him and all was well. I returned home only days after you were wed and was sorry to have missed your nuptials. I have heard grand words of praise on your husband's behalf from your brother when I saw him in Albany. I am anxious to meet David."

"And so you will. My husband has only just gone off to find John."

"God willing, you will be happy in your marriage. I miss my own good wife and would marry again could I find another who would have me."

"I will keep your request in my prayers, Seth."

"I can see the marriage has agreed with you, Peggy. You look as fit as any one of the horses lined up. I am disappointed that you will not ride today, as I was set to place my wager upon your horse with you holding the reigns, but I was forgetting that you are married."

Margaret reddened. "I can see you will get on well with my husband."

Seth's voice became sober. "The race is soon to start, but I would have you walk with me toward the river. Your husband would take no offense if we were to speak alone?"

Margaret studied her childhood friend, the man who as a boy had witnessed her father and mother's marriage. "No, Sir, my husband would take no offense at all."

"I will take but little of your time; there is something that you would want to hear."

Margaret turned to Titus. "Should Master David or Master John come hither, you will tell them I will be back to this place long before the teams face the start."

"Yes, Mistress."

Linking arms, Margaret and her old friend walked off away from the crowd amid a few curious glances, "I have serious news that I must impart to you, dear Peggy."

"What is it, Seth? No sorrows from sickness?"

"No. All of my children fare well, thank God, and I am still fit as any bear. The matter that I would speak with you about is something apart, and what I have to say, I would have you keep to yourself alone."

"Of course, Seth, but what is it? You frighten me."

"Let me come then right away to the heart of it. The countryside is ablaze with what has happened at your manor: the raid, the death of your Negro, and your marriage. All of this naturally, stimulates discourse. Yet, aside from this, since I arrived home from England all I have heard is the hard talk on how John has it in for Tom Kingman. It is common knowledge that John cannot abide the man in his brother's stead and sees him none other than a serpent. There is scarce a soul hereabouts who does not know that you also have little use for Mr. Kingman, though I suspect that you do your best to abide him."

"All of what you say is true, Seth. There is no love between us, and since John's return many terrible atrocities have occurred. John has settled upon Tom Kingman as the man who is at the root of all our troubles."

"I thought as much after talking with him in Albany. Of course, I recall that there was a time Tom Kingman had set about courting you, but you firmly rebuked him, and I can tell you that he did not take the rebuke favorably."

"He did not, but that was long ago."

Seth continued…"After your sister-in-law married Kingman, and as recently as this August, I did not know what to think of all these stories that are often spread, I am sorry to say, without foundation across the tavern tables, but I have come to suspect that John's suspicions may hold water. Though I have no proof, I sorrow to say that I fear Tom Kingman had a hand in the raid upon your plantation."

Margaret's face reflected the horror of Seth's words. "Why do you say such a thing to me? We know not which way things go, Seth."

"This is why I asked that we walk alone. There is more to be said. Although I do not know all who took part in the raid, sadly I know who killed your Negro, the one called Peter. I know the treachery of the killing, and I cannot in all good conscience keep the truth to myself any longer."

Margaret stopped short, visibly shaken. "How can this be? John did tell me that he had met with you whilst in Albany. He said that you told him that you had heard something of two strangers who were thought to have come upon a boy who could have been my slave. Because of the hearsay, many times I set forth a great search."

"I thought that your boy would have been found months ago," Seth mumbled.

"Seth, please speak to me plainly now, or risk our friendship."

Glancing down, Seth replied gently, "I would not wish to cause such a breach. I never meant any harm to you or your family by keeping this knowledge to myself. To the contrary, I only meant to be kind to a poor, distraught woman. And further, the details had not been confirmed at the time."

"Seth, all the same, you should have spoken sooner!"

"I did, at first, hear the news in Albany by way of a trapper as I had said to John. I later came by information first-hand from the mouths of those who did the deed."

Margaret gasped. "What say you?"

"Perhaps a month ago I was on my way to visit my son living near Rensselaerwyck. I stopped at Jonas' Tavern where I encountered two braggarts who were already in a sour drunken way when I arrived. Being much weary, I was ready to take to the nearest bed available, but the tavern keeper, Jonas, had engaged the two, his only customers, in conversation. He seemed anxious that I hear the talk and insisted I join the three of them for a mug of ale. So I quenched my thirst after my long ride, and thanked him for his offer. After I finished my drink I thought I would go straight to bed, but Jonas again bid me stay. It was then that one of his patrons began to brag about how he had rid the valley of trouble."

Seth faced Margaret squarely. "The two in the tavern that night were the Meyndert brothers, Peggy. According to their own words, it was these two bullies who were a part of the raid upon your property, and who sent your Negro into the hands of our Redeeming Savior, though I am convinced," Seth added earnestly, "that the loose-tongued sailors meant only some amusement and not to kill the boy. The one said that a short time after the raid, they came upon the Negro running along the road and ordered him to halt. They said they recognized him as one whom they had seen before in Albany with your overseer unloading goods at the wharf. One of the brothers slapped Peter hard, and when the other took his cruel turn, the boy fell against a rock. Kicking him as he lay there, they bid him rise, but he did not. Your slave's eyes rolled back into his head, and his body continued to shake. The two grew fearful seeing him in such a way, convinced that the boy be possessed by the Devil. Finally he lay silent and ceased to breathe. At this point, the brothers panicked and threw him into the water thinking, I suspect, that all would say he had drowned. They ran away more or less convinced that they had done no intentional wrong.

Margaret quickly wiped away a tear. "Oh, Lord, give me strength for I can not abide another word of this."

Seth gently touched her arm. "I should have told John my full suspicions whilst we spoke in Albany, but did not have all the information at that time and did not want to spread rumors. After all, I have long been acquainted with the culprits' mother. She is a good and virtuous woman. And knowing John's sentiments, I was not in want of igniting a powder keg."

"Ah, Seth," Margaret sighed, composing herself, "though sore to hear the details of the boy's tragic end, it is better to know the truth of it."

Seth nodded. "For you the truth will give resolve, but I think in the end you will agree that it serves no purpose for others, especially the mother of those who murdered your servant. Little over a year ago she suffered the loss of her husband. I know I should have turned them into the officials, and that very night threatened to the tavern keeper that I would do so as soon as the opportunity be presented, but the following day I relented. The tavern keeper swore to me that the poor widow had nothing for her support except the pay of her two sailor sons. Though I am sure that the proprietor wanted not to be known himself as loose-tongued to his patrons, on the basis of the mother, he convinced me to keep silent since the woman is very ill. I had not the heart to send her to an unhappy death on the heels of seeing her only sons arrested."

Tearfully, Margaret studied Seth. "You say the boys were a part of those who raided my farm. Who are the others? Surely they must be brought to justice. Those men left my Moses with loss of ear and limb. He will never be able to work again. They must be held accountable!"

Seth shifted his bulky frame nervously, "Yes, justice should be served, Peggy."

"I understand your compassion. For as long as I have known you, I have realized a most tender heart beats within your chest. But, I am confused. What, pray tell, makes all the difference that you confess all to me now?"

"I am sorry to hear that the injury suffered by another of your servants was so severe. Yet, I still hold as I did. The raiders who came upon your property took no life, Peggy, and nothing could be done to bring back your manservant. I have kept this in my mind all along, and from what I could make of the sailors' drunken talk, the other two who were party to the attack soon made their way to parts unknown by way of a sailboat that was hidden some miles down river."

"And these criminals who escaped by boat, do you know who they be?"

"No names were ever mentioned, though I suspect from the talk that they might be Englishmen bound for the *Hannah* that had sailed. When I pressed upon him, one of the Meyndert's said that they were hired to partake in the raid by a Provincial of great means; they indicated their benefactor was English and not of the Dutch Valley, which brought me to think that Kingman was the one in the shadows."

Margaret deliberated a few minutes before choosing her words. "Of course you know the Meyndert's, therefore you cannot be mistaken as to their identity."

Seth sighed. "I had not seen those boys for many years, and they did not make introduction, nor would they have recognized me even if they had been sober. As to them being the sole support of their widowed mother, I already knew of the woman's grief; I was called upon by the church committee to personally minister to her from the funds of our poor box. Of course, I should not disclose this to you now, but feel you should know how this poor woman suffers."

"Your words have cut through my heart, Seth,"

"Peggy, I would have been happier to cut off my arm than to have to deliver these unhappy tidings. As for the tavern keeper, I doubt that the following morn he recalled much of what his patrons confessed in his tavern or our discourse that night. Later, I prayed to God that I should do right, which brings me to this day, but doing what is right has cut open my own heart as well. Putting all of this upon you today you will learn is of no avail. All the same you should know."

"I do not understand what you mean. The truth is always best to say."

"Nay, not always. Last week I heard that the ship *Maria* went down."

Margaret gasped. "I had not heard."

"'Tis true. The *Maria* took her crew to the bottom. The Meyndert brothers went with it in her belly with the rest. Forgive me, Peggy. You are as dear to me as my own sister, and I hate that I had not come to you sooner."

"'Tis all right, Seth," Margaret whispered. "Knowing your softness for this poor woman, I forgive you for keeping still; I shall do the same, for I too would send her no more grief. I am most glad that I was the one to whom you have unburdened your heart."

Seth's reply was filled with compassion. "When you tell John all of this, as I know you will, his mind may find some small morsel of peace in knowing that the boy's murderers now feed the sea's creatures. Unfortunately, we may never know the names of the others who took part in the raid."

Suddenly they were startled by a great commotion coming from the area of the festivities. The intensity of the shouting was enormous. "What comes now?" Margaret asked nervously.

As the two quickened their steps back toward the track a horrified gasp came from Margaret when in the distance she saw Tom Kingman lying on the ground. His runaway horse was racing at a furious pace without its driver, dragging the cart toward an embankment. She was still more horrified as she realized that one of Kingman's small twin sons lay in the dirt not far from his father. It looked as though he had fallen from the cart when the horse bolted.

"Look!" Seth shouted, pointing. "There's another child still with the cart!"

The two ran in the direction of the screaming little boy gripping the side of the cart, joining several others who had responded to Rachel's frantic hysteria as she sprinted toward the still bodies of her husband and son. Margaret reached her former sister-in-law at the same time she saw John jump onto the back of the runaway cart. Pulling himself over the back he grabbed the reins. Within moments the horse had been halted and the Kingman boy was secure in John's arms.

Margaret stood beside Rachael who cradled her husband in her arms. Clutching his chest, Tom Kingman opened his eyes that met those of his terrified wife. Looking past Rachel to Margaret he struggled with his last words....*Forgive me.*

Chapter 29

The shrill whistle of an incessant blistering March wind angrily drove its way through the snow covered corridor leading to the big house on the knoll. Inside, with many of the rooms closed off for the winter, and the parlor furniture draped for the season, the only sound to be heard was the scraping of iron against the basement floor brick as Margaret poked at the kitchen hearth's smoldering charred wood. She and her elderly companion had spent hours polishing the silver they had brought down from the dining room. Before they had started David and John had gone off to check on the grist mill and the saw mill. Now her servant woman, Eva, sat nearby, dozing. Margaret picked up the sampler she had started the day before and sat quietly in a chair near the fire. After a few minutes she set the sampler aside and rose to again poke at the wood, hoping to rekindle a flame.

Since the tragic death of Tom Kingman last autumn, more heartbreak had befallen Vandenberg Manor. Eva was mourning the loss of her husband as well as her son, Moses, after an infection had developed in the stump of his leg. Months of grieving had settled upon all at the Estate.

Even the little yellow songbirds Margaret had brought home from England four summers ago had lost their voice. The pair watched her from within their bamboo cage as she meandered around the warmth of the kitchen fire. Perched protectively, their necks sunk low into tiny-feathered bodies; she again wished the wind away and the return of blue sky. Margaret approached the birds and attempted coaching them into animation by tapping lightly on the side of their cage. Tiny black dots stared back, but the little bodies remained still. Margaret's concern rose. Once again she tapped. "Come now, my little ones," she cooed, "be brave for spring is but a breath away and summer not far behind."

She walked over to the colored threads stored in a basket near the chair. As she picked through the strands, the events of the last year played through her mind, a medley of various high and low notes reflecting the tempo of the happiness and despair that she had felt at various times. Her moods bounced between the euphoria of her own glorious wedding to the anguish she had felt upon the death of each of her loved ones, most especially Zebulon.

Glancing at Eva, she resumed her chair and tried to shut away the morbid tones of death by focusing upon the joy of her marriage day. She also thought of Clare who now sat unassisted and who was beginning to voice her own babyish interpretation of the Dutch language. Throughout the darkness, blessings had been bestowed.

Rachel, no doubt grateful to John for saving the life of one of her small sons, no longer ignored them when they met at church. Her slight smile seemed genuine; but sadly Margaret had concluded that the close friendship they had once shared would never be the same. Margaret wondered if John understood now how harsh he had been in his condemnation of Tom Kingman. Though surely neither she nor her brother had ever wished Rachel's husband dead, Margaret had come to acknowledge that she too was guilty of being hard-hearted. She had often prayed that Tom Kingman would sail home to his native England and never return or that the Lord would work a miracle and simply make Kingman disappear. She shuttered to think that her prayer had been answered with such severity. Justice was meant to be held within the hands of the Almighty, but that she had through her own supplications called down Rachel's husband's death was sometimes more than she thought she could bear.

Divine forgiveness was not easily begot. Only letting go of the anger she still held within her breast would allow God's grace to enter into her soul, but how could she forgive when she still blamed a dead man for fanning the fire that turned Teunis' children against her. Once she had lovingly bounced them all on her knee, and now all but two stared at her from their church pews in blank silence. She had thought her prayer to be rid of Tom Kingman would bring justice, and thereupon peace would dwell within her soul. But on race day when she had looked down upon Tom's still body, even though justice seemed to have been served, her heart was filled with only heavy remorse.

Throughout the winter months, despite her husband's enduring strength and their dear friend, Phillip Lansing's steadfast and compassionate company, Margaret and her household had struggled to reach for cracks of light. The first ray broke through during the New Year week visiting period when they had learned that Rachel's small son had recovered completely and fared well. Rachel had sent Hatter to give them the joyous news. Following the open accusations that John had made against Kingman, Margaret had feared that his death had put an end to any step toward amicability between families.

Reaching for a caraway cookie, she was hopeful that it, and a cup of Eva's tea, would rest easy in her stomach. After weeks of battling a wretched nausea, yesterday, quite suddenly, the sickness had left, yet she knew that she must take care not to put any further distress upon her person. What she had suspected, and had kept to herself, she now believed. She was certain that she was with child.

To present her husband with a son or daughter was something that she wanted above all else. It was a miracle beyond the greatest of miracles, and she could imagine David's roar of delight when she would tell him.

Thinking back to Rachel as a young woman expecting her first child, Margaret was startled as her two feathered companions fluttered their wings, and began to chirp wildly as if providing their own accompaniment. Margaret smiled to herself. *Perhaps they can read my joyous thoughts.* She knew the importance of keeping all calamity and any morose thoughts at bay if she was to be able to carry, and then be delivered of, a healthy baby. A long laying-in time would be difficult for her, but she promised herself she would not fight her quiet time for a fine babe would be the result. By her calculations the child should be born in the autumn, close to apple celebrations. October and November apple-bees as they made the fruits ready for drying were always one of her favorites. How she and Rachel had enjoyed being together during that season.

The fire in the hearth had taken hold again, and after adding another log to the flame it grew into a significant orange blaze filling the surrounding space with renewed warmth. It brought to mind those afternoons this past January when she and David had huddled together in the big sleigh under piles of fur. Still, despite pleasant memories and the comfort of the heat, Margaret was finding the unusual quiet of the house nearly as chilling as the cold. *If only Marie were here*, she thought, *surely I could talk her into a good game of thirty-six-card Piquet.*

Margaret sat down and adjusted her sampler. How she longed to hear David's melodic voice trailing through the rooms. They had been blessed, for without question each had found in the other a good match.

Glancing at the clock, she wondered where Sally had hidden herself. She had not seen her in hours, and it would soon be dark. She had distinctly heard Marie instruct the girl that she should keep her Mistress company until she returned from Henry's cabin.

But what silent complaint could be made, for indeed it was she who had encouraged Marie to spend the Sunday afternoon with her brother and his wife. Marie's comforting strong arms would be a blessing to Peter's mother. She poured herself another cup of tea, recalling the rainbow everyone had witnessed the day Peter's remains were put into the ground. Margaret supposed that the once dreaded separations from her dearest did have some merit: the man's absence provided opportunity for quiet, womanish reflection.

Surveying the polished silver laid out on the long table, Margaret rose to further inspect a double-handled cup that had been a wedding gift. Spotting a smudge, she pulled up the edge of her apron, quickly wiping a finger print away. *To all of life there is a beginning, a middle, and an end;* Catharina had said so when she lovingly presented her and Peter's gift.

Holding the glistening cup brought to mind another Waldron family story of Peter's Aunt Aeltje, who as a small child had charmed Peter Stuyvesant by telling the Dutch Director of the Colony that the ornate silver bands on his wooden peg leg were pretty. Margaret promised herself that the first note she would pen extolling her good news would be to Aeltje Vermilye, now a grandmother many times over.

Margaret smiled recalling her impatience with Benjamin as he completed her portrait and how David had praised her grandness when her likeness was unveiled to him. Margaret thought that it felt as if she had known her husband far longer than she actually had. Sometimes it seemed there was never a time before David. Together they were as one in both body and mind—except for her stubborn reservations over his intention to purchase still more slaves to work the foundry.

Tracing the ornately scrolled "K" that was etched deeply into the silver cup, she read the inscription out loud, briefly awakening Eva from her slumber, "*When this you see, remember me*". The old woman starred incoherently at her for a moment before her eyelids dropped. Margaret suppressed a giggle and continued to envision the guests who had attended her wedding, beginning with Peter Waldron and his stout, jolly wife. Her cousin, Catharina, had dressed herself in a most vivid purple stomacher, which her clever seamstress had colorfully fashioned to match that of her husband's own velvet waistcoat. Margaret had begun to notice several other married couples who enjoyed coordinating the colors of their attire; the lot of them she supposed wishing to present themselves as a pair—much like her songbirds.

Placing the cup back on the table with the other pieces, Margaret thought upon the intricacies that drew together

God's children, weaving families as one, colorful threads binding a tapestry that many times spanned the decades.

This afternoon her thoughts turned to Zebulon and so many others who had long been with her. Had Resolved Waldron not been friend and neighbor to her father from the olden Dutch times near Horne Hook at Harlem, Zebulon would not have come to them. How different Vandenberg Manor would have been without Zebulon and Eva's family. Had there been no Zebulon, there would have been no Marie. Margaret could scarce imagine her life without Marie's constant companionship.

Had her father not come to know Matty Thomas, he would probably not have been induced northward, and of course, he would never have met her mother, Gentle Heart. Thinking of Matty, she shivered. After fathering fourteen children with his Indian wife he had once again grown tired of civilization. At the advanced age of sixty two, his wife dead, Matty had packed up his three youngest, left the New York Colony, and traveled westward into hostile Shawnee lands. Neither Matty nor those who went with him were ever heard from again.

Margaret pulled from her apron pocket a recent response to a letter she had written to Benjamin Lapett in which she had conveyed the sad details of the death of Zebulon and Moses. Benjamin had written back remembering Zeb with kind words and offering sympathies to be conveyed to Marie and her extended family. He had recalled that he knew that Zebulon had been with the Waldron's for some years prior to being purchased by her father. Lapett had remarked of how impressed his girls had been with Captain Waldron's tale-telling at her wedding; the Captain saying that Resolved Waldron's family had settled at New Amsterdam with three children when first arriving from Holland, Captain Will's father being the eldest boy.

In addition to his wife and children from a first marriage, a younger brother had accompanied Resolved Waldron on his voyage. The brother's name was Joseph. After a time living in New Amsterdam Joseph Waldron and the house servant had struck out on their own when the English took the colony in 1664. No one knew of their whereabouts for years, most likely presuming the couple had perished at the hands of hostiles. The way Benjamin understood it, old Mr. Waldron rarely mentioned his younger brother. It seemed that the two had parted after bitter words. Resolved died without ever knowing what had happened to Joseph. Had the story ended there, no one would have thought it so unusual, for many settlers went off to make another life and never looked back to the kin left behind. But now, over thirty years after Joseph Waldron had left New Amsterdam, new information surfaced which oddly enough touched Margaret's household directly. Lapett's letter provided the most astonishing weave to the cloth that blanketed Margaret's shoulders.

Benjamin wrote that three weeks prior, his wife had delivered three fancy bonnets to Ann Delameter, wife to John, and a granddaughter of the departed, Resolved Waldron. After business had been tended between the two women, the subject of Resolved Waldron's one time slave came up after Mrs. Delameter had invited Mrs. Lapett for a cup of tea. Expressing both shock and sorrow over the treachery that had occurred at the Vandenberg farm last summer, Mrs. Delameter had proceeded to share a fascinating slice of Waldron news that had been revealed during the New Year's week of visiting. By way of an aged French Jesuit, who had said that he had spent many decades preaching amongst the Iroquois, Huron, and the Shawnee Indians, the Waldron family had learned that there was a possibility Resolved Waldron's younger brother had not been killed by the savages as all had thought, but indeed had survived and prospered.

The Jesuit had told John Delameter that when he was very young, he had once known a man by the name of Joseph Waldron. The Waldron he knew, and a woman called Sarah who Waldron called his wife, operated a frontier trading post deep in Shawnee territory, on the other side of the Great Falls. They were a kindly couple who he called friends. They had no offspring as far as the old priest knew that were of their own, but had taken in several orphaned natives. The Jesuit claimed to have baptized two of these children himself.

The Jesuit said that the trading post proprietor once told him that he had come from the east where he had been a printer. He had traveled westward for nearly four hundred miles between September and early November of 1664. After passing the Great Falls the Waldron's had stopped and built a camp near the edge of the wide Red River, which is almost the size of the North River.

In time the unlikely friendship between the young French Jesuit and middle-aged Dutchman with the English name had grown, and the priest learned that there had been little doubt in Joseph Waldron's mind that he and the woman would have frozen to death during the snows of their first winter if a local fur trader, Paul Karski, had not found them and brought them to the shelter of his log home.

In the spring, the two had recovered fully from their ordeal, and Waldron and his wife had returned to the Red River where, assisted by friendly Indian neighbors, they had built a one-room cabin on land Waldron purchased from natives known as those of the Cat Nation. For the trade

Waldron used the glass buttons that he had torn from his red jacket. Also included in the bargain was a much treasured silver funeral spoon, and later Waldron had told the Jesuit that he traded his wife's looking glass for ten excellent beaver pelts.

Margaret folded away the letter. She had confronted David immediately after reading Benjamin's correspondence. What her husband confessed had nearly taken her breath away.

David said that he had suspected a connection between the Waldron's of whom Margaret's family were acquainted, and the Waldron known by his own family, ever since the evening prior to the tragic race day. When John talked about his father's early days of settlement in this country, relating the tale of a man by the name of Joseph Waldron who had departed New Amsterdam years before, taking with him his brother's slave woman, something had flashed in David's mind, yet he thought the possibility of such a connection far too unreasonable to consider. However, Lapett's letter, and the mention of Paul Karski, had made it clear to him that Joseph Waldron of the frontier and Joseph Waldron of New Amsterdam were one and the same.

David recalled the stories told to him when he had been a young man of the tall, slender Joseph Waldron and his industrious little wife. He remembered well how his stepmother, being Holland born, had said she enjoyed talking the Dutch with the Waldrons. Waldron's wife's name was Sarah, but he did not recall his step-mother or anyone else saying anything about the woman being a Negro.

Jesuits, David had said, often ministered to both Indian and whites on the frontier. Finally, and most shockingly of all to Margaret was David's disclosure that Paul Karski was his grandfather, and that it was he who had originally established a trading post with a Waldron. Joseph Waldron, his wife, and David's grandfather were all long dead, but the Karski family, David had insisted, operated the post to this day.

Margaret rose and picked up a poker addressing a faltering log. "Papists" she muttered disgustedly and spat into the fire. What is wrong with Delameter? Why would he be so open as to engage in discourse with a Jesuit? He might as well have handed his sharpest blade to the French enemy, and invited them to come hither to slit the throats of his and his wife's children whilst the little innocents slept. Critically she wondered if those who had been baptized by the Jesuit had later been baptized into the true faith.

Ah well, Margaret sighed, her country was growing, and the sentiments of the people ever changing; the past soon forgotten. She must pray to God for tolerance of people whose foolish actions she could not understand, whilst at the same time asking for wisdom that she may know the true enemy.

The sound of approaching horses broke the stillness—and her thoughts.

"Sally, are you there?" Margaret called out. Ascending the narrow servant's stairs on the side of the hearth, she poked her head out into the barren dining room. "Sally!"

There was no answer and nothing to be done but go to the door herself, muttering as she went that Sally was a poor substitute for her Marie. As she passed the parlor window she saw that David and John had dismounted, and Titus was already leading their horses away to the stable. Brownie, visiting again, sat nearby unusually patient. The only sign of a soon to be eager welcoming was the dog's tail pounding hard against the dirt. *Unconditional love*, Margaret thought.

While her husband and brother ascended the steps of the stoop, Margaret paused, placing both her hands upon her stomach. She smiled, thinking that she and the precious new life that grew within her would hold onto their secret a little longer. Perhaps tomorrow she would tell David that if the Lord willed it, he would be a father before St. Nicholas Day.

Opening the top half of the front door she called out, "Welcome home!"

1 Corinthians 12:13

Some of us are Jews, some are Gentiles, some are slaves, and some are free. But we have all been baptized into Christ's body by one Spirit and we have all received the same Spirit.

Peter Waldron
1675 – 1725
Albany Resident

The following is a translation of excerpts from the will of Peter Waldron:

"In The Name Of God Amen I Peter Waldron of the City of Albany, bricklayer do make and declare this my Last Will and Testament in manner and form following:
I bequeath my soul into the hands of All Mighty God believing remissions of sins and everlasting life by the merits death and passion, of Jesus Christ my Lord and only Savior."

"ITEM I give and bequeath unto my oldest son William my great Dutch Bible....."

"ITEM I give and devise unto my beloved wife Tryntie my house and land at the Halfmoon and also one moiety or just half part of my house and lott of ground on the west side of the low street in the said City of Albany....."
"I also give and bequeath unto my said beloved wife Tryntie my Negro wooman called Sarah...."

"LASTLY I do nominate and appoint my said beloved wife Tryntie and my son Cornelius to be Executors of this my last Will and Testament. In witness whereof I have hereunto set my hand and seal this 28th day of April anno dom 1725."

"Sealed Signed Published   "his
and Declared in the Presence   Peter   *P W* Waldron
of *Gerrit Lansingh, Jr.*   mark"
Joseph Vandeusen
John Collins"

ACKNOWLEDGEMENTS

First, I acknowledge and thank my husband, Andrew Perreault, who through his unending patience, editorial skill, creative suggestions, and strong support has made it possible for the completion of three novels within three years...hence, the Waldron Series.

* * * *

I thank old and new friends at the Knickerbocker Society, Schaghticoke, New York, the Albany Dutch Settlers Society, Bradt Family Society, Mayflower Society, Albany Jewish Community Center, and various chapters of the National Society of the Daughters of the American Revolution for their gracious invitations allowing me to share a unique slice of New York State history through story. A special heartfelt thank you goes out to the ladies of my own DAR Ft. Crailo Chapter, for their support.

* * * *

As always I thank friends at the libraries who shelve those reference building blocks that form the foundation of my books.

* * * *

Finally, and most importantly, thanks to all my readers who took the time to write emails or to send posts.

Remembering fondly Mr. Dick Ross who passed away in California March 14, 2009

About the Author....

This is a third novel for Gloria Waldron Hukle. She and her husband, Andrew, reside in Averill Park, New York. For information on event schedules or author speaking engagements, please visit:

www.authorgloriawaldronhukle.com
Email: ghukle@nycap.rr.com

Made in the USA
Middletown, DE
18 November 2017